870812

SNOW
ON THE
WIND

Previous novels by Hugh Miller:

The District Nurse
The Rejuvenators
The Dissector
Ambulance

SNOW
ON THE
WIND

HUGH
MILLER

St. Martin's Press
New York

Library of Congress Cataloging-in-Publication Data

Miller, Hugh, 1937–
    Snow on the wind.

    Sequel to: The district nurse.
    I. Title.
PR6063.I373S6 1987   823'.914   87-85
ISBN 0-312-00682-9

First published in Great Britain by Transworld Publishers Ltd. as a Corgi edition.

First U.S. Edition

10 9 8 7 6 5 4 3 2 1

SNOW
ON THE
WIND

CHAPTER ONE

MEGAN sat down opposite the desk, breathing the room's permanent odour of ether and antiseptic. Dr O'Casey smiled and touched his cap of dense, smooth-winged grey hair, as if to make sure it was still there.

'I'm sorry to interrupt your rounds like this,' he said, 'but there's something I felt you should know as soon as possible.' He pointed to a letter on the desk. Megan noticed the tremor in his fingers. 'I've managed to find myself a locum, so you'll be dealing with a new man for a while.'

'You're going away, then?'

The doctor nodded. 'I'm taking myself off on an enforced and prolonged holiday.'

'It's about time you did.'

'I could say the same to you.'

Megan shrugged. He could say it and she would give him the answer she gave everyone else. There wasn't the time. People needed her and there was no one to do her job if she took time off. 'Enforced, you say?'

'By the state of my health, Megan.' O'Casey touched his chest. 'My souvenir from the war has been plaguing me for the past couple of months. It's not threatening my life, mind you. But I get so tired . . .'

Megan knew his condition had been growing worse. It had been noticeable for a long time. 'Tired's hardly the word for it. You get downright exhausted.'

Ten years ago a fragment of shrapnel had torn away a piece of Dr O'Casey's left lung; battlefield surgery had left him with an internal deformity that caused him recurring pain and debility. During the two years that Megan had been District Nurse in Pencwm, she had seen the attacks grow

7

more frequent and persistent. On the occasions when she had suggested he take a holiday, Dr O'Casey had given her the same answer she would have given him.

'I took my rattling wheeze-box to a specialist in Cardiff a few weeks ago,' he explained. 'A very bright old boy who's always writing papers for the *Lancet*. He tapped and prodded and listened, and finally he counselled rest. Lots of it, a year at least.'

Megan stared at him. 'That long?'

'The alternative, he assured me, would be early retirement. Since I intend to drop dead in harness, I decided to take his advice.' O'Casey smiled again, deepening the weary lines around his eyes. 'Now I've accepted the idea, I'm quite looking forward to going away.'

Megan tried to picture a whole year without him, a year devoid of his reassuring presence. She couldn't. 'Where will you go?' she asked.

'To the sun for a few weeks. Greece, if it can be arranged. After that, I'll go and stay with my brother in Ireland.'

Megan looked round the consulting room, imagining it occupied by a stranger. That was hard to picture, too.

'The new man . . .' his name is Morris. He's thirty-seven and he's from Newport – though I understand he trained in London and was conditioned there. That's where he is now, in a well-heeled joint practice in Kensington. My decision, it seems, coincided with one of his. He wanted to come back to Wales and work in one of the poorer communities.' O'Casey sighed softly. 'He'll find this place poor enough, God knows.'

'And a bit of a shock after Kensington.' Megan was beginning to feel uneasy. It was bad enough that Dr O'Casey would be gone for so long. But to have some hoity-toity London man in his place, full of lofty pretensions and do-gooding ideals – that was a prospect she didn't relish.

'Try not to prejudge Dr Morris,' O'Casey said, as if he had read Megan's mind. 'He'll most likely find it hard to adjust, at first. He'll need your guidance – and your patience.'

'Of course.' Megan forced a smile. 'When will you be leaving?'

8

'At the end of the month. Doctor Morris will spend a week here with me before I leave. It's not a long time, but going in at the deep end's the best way of learning to swim, eh?'

And to drown, Megan thought. 'Well, thanks for telling me.' She stood up, smoothing her long blue uniform coat and squaring her hat. 'I've got to be going now. I should have been at the Prentice's ten minutes ago.'

O'Casey went out to the hall with her. 'We'll have a little get-together before I go,' he said. 'Sherry and small talk, that kind of thing.'

'I'll look forward to it,' Megan assured him. As she opened the door and stepped out into the pale October sunlight, she wondered again what it would be like to cope without Dr O'Casey. And to put up with the new man. It could be like losing a limb, she supposed, and having to live with a cumbersome wooden replacement.

In the world at large, 1927 had been eventful, a year full of progress, innovation, upheaval and change. In the spring an American aviator, Charles Lindbergh, made the first solo flight across the Atlantic. Another American, Jacob Schick, had invented an electric razor. In China a general called Chiang Kai-Shek purged the communists and set up a Government at Nanking. A Scottish scientist, Alexander Fleming, had discovered a substance called Penicillin, which was beginning to look like the most significant medical breakthrough since the turn of the century. Across the globe wars began and others ended, politicians spoke of narrowly-avoided disasters and fresh ones on the horizon. Famine struck in Africa while elsewhere industries and economies boomed. In Britain, if the press was to be believed, the main social preoccupations were sex, fashion and the latest dance craze, the Charleston.

Among the people of Pencwm, the preoccupations were of a more sombre tinge. Flippancy and the pursuit of pleasure were, after all, for men and women who had secured a foothold on survival. To a mining community dominated by

9

poverty and the countless legacies of a seven-month national coal strike, few pleasures were imaginable that could eclipse the occasional certainty of a week free from hardship.

Pencwm seemed to have been designed to attract adversity and affliction. Row upon rising row of flinty, dour-fronted cottages merged their greyness with the darker backdrop of mine buildings and looming black tips. A stubborn overlay of coal dust and soot clung to everything, even the swell of windy fields to the west, giving the town a cloak of drabness that even sunlight could never relieve.

Pencwm's people, for the most part as colourless as their surroundings, existed within a framework of life that city dwellers, even the poorer of them, would call stunted. Male adult recreation was to be found only in the pub or in the occasional improvised game of street football. The women mainly found their distraction in gossip, the primary topics of their prattle being illness, promiscuous neighbours, gone-wrong children and newcomers. In spite of two years' intensive work there, Megan Roberts was still regarded as a stranger by a lot of people; that afternoon, as she pushed her bicycle to the top of Cardower Road and leaned it outside the Prentice's house, women at doorways nudged each other and stared. Megan nodded brightly to a couple of them as she unstrapped her black bag from the rack. One woman sent back a tentative smile. The other turned away.

Mrs Prentice answered Megan's knock. She was a small woman in her late thirties with greying hair and a constant expression of wariness.

'Sorry I'm a bit late,' Megan said as she followed Mrs Prentice indoors.

'That's all right.' The woman always gave Megan the impression that she expected hold-ups, setbacks, and general misfortune as deserved features of her life. She never complained. She accepted.

Megan set down her bag on the living room table. 'How has Gareth been today, then?'

'The same.'

'Has he been taking the medicine?'

10

Mrs Prentice shrugged, which caused her thin collarbone to make a soft, cracking sound. 'I told him to. And I told him what you said, about it being terrible tasting, like, but good for him all the same.'

'It's very important he takes it all, Mrs Prentice.' Megan opened the bag and took out a bottle of cloudy liquid. 'I've brought some more, he should be needing it by now.' She put the bottle down and closed her bag again. 'Let's go and have a look at him, shall we?'

The bedroom across the narrow lobby was small and airless. A dusty shaft of sunlight threw an oblong on the grey-blanketed bed and the folded hands of Gareth Prentice. He was sitting up, propped by a coverless pillow and a folded bolster. His face was so thin that his cheek bones looked as if they had been stuck on as an afterthought. Gareth was eighteen and weighed no more than a healthy twelve-year-old.

'Now then, Gareth . . .' Megan went to the bedside and showed him her firm, confident look, the one she kept for patients who were disheartened and rather afraid of their illness. 'How have you been feeling since I saw you last?'

'No different.'

'Been taking the medicine, have you?'

His deep-set eyes flickered away from Megan's. 'Some of it,' he said. 'I don't like it much.'

'You're not supposed to like it.'

'It makes me sick.' Gareth looked at his mother, who was hovering at Megan's side. 'Tell her how bad I was, first thing Saturday.'

'He was terrible,' Mrs Prentice said dutifully. 'His dad had to hold his head, he got that weak from retching.'

Megan frowned at Gareth. 'You remembered what I told you – about taking the medicine after you've eaten something?'

Again his eyes flickered aside. He pursed his lips and stared at the blanket. He was a petulant boy, given to black moods and tantrums even in the days before he become ill.

'I can't see how it made you sick if you took it the way you

11

were told.' Megan turned to his mother. 'It would be better if you gave it to him, Mrs Prentice, rather than relying on him to take it himself.'

'He . . .' The woman looked cautiously at her son. 'He doesn't want me giving it him.'

'I'm not some baby,' Gareth grunted, without raising his eyes.

'I know you're not,' Megan said. 'But you have to follow instructions if you're to get better.'

His condition was a tenacious combination of vitamin deficiency and gastritis. Dr O'Casey had taken advice on the case and was told that a liquid diet supplement was the only treatment known, so far. The condition had been aggravated, and perhaps caused, by Gareth's refusal to eat fresh vegetables, even when his mother could afford them; to make matters worse he would only eat meat that had been fried, he disdained all fruit and would only drink milk when it was in tea. As matters stood, the supplement was practically the only worthwhile contribution being made to his diet. That and bread.

'I'm not getting any better, am I?' Gareth fired the question suddenly, glaring up at Megan. 'All that weight I lost, it's not come back. And my stomach still hurts all the time. It hurts worse when I swallow that medicine.' Fear was in his eyes again, just as Megan had seen it on previous visits. 'It's something terrible I've got and the medicine's no good.'

'Shush now, Gareth,' Mrs Prentice breathed.

'Bob Malcolm's dad had this.' A tear glinted in the corner of the boy's eye as he looked at his mother. 'Just the same, it was. He got all thin an' his belly hurt day and night and he kept being sick.'

'Listen to me,' Megan snapped. 'Mr Malcolm's illness was nothing like yours.' The man had died of a liver cancer eight months after Megan arrived in Pencwm. 'You can get well again. He couldn't.'

'But it was the same!'

'It was *not*!'

12

Gareth wiped a tear from his cheek with the sleeve of his shirt. 'You wouldn't let Mr Malcolm see Nesta Mogg, just like you'll not let my mam get her in—'

'That's enough, Gareth!' Megan strode to the window and opened it a crack while Mrs Prentice backed towards the door. She was eyeing her son with as much reproach as she dared. Megan had heard that he once hit his mother when she refused him money to go down to the pub. In a house where the mother was weak and the father ineffectual and soft, even someone like Gareth could become a tyrant when he wanted to.

'Now.' Megan came back to the side of the bed and folded her arms. 'I'll make this clear to you. You're suffering from nothing deadly. It can be cleared up if you'll take the medicine and if you'll eat more vegetables and drink more milk. As for Nesta Mogg, I don't want her interfering in your treatment because she's an ignorant, dangerous witch-woman.' She glanced at the brown pharmacy bottle on the chair by the bed. 'I can see from here that you've *not* been taking your medicine – not nearly as much as you're supposed to anyway, and not in the proper way, if it's been making you sick.'

Gareth gestured impatiently. 'How long's it going to take, anyway?'

'Two, three weeks, if you follow instructions.' There was no point in discouraging him. In three weeks he could be back on his feet, but it would be a further month, at least, before he made up his weight loss and his general stamina. 'And when you're better,' Megan added, 'you'll have to keep up the improvement in your eating habits, or you'll wind up bad as ever.'

Gareth leaned back and turned his face towards the window, sulking. Megan and Mrs Prentice went back to the living room.

'You'll have to be more firm with him,' Megan said, knowing the advice was wasted.

'He's not a bad boy, really . . .' The little woman's eyes betrayed the kind of despairing affection whipped dogs show

13

their owners. 'He just finds it hard to believe he's going to get better again.' After a moment's hesitation she said, 'I find it kind of hard myself, sometimes. I mean – it's a wasting thing he has, isn't it?'

Megan felt she was too often in the presence of the same spectre, a black-cloaked, hooded beast called ignorance that hovered and held sway in house after house across that gnarled town. People would sooner trust their prejudices and ingrained fallacies than let in a single ray of enlightenment. 'I've told you time and again,' she sighed. 'It's going to be a fairly slow business, but we *will* get him better. Forget all that twaddle about wasting diseases. The answer's in your hands – or his, since you're so lenient.'

'His dad . . .' Mrs Prentice gestured to an empty chair, the back greased dark from years of contact with Mr Prentice's hair. 'Well, him and his dad both, I suppose – they've been on at me so much about Nesta Mogg . . .'

'Now you know what I feel about that creature.'

'Yes, but they've heard tales about things she's done . . .'

'Exaggerated, superstitious tittle-tattle,' Megan snapped. 'And all her failures and disasters get conveniently forgotten, I've noticed. Listen. Half the time it's nature itself that cures people she gets her hands on – the ones she doesn't push beyond the reach of cure, that is.'

'I just wish they'd stop going on at me,' Mrs Prentice sighed.

'Because if they do for long enough, you'll give in and go to Nesta for help – is that what you're saying?' Megan snatched up her bag. 'The woman is dangerous. Can you please get that into your head? She's a menace. In her time she's blinded, poisoned and maimed people with her mumbo-jumbo and her filthy so-called remedies. She should be locked away where she can't do any more harm.' Megan turned and strode to the door with Mrs Prentice behind her.

'It's taking so terrible long, Nurse. That's the trouble. Young folk don't like having to wait.' She spoke as if there was a wide span of time separating her own youth from the present.

14

Megan stepped outside and began fastening her bag to the bicycle again. 'If Gareth's weakness had been reported to the doctor weeks before it was,' she pointed out, 'that lad would have been up and about long ago and going to his work again. As things stand, he'll just have to be patient and do as I've told him.'

As she cycled away, Megan carried the image of Mrs Prentice standing in the doorway, round-shouldered and dejected. She should have been less abrupt with her. It wasn't as if the woman could help being the victim of an ill-natured son and the handmaiden of a dithering husband. She couldn't help being ignorant and benighted, either. Megan could have shown her sympathy and understanding – which was part of her professional duty, after all.

As she pedalled round the corner and down past the methodist chapel she realized why her compassion had been on a low flame back there at the Prentice's. It wasn't her resentment at knowing she was automatically distrusted by a lot of people in Pencwm, because she was from the north of Wales and anglicised to boot. It hadn't been Gareth's attitude, either, or his infuriating desire to consult that witch Nesta Mogg. Underlying all that had been a sharper annoyance, the knowledge that soon Dr O'Casey would be leaving the town.

She still couldn't imagine what it would be like. The man was both comforter and sparring partner, he was her guide and benign critic. He was her friend. It was only now dawning on Megan how large a part of her life he had become. The gap left by his going would be hard to bear – and it would be there for an entire year or more. She felt her spirits come down one more notch.

Turning another corner she lowered her shoulders and began pedalling grimly up the hill towards her next call. The miserable prospect persisted. The doctor was taking leave and she would have to live with that. What she might find intolerable was accepting the new man. He could certainly never replace Dr O'Casey. How could he? He was some upstart from London, a man practically her own age and

15

completely unprepared for practice among these people. How could she possibly respect him, let alone work with him?

Don't prejudge, she reminded herself. Patience and understanding were what Dr Morris would need, whether she took to him or not. She, of all people, knew how it felt to be rejected out of hand. Beginning to pant with the effort she turned one more corner and braked outside a house with a yapping dog standing in the doorway.

As she leaned the bicycle on the wall she looked up and saw Dr O'Casey's car cross the junction twenty yards ahead. Her heart sank further at the sight of it. For a long moment Megan stood there, staring as the car disappeared. In spite of herself she entertained a sudden and uncharitable image of Dr Morris. He would be some glassy-eyed, witless, faltering drip who would hand out silly orders to her, expect her to kow-tow and to cover up his blunders. He would be some medical buffoon with the effrontery to think he could hold a candle to Dr O'Casey.

'We'll see about that,' Megan muttered, snatching her bag off the rack and abandoning every notion of patience or understanding.

CHAPTER TWO

THE woman was tall and slender, with Eton-cropped brown hair peeping from the edge of her cloche hat. She crossed the waiting room with a self-assured grace, emphasized by high-heeled court shoes and a wrapover coat, its long sweep fastened by a single large button at the hip. She was a person of evident wealth and breeding, a fact which was not only apparent from her style and bearing; her mere presence in those consulting rooms was solid proof that life was a lot easier for her than for most of the people on the busy street outside.

She threw open the big oak door and stepped into the well-furnished room beyond. 'Doctor!' she cried, as if it were surprising to find a medical man in there. 'How lovely to see you!'

Dr Morris smiled as he stepped forward, extending his hand. 'And it's always a pleasure to see you, Mrs Burke.' He closed his fingers around hers for an instant, then waved towards a chair. 'Do sit down.'

There was a neat formality in the way he stood to one side, almost like a waiter, as the woman lowered her elegant length on to the chair. It seemed he would only be prepared to take his own seat when he was entirely satisfied she was comfortable.

'It's good of you to see me at such short notice,' Mrs Burke said as the doctor sat down behind the desk.

'I had a cancellation this morning,' he said. 'And even if I hadn't, I'm sure I could have found a way to accommodate you.' His dark eyes narrowed slightly, showing a touch of professional concern. 'It's nothing serious, I hope?'

Mrs Burke sighed. 'It's something that's been preying on

17

my mind, Doctor.' She drew back one sleeve of her coat and laid her hand on the desk, palm upward. 'This bump . . .' She pointed to a swelling the size of a bird's egg on her wrist. 'I've ignored it for months, but lately it's become larger, and when I woke up this morning it was actually hurting – well, throbbing a little. That's why I called you for a consultation.'

Dr Morris leaned forward and touched the lump. It was soft, and it moved aside under the pressure of his finger. 'Hmm,' he said.

'You know what we women are like,' Mrs Burke murmured. 'We'd rather pretend some things aren't there, rather than face them.'

Morris sat back. His patient gave him a questioning look. The square, strong-featured face told her nothing. 'Flex your fingers a few times, would you?' he said. As Mrs Burke did that he watched the wrist tendons move. The swelling seemed to stay where it was, floating on the mobile structures underneath. 'Fine.' Morris looked up. 'It's just what I thought it was.'

'What?'

'A ganglion.'

'Is it serious?'

Morris shook his head. 'It's completely benign.'

Mrs Burke didn't look reassured. 'Will it go away, or will I need to have it removed?'

'It won't go away by itself – well, it's not likely to, anyway. But I can remove it for you. Before you leave, in fact.'

'Oh dear . . .' Now the woman began to look alarmed. 'I don't think I could go through with that, not without preparing myself in my mind, you understand. I mean, a surgical operation's quite a major thing, however straight-forward . . .'

'There's no question of surgery,' Morris said. 'Of course, it'll do no harm to keep the lump, if you'd rather. But a sharp smack with a heavy book will get rid of it for good.'

She stared at him. 'Is that all?'

'That's all.'

She seemed disappointed. There was scarcely dramatic

18

possibility in the situation. She couldn't rivet her friends with the story of an ominous lump that vanished with one whack from a book. 'Well, I suppose you'd better go ahead . . .'

Dr Morris chose Stewart's *Principles and Practice of Surgery*. He told Mrs Burke to set her arm firmly on the desk, and when she had screwed her eyes tight shut he brought down the volume sharply. When he removed it there was no trace of the swelling, only a pink blotch where the book had made contact.

'There we are.' He put down the book as Mrs Burke opened her eyes. 'You're completely cured.'

She fingered the smooth skin. 'And to think I've been fretting about it all these weeks.' She looked at Morris. 'I came here half-expecting some serious news, you know.'

'People frequently do.' He took a step away from the desk, subtly suggesting it was time for her to go. 'It's always a pleasure to put someone's mind at rest.'

Mrs Burke pulled down her sleeve and stood up. 'I'm grateful to you, Doctor.' At the door she turned and shook his hand again. 'I don't know what we shall all do when you've gone.'

'You've heard, then.'

'Oh, I've been told by more than one distressed lady.' She fluttered her eyes at him. 'You've a fair-sized band of admirers. They'll all miss you terribly.'

'And I shall miss them,' Dr Morris said quietly. 'Yourself no less than the others.' He led the way across the waiting room and opened the door.

'How long will it be before you leave?'

'A couple of weeks.'

'Then you must come round and have drinks with us before you go.'

'That would be very nice.'

When Mrs Burke had gone, Morris tapped the door to his partner's consulting room and went in. Geoffrey Lloyd was pouring coffee.

'I heard your patient leaving,' he grunted. 'Thought you'd be ready for this.' He turned and handed the cup and saucer

19

to Morris. 'Another large-scale emergency was it?'

'Oh, the whole morning's been like that.' Morris sat on a leather easy chair by the window. 'I've had Mr Priors with a splinter under his thumb nail, Mrs Ingoldsby at death's door with a head cold, a lady complaining of severe heart pain on the wrong side of her chest and Mrs Burke with a ganglion.' He sipped his coffee. 'It's hell out here on the frontiers of medicine, isn't it? Dealing with the desperately sick, tackling one crisis-ridden soul after another . . .' He shook his head with overdone sadness.

'Come on now, Timothy.' Dr Lloyd sat on the window seat, smiling faintly. He was older than Morris, a short, well-padded man with sandy hair and skin that shone with health. 'They're our bread and butter, remember.'

'Yes,' Morris sighed. 'They've been mine for too long.' He drank some more coffee. 'I'll tell you something. I've been listening to myself lately. Listening to all the hollow responses I make, the oily little flatteries, the civilised snobberies that are second nature now. My whole style embarrasses me. I'm turning into the kind of man I can't stomach. And *they've* done it to me, all those neurotic, self-preoccupied, idle-rich patients of mine.'

'They're not all like that.'

'Most of them are,' Morris insisted. 'I can't remember when I last practised any real medicine. I haven't been face to face with a decent challenge in months.'

It was Dr Lloyd's opinion, though he never voiced it, that Morris had only begun talking this way because he had to keep convincing himself that going to Wales was a practical move. 'You'll soon be facing more challenges than you'll know what to do with, Tim.'

'Yes, and I'll thank God for that.'

'I think you'll have cause for regret,' Lloyd said. 'Deep regret. But you know my views in that direction.'

Morris did. They had argued many times about his resignation from the practice, until a point was reached where neither was prepared to say any more, simply because both points of view were too firmly rooted to be budged.

'Geoffrey, I know there are things I'll miss. Personalities I'll miss. Some of my patients are lovely people, it's not a fact I can deny. But taken over all, I see myself as a doctor who's abandoned medicine for the practice of mollycoddling. It's not a fact I'm prepared to live with any longer.'

'Do you see me in that light?'

'What light?'

'A licensed pamperer.'

Morris shook his head. 'I've told you before, I make no judgements where you're concerned.'

'None at all?'

'No. None.'

'But you're bound to . . .' Lloyd grinned suddenly to dispel the stiffness that was growing between them. 'Here we go again. Arguing to no point.' He stared at his partner with open affection. 'You can't blame me for believing you're deluding yourself. I mean, look at the picture squarely. You've been eight years here, firmly entrenched at the comfortable end of the profession, securing a solid, comfortable future for yourself. you could—'

'Please, Geoffrey, let's not go through it again. We'd agreed to differ, remember? Let it rest there.'

'Just hear me out, then I'll say no more on the topic. Ever.' Lloyd leaned forward, propping his elbows on his knees. 'You're not only going to get a terrible shock when you go out into the wilds and start roughing it, you'll find you're totally unsuited. You're too accustomed to the luxuries and the easy hours and all the conveniences of a West End practice. You won't be doing those new patients of yours any favours. You're not the man they need.'

'I'll make myself their man. I've got the tools, after all. There's my training, which I've been wasting for years, and my determination. I've no illusions about what I'm taking on, which is another asset. There'll be hurdles and a lot of serious problems at first. But you know my motto – problems are only opportunities with thorns on them.'

Dr Lloyd sat back, staring out of the window. 'Fine words,' he murmured. He wished, as he had often wished in the past

21

weeks, that he could see Morris's real motive. Lloyd was sure it had never been stated. All the arguments were too pat, too tidy, as if they were designed to obscure the fundamental truth.

'I've a call to make,' Morris said. He stood and drained his coffee cup. 'After that I'm sitting in on a lecture over at Guy's.'

Lloyd nodded. 'Compound respiratory ailments and their treatment – right?'

Morris laughed softly. 'Do you have a crystal ball tucked away in your desk, or what?'

'I've seen this month's programme of post-graduate lectures. You were bound to be attending that one, weren't you? The only sound that travels clearly across the Welsh valleys and hillsides, apart from the screeching of the wind, is the coughing and hacking of coal miners.'

Twenty minutes later Dr Morris stood on Chelsea Bridge, watching small boats bob on their moorings and listening to the city sounds beyond the quiet waterside. He had no call to make, as he had told Dr Lloyd, and his lecture session wasn't for hours yet. He had come down here to gaze across the grease-streaked waters of the Thames and to reinforce another layer of memory.

He had first met Lucinda Gregg on this bridge, on a windy afternoon in 1926. She had asked him, in her tinkling, breathless voice, if he knew of a houseboat called *Osprey*. He had never heard of it, nor of any of the other houseboats tethered along the river wall. But befriending Lucinda was so easy, and seemingly so appropriate on an otherwise pointless day, that he had gone with her to seek out the boat. After ten minutes they found it, and within another three minutes they were inside, clutching glasses of white wine in the cramped quarters while a small, carefree party took place around them.

That had been their best time together, Morris realised, that day when they discovered what they later called, rather misguidedly, their special harmony. While a handful of debutantes and their young men whooped, sang, cavorted

22

and giggled around them, making the boat bob alarmingly, Timothy and Lucinda agreed to meet again, soon, in surroundings where they could comfortably explore their attraction to one another.

The relationship foundered after fourteen months, after a love affair that had begun with intensity and then gradually thinned into sullen decline. The dying-off had been brought about by Lucinda's restlessness, and by Timothy's discomfort over their social differences and their opposing views on almost everything. What had united them, he later realised, had been no more than sexual novelty. There had been no harmony beyond the bedroom. They parted after an hour-long row which brought every buried resentment and displeasure screeching to the surface. They never saw each other again.

At the time of their parting Timothy had felt relief. Now, smelling the oil-tainted breeze and recalling that day they met, he felt a tug of sadness. There had been golden moments, and they were all he remembered now. They would form the glinting highlights of this skein of memory; the rest would be carefully set in shadow.

He turned up his coat collar and began walking towards the far end of the bridge. Gulls swooped for meagre pickings and somewhere round the bend of the river a horn sounded. Timothy thought of how the wind ruffled Lucinda's pale hair. He saw her climbing down on to the houseboat, laughing and holding tightly to his hand as the deck swayed. It was one more thin ply of remembrance, one of the many he was restoring, day by day, as the sad time of leaving drew nearer.

Less than a mile away Dr Lloyd stopped what he was writing, his pen hovering over a case card as he wondered, again, just why his partner was leaving the London he loved. He sighed and began writing again. Probably no one but Timothy himself would ever know why.

CHAPTER THREE

MEGAN picked up the envelope from behind the door as she greeted her dog, Scratch. She took off her wet cape and dropped it by the coat stand. It felt like a book in the envelope. The disheartened feeling she had brought in with her lifted a little, both at the sight of her pet and the comfortable heft of this gift. She tore open the envelope and tipped it up. Yes, a book, smelling brand new. Miss Williams's note said *I hope you enjoy it.*

It was called *Tarka the Otter*, written by a man called Henry Williamson. Miss Williams had mentioned it when they met on the street a couple of weeks before. She told Megan that she had read a good review of the novel in her daily newspaper and was thinking of ordering a copy. She had clearly ordered two. Megan fingered the spine, feeling her low spirits lift a shade higher still. The kindness of people, especially such instinctively generous people as Miss Williams, could be a tonic.

'We've got something new to read in bed,' Megan told Scratch. He was bounding around her ankles, wagging his tail and gazing up open-mouthed, panting his gladness to see her. 'She's terribly good to us, our Miss Williams, isn't she?' Megan bent and patted Scratch briskly, then put the book on the table. 'Let's get you something to drink, eh? Then I'll brew up something for myself.'

The cottage was small, well-aired and light. It had modest, comfortable furniture and more bookshelves than were usually to be found in the houses of that region, even the more opulent of them. The place had once belonged to a schoolteacher called Dylan Roderick. When he moved out, the Charity Committee which employed Megan had arranged for her to move in – another act of kindness engineered by Miss Williams, who headed the Committee.

'We'll send her a thank-you note when I've read the book,' Megan told the dog. At the sink she filled a bowl with fresh tapwater and put it in front of Scratch. She grinned at him fondly as he lapped it up. He was a brown terrier of no official breed, Megan's only close companion, and on occasion her confidant, too.

It was ten past three and raining. The dismal curtain of drizzle had been falling from low, hummocked clouds since early morning. Megan had seen one or two people snigger at her as she cycled past them in her voluminous home-made cape. They could go on tittering for all she cared. That circle of oilskin, with a head-hole cut in it and a stitched-on hood, kept her nice and dry. As she filled the kettle she stared out at the puddles in the yard. Some days it seemed the rain would never stop. It was the same when the sleet came. And the snow. She remembered somebody had written that the weather could have as much effect on the constitution as real blessings or misfortunes. Megan was sure that was true. The glowering days of autumn and winter around Pencwm were the last straw for a lot of people already saddled with too much hardship.

'Another rotten old day, Scratch.'

She turned to the hob and almost dropped the kettle with fright as something crashed against the front door.

'What in the name of God is that?'

Scratch was barking, droplets of water flying from his muzzle. The crash came again, then again, harder. The dog barked louder and began running around the room. It dawned on Megan that a human fist – barely human, by the force of it – was making all that noise.

She slammed the kettle on the hob and strode to the door. As she jerked it open a man's bulk stepped forward, nearly filling the frame.

'I want a word with you!' he shouted. His breath wafted beer and onions in Megan's face.

'You'll behave in a civilised manner or you'll be having a

25

word with the Constable, double quick!' She knew who he was, though she had never spoken to him before. He was Owen Clark, a big, brawling boozer of a man, wild-eyed and ape-featured. 'Kindly step back on to the path,' Megan snapped, 'and state your business in a respectful tone of voice.'

'Oh-ho.' Clark's mouth curled in a sneer but his eyes had turned uncertain. Probably no one had ever talked back at him like that, Megan thought. Certainly never a woman. 'It's respect you want, is it? I'd no idea I was talkin' to somebody special.'

'I want the respect due from a stranger to any woman – any man, for that matter!'

Clark's lips worked but he couldn't raise a retort. His fists, Megan knew, were his only tools of argument. She watched him take a couple of steps back, trying to call up his rage again, blinking as the rain streamed across his face and into his eyes.

'Well? Why have you come?' She believed she knew.

'My Rose,' he growled, putting his fists on his hips, since there was nothing else to do with them. 'I don't want you interferin'. There's nothin' the matter with her.'

'I haven't interfered, Mr Clark. I was sent for.'

'That's a damn bloody lie!'

'Don't you swear at me!'

'Nobody sent for you!' The strain of even simple dispute was pinkening his cheeks. In any other confrontation he would have been throwing punches by now. 'We stay on our own, me an' her. I know she didn't send for you.'

'I didn't say she sent the message.' Megan thought of Rose Clark. She was small, thin and dark-haired. She was four-teen, a girl with the face of a picture-book angel, except that her eyes showed no serenity.

'I want to know who put you up to stickin' your nose in.'

Megan stared at him, imagining him capable of almost any badness or wrongdoing. 'What is it I'm supposed to have stuck my nose into, Mr Clark?'

'Well you'd know that!' he blustered, his eyes wary now.

26

'And you don't?'

'All I know is, you been talkin' to my Rose, an'—'

'I can't imagine what you have to be annoyed about.' Megan moderated her voice deliberately. She delivered the voice of reason, with an edge of authority. 'It's not my place to do harm. People have nothing to fear from me. I'm in this job of mine to *help*.'

'Just keep away.' One hand came off Clark's hip, a balled warning that said, *I'm not above hitting a woman*. 'Hear what I say, now?'

'Yes, I hear you.' The rain had flattened his wiry hair, making him look even more neanderthal than usual. Megan considered her position, wondering how much risk there was if she followed her impulse. She decided he was sufficiently off-balance. She *hoped* he was. 'Mr Clark . . .' She took a step nearer him, feeling the rain strike the shoulder of her uniform dress. 'Would you have anything to hide, by any chance?'

For a terrible second it looked as if she had misjudged. Rage flared in the yellow-rimmed eyes and Clark's shoulders hunched forward. In that instant, feeling sure he would strike her, Megan knew she was right. The suspicion that had been pricking her mind since she saw Rose, the black hunch that had been growing since she looked closely at Owen Clark, was a certainty now. She read it in his response, in those awful eyes, in the set of the hairy jaw and in the scowling mouth that looked like a split, decaying, obscene fruit. Megan tensed herself, hearing Scratch begin to bark again at her heels. Clark brought up one fist sharply. Megan tried not to shut her eyes or shield her face.

But Clark didn't hit her. Instead he waved the fist in a tight eclipse under her chin. 'You're askin' for more trouble than you can cope with,' he snarled, wafting beer and onions again. 'Stay away, or else.'

Megan felt herself begin to shake as he strode away. Against every impulse of safety, almost without realizing she was doing it, she said, 'Mr Clark – listen.'

He stopped, his head turned but not facing her.

'See that nothing bad happens to Rose, or *you'll* be in more trouble than you could ever imagine.'

Clark's head drew back. He hawked gutturally and spat on the ground. As Megan turned back into the cottage she heard his boots crunch away on the gravel.

It took her ten minutes to stop shaking enough to make the tea. When she did she sat down by the fireplace with both hands around the cup and Scratch curled at her feet.

'Poor child,' she whispered at the grate.

The fear in the girl had been specific, the neighbour who spoke to Megan hadn't overstated a thing.

'Haunted looking she is, Nurse. Never goes further than the yard, but I see her now and again, through the slats, like. Just stands and stares at nothin'. There's somethin' terrible wrong. She's not been seen out since her mam died a year since – that's bad enough itself, isn't it? A young girl shut up with no company but her drunken layabout of a father. And her lookin' so frightened – I had to say somethin' to somebody about it . . .'

It was the fear of the imprisoned that Megan saw, the captive's near-certain knowledge that there was no escape, no remaining contact with the life outside. Megan had no right to enter a house where she wasn't invited, so she had interpreted the rule ambiguously and had spoken to Rose in the back yard. That had turned out to be an advantage, for it was harder for the girl to hide her despair in daylight.

'Yes, I've got friends. I go out with them a lot . . .'

The scarcely-used voice and light-starved skin said otherwise.

'I do the housework. That keeps me busy . . .'

The house's unclean breath was unmistakeable, even at a distance from the half-open back door. It was an untended place, a dank little prison where a despairing child spent her days in awful stillness.

'No, I've not been sick. I feel all right. Never been sick since I was a baby . . .'

Her pallor went beyond the colour of hunger. The tremor in the thin shoulders and hands was more than nervousness

28

at talking to a stranger. Those pained eyes, older than their setting, mirrored far more than fatigue. Megan had seen the total picture more than once before, in Liverpool when she was training. Looking at Rose her suspicion had been inevitable, it was a reaction to indelible experience. It hardened a trace as Rose turned and went back into the house, leaving Megan with the shadow of her misery.

The father's visit put urgency into the case. There was no saying what he might do now, especially if he fanned his new vexation with drink. Megan had planned to talk it over with Dr O'Casey the following day. Now she stood up, emptied her two-thirds full teacup into the sink and reached for her coat and cape.

'The woman had an almost . . .' O'Casey paused, searching for the apt word. ' . . . *serene* acceptance of her condition. I've seen a lot of women behave a lot of different ways when they knew they were slipping in the direction of the grave. But Mrs Clark – she was different. I got the feeling sometimes she looked on her death-sentence as something she deserved. But as a reward, not a punishment.'

It wasn't yet four o'clock, but it had turned so dark outside that the doctor had turned on the desk lamp in order to read the Clark family's case records. He looked up from Rose's mother's card and stared at Megan. His eyes threw back the light from the lamp at her in sharp glints. 'So there we have it. A woman who virtually welcomed the embrace of death, and a daughter who sounds, from your description, to have the burgeoning qualities of a replica.'

'More afraid of living than dying,' Megan said. 'Maybe that's a bit fanciful, but . . .'

'But we both know about Owen Clark, don't we? His wife lived in terror of the man.'

'I never met him face to face before today. But it didn't take long to size him up – and his reputation came before him, anyway.'

O'Casey put the case records in a squared bundle before

him. 'I've only attended young Rose a handful of times over the years. According to the record I've not seen her professionally for three years. So, to be fair and even-handed, even though I'm more than half-persuaded that your concern's well-founded—'

'You mean you're not going to do anything?'

O'Casey sighed. 'You're tendency to interrupt, my dear, could be construed as unprofessional. People in your profession mustn't jump guns.'

Megan glared at him. The generosity of her lips narrowed to impatience. 'It's what you're about to say, though, isn't it?'

The doctor nodded. 'But you shouldn't anticipate me.' He tapped the case cards. 'I have to say that there's no solid evidence on hand to justify me taking action.'

'What do I have to do to get some action, then?'

'Find me specific evidence that Rose Clark is being mistreated, or neglected, or both. Then I can have her removed from that squalid little house.'

Megan tutted. 'Surely there are *some* steps you can take?'

'No, there aren't.' O'Casey spread his hands, signifying his helplessness. 'I can't just go barging in there to see for myself. Besides, even if I did go to the house, what would I find? There are plenty of undernourished, listless-looking children around this place. That's not evidence of any wrongdoing on their parents' part.'

Megan chewed her lip for a moment. 'Doctor . . .' Her eyes darted uncertainly. 'I've told you my feeling is that Rose is at terrible risk—'

'You may be right, but a feeling is nothing I can act upon.'

'The truth is,' Megan went on, 'I think it's far worse than risk.'

O'Casey sat back, his face going into shadow. 'Worse?'

'Yes.'

He gazed at Megan patiently. 'Are you saying that what you told me earlier isn't the whole story?'

'I knew you'd respond the way you usually do when I get a feeling about something.' Megan brushed aside a wisp of dark hair and looked at the doctor squarely. 'You'd resist and argue. I didn't want to tell you anything you'd think was so far-fetched that you'd reject it out of hand . . .'

'I do trust your instincts, Megan.' He didn't often use her first name. 'But I also know you're impulsive. So I'm inclined to interrogate you, just to be sure that *you're* really sure.' He folded his hands across his waistcoat. 'Now tell me what it is you think I'll find far-fetched.'

'Well,' she began hesitantly, 'you remember the game young doctors often play in clinics – nurses do it too – you see a patient come in and you try to make a diagnosis, just from their appearance?'

O'Casey nodded. 'Interpretation from landmarks. Not too reliable, is it?'

'But you get better with experience. I can spot certain conditions straight away. So can you. I spotted something about Rose Clark. It's not something I've seen hundreds of times, not even dozens, but it's a picture so . . .' She hesitated.

'Profound?'

'Yes. So profound it has been printed deeply in me.' She paused, reluctant to go on.

'I won't start laughing at you,' O'Casey said gently. 'Tell me what it is you suspect.'

'It's more than suspicion. I'm sure. Rose is being maltreated.' She paused. 'Sexually.'

The doctor was gazing steadily, reading the intensity in Megan's expression. 'By whom?'

'Her father.'

O'Casey closed his eyes and didn't open them again for several seconds. 'You say you're convinced?'

'As convinced as I've ever been of anything.'

'I can't see how you can arrive at that conclusion after only a minute or so with the girl. I mean you didn't even examine her, did you?'

'I've told you.' Megan frowned at the desk, making little creases at the corners of her eyes as she scanned her inner certainty. 'It's not a picture I could mistake. It has a special, terrible quality, Doctor.'

It was a minute before either of them spoke. Finally

O'Casey said, 'I've seen it too, I have to admit. The look. Especially in good, modest girls, schooled to know the rules of morality and to live by them.' He sighed softly. 'I've never made a diagnosis purely on the basis of the way they looked though, Megan. I learned to read the picture after the crime had been uncovered, when I had to examine the poor creatures.'

'So you're still saying you can do nothing?'

O'Casey leaned forward again, his face coming back into the fan of light above the desk. 'I'm strongly inclined to believe you're right – especially since I know a thing or two about Owen Clark's horrendous past.'

'So why don't you—'

'We're still talking about a feeling, Megan. There's no evidence. No policeman, no Child Welfare Committee is going to pay a blind bit of notice to me. Not on the basis of what I have. You're own Committee would be just as unresponsive, you're bound to know that.'

Megan stood suddenly, tightening her coat belt. 'If we need proof before anybody'll do anything, I'll damned well get it.' Her round, strong face was flushed as she squared her cap and strode to the door.

'Now don't go doing anything rash,' O'Casey warned, rising. 'You've been in enough scrapes with this and that authority since you came here. Don't go destroying your career just because of . . .' He tailed off, seeing her glare.

'Just because of a child who's been through purgatory and probably still goes through it regularly? Is that what you were going to say, Doctor?' Megan opened the door sharply. 'Or were you going to tell me I shouldn't destroy my career for some worthless kid who wouldn't amount to much anyway?'

The doctor came round the desk and stood before her. 'I was going to say, don't risk everything just because of an instinct. Think it over calmly. There might be a flaw in your intuition.'

'And if I find there isn't?'

'Well . . .' Dr O'Casey shrugged. 'I don't know . . .' He looked at her helplessly. 'Cases like this aren't easy.'

32

'I'll make it easy,' Megan said firmly.

As she turned to go the doctor touched her arm. Almost apologetically he said, 'You'll remember Doctor Morris is joining us tomorrow? I'm expecting him at my house tonight. I'd like you to come in first thing after morning surgery and be introduced.'

Megan had forgotten. 'Of course,' she snapped. 'I'll be there at half-past eleven.'

Striding out into the rain, struggling with her billowing cape, she wondered desperately what she was going to do to get her proof. Alongside that dilemma was the miserable prospect of meeting Dr La-di-da Morris. It felt like having a toothache challenging a far greater pain.

Megan jammed her head through the hole in the stiff material, flipped up the hood, then grasped the handlebars of her bicycle and pushed it along the path. All things could be overcome, she reminded herself. All obstacles, all adversity. She only wished she could find proof of that, too.

CHAPTER FOUR

GLADYS and Wyn Brewster were good friends of Megan Roberts. Six months after she had come to Pencwm, the Brewsters, shrewd observers of life in the region, decided something should be done to counteract the hostility being directed at the District Nurse by a large proportion of the population. So Wyn prompted his sister Gladys to approach Megan and invite her round to tea. From that day on their meetings had been regular and cordial, and a firm friendship had been cemented.

Gladys was forty, a maiden lady of rather more than comfortable proportions. She had glossy black hair, a mouth that smiled more readily than it scowled and eyes that seemed to dance when she talked. Gladys had never married, simply because she had never wanted to. Even if she had, there were no prospects around Pencwm, or none she would have considered.

'I'm no snob,' she had told Megan when they first met, 'I'm in no position to be one, but the men round here – oh, such pigs they can be. They've no interest in anything, except drink and the other thing. I could never see myself narrowing my life to match that paltry pattern.'

Gladys drew her fulfilment from looking after Wyn, which she had done since they were orphaned twenty years before. Wyn was thirty-eight and a bachelor, though not from any special desire to stay single. Life had always seemed to be flying by, and the opportunities to pursue the girls had to be weighed against the opportunities for self-improvement. He was a miner, but he was also Secretary of the Pencwm Widows' and Orphans' Aid Association, a pigeon fancier, and at the local school and various Miners' Institutes he

34

lectured regularly on his lifelong passion, the Crusades.

'Not a likely enthusiasm for an agnostic,' he freely admitted, 'but then they weren't all that Christlike, the Crusaders.'

Gladys and Wyn lived in an end-of-terrace house on Vaughan Road, a curve of single-storey buildings on the north-east ridge of Pencwm. Their back windows overlooked the deep, rocky slope that led down to the cluster of wizened trees known as Colwen Wood. A tiny window on the gable looked directly at a trio of unsightly tips Wyn had christened The Three Sisters, in the manner of Englishmen who frequently gave romantic names to the uglier of their landmarks.

On the breezy, watery-sunlit morning of the day she was to meet Dr O'Casey's locum, Megan took the steep path past Colwen Wood to the Brewsters' house and leaned her bicycle against the wall of their tiny front garden.

Gladys had the door open before Megan reached it. 'I saw you out the back, love. You must be exhausted, pedalling all that way up. What made you take the hard way?'

Megan followed Gladys along the short lobby, unbuttoning her coat as she went. 'I had to look in on the Rawlings' baby,' she said, pausing by the living room door to catch her breath. 'I didn't know I was coming to see you. It was an impulse, so I took the shortest road up from the Rawlings' house.'

Wyn looked up from the book on the chenille-covered table as Megan came into the living room behind Gladys. His eyebrows went up. 'Well now, here's a pleasant surprise.' He stood and pulled out a chair from the end of the table. It was always their custom to sit round the table when Megan called.

'I'll get the kettle on,' Gladys said, and bustled off to the tiny kitchen at the back.

Megan sat down and took a deep, grateful breath of the lavender-scented air. This room was one of her favourites, a tidy, low-ceilinged little haven, the abode of gentle, intelligent people who treated her as one of their own. She smiled

35

at Wyn, not missing the particular warmth of his own smile.

'I don't think we've seen you this early in the day before,' he said, sitting down again. 'It's a pleasure at any time, mind you.' His big soft eyes lingered on Megan for a second before he closed his book and pushed it away. 'Gladys was just sayin', last night when we were havin' our cocoa, what a pity it is you're so busy, or we'd have you round to tea more often.'

Again Megan observed the tight pleasure of his smile. The Crusades were not Wyn's only passion. His special feeling for her was never given voice, though, and Megan was grateful for that. She never wanted to hurt him with a rejection.

'I'm not here strictly for social reasons, Wyn. I've got a problem and I thought maybe you could help me.'

'Well if I can, you know I will. What is it?'

'Can we wait till Gladys comes back? It's something I want to talk to you both about.' Megan pointed to the book on the table. 'What are you reading?'

'It's a manual of Chinese cultural pastimes.'

'Oh! I'm impressed.'

'I picked it up for a tanner when I was in Cardiff for the welfare administration conference.' He patted the faded cover of the thick book. 'It's fascinatin' stuff, Megan. You'd like it.'

'Given up on the Crusades then, have you?'

Wyn wrinkled his forehead. 'No, nothing like that.' His coal-scarred hands came together in a tent. 'A person's got to avoid obsession, hasn't he? You have to take a broad view or you turn into a bit of an oddity.' He grinned, his teeth showing large and strong beneath the fringe of his thick moustache. 'You know what they say – the world's leading expert on one subject is the world's leading numbskull on just about everything else.' He nodded at the book. 'I've been widenin' my horizons for an hour or more now. When you came in I was learnin' how to tell folks' fortunes from the number of strokes in their names.'

Megan frowned. 'I don't think I'd want to know about that.'

'There's a chapter on how to judge people by their habitual

36

actions – but I think I can do that already.' Wyn untented his fingers and tapped the book again. 'Every pastime or game they have, it seems, revolves around human character or personality, an' yet they seem sort of – well, characterless themselves. The one or two I've seen anyway.'

In Wyn's intelligence and enthusiasm Megan detected echoes of Alun. She noted now that even the movements of his head – dipping for emphasis, rising stiff-necked when he expressed surprise – had an unsettling similarity to her dead fiancé's. She pushed the observation aside swiftly as memories began to poke through the wall she had put around them.

'Other cultures, other lands,' Wyn was saying, 'Oh, Megan, I'd love to travel. Books can only tell you so much.'

'But we'd be poor lost souls without them.' It was resoundingly true in Megan's own case. Books had liberated her. Wisdom from the inert printed page had put life into areas of her mind that would otherwise have lain dormant forever. 'I'd like to travel some day too, mind you. It's like what you said about avoiding the narrow view of life. Staying in one place too long can diminish a person.'

Wyn nodded slowly, thought over what she said, then nodded again. 'Greece. Now there's a place I'd like to go. I'd love to sail all the way down to Rhodes an' walk round the Crusader castle at Lindos.'

Greece, Megan thought. Dr O'Casey was going to Greece. And a new man would be in his place, for one whole endless year, at least. She was grateful that Gladys came back from the kitchen at that moment, bringing the distracting clank and rattle of cups and saucers.

'Tea'll be ready in a couple of minutes,' Gladys said. She put the scones on the table and sat down opposite Megan. 'Got a break in your rounds, have you?'

'She's got a problem,' Wyn said. 'Wants us to help.'

Gladys immediately folded her hands in her lap and looked attentively at Megan.

'It's about the Clarks, down on Trevor Street . . .'

'Owen the Bear,' Wyn grunted.

37

'And that poor daughter of his.' Gladys shook her head. 'The lamb can't have much of a life.'

'It's her I'm concerned about,' Megan said. 'Do you know if anybody else ever goes near their house, Gladys?' Among other talents, Gladys had an aptitude for collecting and storing seemingly trivial information about the inhabitants' movements which, in oblique ways, often proved valuable to Megan. 'Do other men go there, for instance?'

Gladys pursed her lips for a moment, thinking. 'No,' she said at last. 'I'm pretty sure he's never let anyone else over that doorstep. Not even in the days when his wife was alive.' She sniffed. 'Like as not he doesn't want other folk seein' what a shambles it is.'

'And the girl, Rose – does she ever go out?'

'That's the real scandal, if you ask me. The girl's not been seen for a year or more, not out on the street, anyway.'

Which confirmed what the neighbour had said. The night before, Megan had calmed down enough to take Dr O'Casey's advice. She had sat and thought things over carefully. Her conclusion, finally, had been that her instinct was accurate. What she had to do, though, was be sure she was pointing her finger at the real culprit. Now she was sure, thoroughly sure.

'Is it somethin' you can talk about, Megan?' Wyn asked.

'Not in any detail, no.'

Gladys stood up. 'I'll bring the tea.' She waddled off back to the kitchen.

Megan leaaned her elbows on the table and looked at Wyn. 'What kind of hours is Owen Clark working this week?'

'You mean what hours is he doin' as little as he can get away with? Well, let me see now.' Wyn stroked his nose, another of Alun's characteristics. 'I saw him goin' in the pub when I was goin' up the pit yesterday. He don't work nights, because of the girl bein' on her own. So he must be on early turn.' He thought for a moment then said, 'Yes, it's bound to be early turn. I mean, he might have been takin' a day off sick, like he does a lot, but he had coal muck on him when I saw him.' Wyn wrinkled his nose. 'He doesn't even have a wash after work, most days, except Saturday.'

'So Rose would be on her own until half-past one or two o'clock every day this week?'

Wyn nodded.

'Good. I just wanted to be sure.'

'That's if Owen goes to work, of course.'

Megan sighed. 'There's always that, of course.'

'Look,' Wyn said, 'I'm not pryin', but it's obvious you want to catch the girl on her own. An' in my opinion, if you go knockin' at that door an' Owen's in, you'll collect a double earful of abuse, at the very least. But there's a way to tell if he's in or not.'

'What's that?'

Wyn winked. 'He always leaves his stinkin' pit boots in the back yard when he's at home. It's his only concession to hygiene, as far as I know.'

Gladys came back with the blue and white china teapot. She poured three cups and brought the milk and sugar from the sideboard. When she sat down again she was looking at Megan, frowning.

Megan sipped her tea and smacked her lips. 'That's grand, Gladys. Just what I needed.'

'If you go near the Clarks' house,' Gladys said, her voice sounding grave, 'just you be careful. He's a bad man, that Owen. I wouldn't put anything past him.'

'Neither would I,' Megan said, and drank some more tea.

Surgery was over by twenty-past eleven. Mrs Colville, who came in every day to clean, had made tea for the doctors and this morning she had added a plate of her home-baked scones – 'To make the new doctor welcome, like,' she explained demurely, offering Timothy Morris a winsome, half-toothless smile before she hurried out.

'Don't touch the scones,' Dr O'Casey warned as the door closed. 'I had a colonic obstruction for days after eating one.' He took a sheet of foolscap paper from the desk drawer and wrapped the scones carefully in it. 'I'll smuggle them home and put them in my dustbin where they can't do any harm.'

39

Timothy poured the tea while O'Casey tidied the desk and sat down in his old swivel chair. 'Well then,' he said, absently rubbing the stiff side of his chest, 'what do you think?'

Timothy turned with the cups and put one in front of Dr O'Casey. 'I'm a little shaken. I was prepared for the sight of some hardship, but . . .' He waved a hand at the waiting room door.

'Not much call for the niceties of medicine here,' O'Casey said. 'I've often thought, since I've been in Pencwm, that the subtle diseases only ever attack well-fed, comfortably housed people. Poor people are immune.'

'The cruder ailments certainly seem to be to the fore.'

That morning, Timothy had stood by as Dr O'Casey attended to a woman with suppurating Paget's disease of the nipple, two men with massive groin hernias, a child whose head was covered with ringworm, a girl with a Colle's fracture that had been left unattended for three days, plus two cases of pneumoconiosis, one of pleurisy, a progressive tongue cancer, three unconfirmed cases of tuberculosis and a horrendous case of late-stage syphilis in a sixty-year-old man.

'And that was only morning surgery, remember. Plenty of men with really serious chest and joint conditions don't come in until their shift at the pit's over. And a lot of women can't get here until their husbands are home to look after the children. You'll witness some sad and tragic cases tonight.'

'I've seen more genuinely ill people in the last couple of hours,' Timothy murmured, 'than I have in the past three years.'

What struck him most forcibly had been the stoicism of the patients. Nobody complained, some even seemed apologetic, as if their bodies had shamed them by getting sick.

'Poverty and ignorance are your greatest enemies in Pencwm,' O'Casey said. 'Prejudice too, of course. Disease thrives as much around stupidity and bigotry as it does in a half-starved household.' O'Casey twiddled his teacup thoughtfully. 'There are people in this town who actually believe that illness is sent as a punishment and must be borne. That's quite a God they worship.' He looked up at Timothy, who was leaning by the window, looking along the road outside. 'That's enough philosophy for one morning though, eh?' He smiled as Timothy came and sat opposite him. 'What do you think they thought of you, then? Did any impressions come across.'

Timothy shrugged. 'Hard to tell. I felt one or two needles of distrust, not much else.'

'Inevitable,' O'Casey said flatly. 'I did feel, though, that a few of them were flattered when you asked questions, instead of barking orders and rebukes at them the way I'm inclined to do.'

Timothy was about to say something when the door was tapped and Megan put her head round the side. She looked solemn.

'Ah, come in, Megan, come in.' O'Casey got up and ushered her across the room. 'Doctor Morris, this is our District Nurse, Megan Roberts.'

As Timothy got to his feet he saw distrust again, even hostility. The nurse eyed him swiftly, up and down and up again, taking in his smart pinstriped suit, his crisp white shirt and dark silk tie. Her perusal of his face was slower as she touched the hand he offered. He felt she was trying, without much hope, to find something about him she liked.

'It's a pleasure to meet you, Nurse Roberts.'

She muttered something, then turned sharply to Dr O'Casey. In her hand she had a metal instrument case, which she held out to him.

'What's this?' O'Casey frowned at her, both from curiosity and as a rebuke for her abruptness to Dr Morris.

'Look at it,' she said.

Timothy came and stood beside them as O'Casey took off the lid.

'Good God!' Timothy breathed.

O'Casey stared for a long moment, then looked at Megan. 'Where did you find this?'

'At the Clark house. Half an hour ago.'

'You went there? You went in?'

41

'How else was I to get any kind of proof?' She looked down into the box. 'I didn't expect anything like this, mind you. Nothing as conclusive . . .'

It had been dark inside the Clark house, the dirty curtains half-drawn across sooty windows. The gloom of the place matched its odour, a stale blend of old cooking smells, damp brickwork and human sweat. Megan stood for a moment after she let herself in, blinking as her eyes grew accustomed to the faint light. She went from the scullery through to the living room, softly calling the girl's name.

Rose appeared in her bare feet, from a room across the narrow hallway. 'My da says I'm not to talk to you.'

Megan smiled. 'I only want to be sure you're all right, Rose.'

The girl pulled her torn cardigan closer about her and stared sullenly at the floor.

'Is that your room?'

Rose nodded.

'Can I see it?'

'No.' Rose's voice had a crack of apprehension as she looked up at Megan. 'Da doesn't want nobody in the house. You better go.'

Megan touched the girl's shoulder, feeling scarcely any flesh under the rough wool. 'Just a little look, my love. I want to see you've got a proper warm bed to sleep in.' She had no idea what she wanted to see. All she could do was acquaint herself with the living conditions and try to make the girl talk to her. 'I promise I won't harm anything.'

Megan crossed the hall and pushed open the bedroom door. It was even darker in there. The odour was stronger, a keener mingling of unwholesome scents. There was a narrow unmade bed, a spindly chair, a tiny dresser with chipped varnish and a bundle of clothes lying in a corner. As Megan stood looking Rose came in and stood beside her. Her fingers were working nervously.

'Please, miss, you should go . . .'

'In a minute, Rose. Don't fret.' Megan went to the dresser. There was a solitary picture book lying there. 'Do you have other books?'

'No. Just that one.'

'So you don't spend your time reading?'

Rose shook her head.

'What do you do all day, love?'

Rose shrugged.

'Are there things you want to do?'

Deep uneasiness showed as Rose struggled with the question. She obviously didn't want Megan to stay in the room.

'Wouldn't you like to go out more and get the fresh air about you? Play with friends you knew at school, maybe?' It was dawning on Megan that she would get nowhere by simply questioning the girl. Answers about her bleak life would only ever emerge, they couldn't be drawn from her.

'Miss, you better go, please . . .'

Megan sighed. 'Very well, Rose.' As she turned she saw something under the edge of the bed. It looked like an old sweet tin. She stooped to pick it up and Rose darted forward.

'No! Don't!' She looked terrified.

'I'm only looking,' Megan breathed, trying to calm the child. 'What's wrong? Why can't I touch it? It's such a pretty old box, with those pictures painted on it . . .'

'Don't!' Rose tried to snatch the tin away as Megan handled it. 'It's mine!' The change in her was astonishing. 'Give me it!' She was agitated, breathing in gulps, trying to pull the box from Megan's hands.

'I won't hurt it, love.' Megan knew she should give Rose the box, but her curiosity was swelling. That box, she was sure, was the reason why the girl hadn't wanted her to come into the room. 'What's in it? Is it something valuable?'

'*Give* me it!' Rose tugged with her small bony fingers. 'It's mine!' The lid sprang off suddenly and she jumped back, her hands flying to her mouth.

Megan looked down. For a moment she didn't know what she was seeing. Then she realised. 'Dear God . . .' Its appearance suggested it had been in the box a long time. Natural decay had shrivelled it and changed its colour. But to Megan's experienced eye it was unmistakably a human foetus.

She looked at the pathetic child, whimpering now into her

43

cupped hands. 'Don't be frightened, Rose. Everything's going to be all right.'

To Dr O'Casey, Timothy Morris said, 'It looks as if it's partially mummified.'

O'Casey nodded. 'Otherwise, we'd be without our evidence.' He closed the box and looked at Megan. 'Where is the girl now?'

'With Gladys Brewster. She'll be well looked after there, until proper arrangements can be made.' She shook her head at the box 'She's been hanging on to that for three months. It's the only thing she's trusted, I think. Didn't want to part with it.'

'She must have been very ill,' Dr O'Casey said.

'We'll never know what she went through.' Megan shuddered, picturing the child alone in that awful house, huddled in the dark with her fear and her pain.

'That man's a monster,' O'Casey grunted.

'From the look on Constable Davis's face when I reported this, I'd say Owen Clark will have a few lumps on him before his cell door bangs shut.'

'This is an incredible case,' Dr Morris said. 'I've never come across anything like it.'

Megan looked at him coldly. 'Well, you wouldn't have, would you?'

That one remark said a good deal to Timothy Morris. He had been rebuked for his background and for his inappropriate presence in Pencwm. He had also been handed a clear warning about the quality of his forthcoming professional relationship with Nurse Roberts.

He smiled at Megan. 'I'll obviously have to rely on you to put me in the picture on a few things,' he said.

'On a lot of things, I shouldn't doubt.' Megan buttoned her coat and moved to the door. 'I'll try to see you don't get too many shocks at once, Doctor.' She opened the door. 'I have to go now, I'm behind with my rounds. I'll drop by later, Doctor O'Casey.'

Her parting look, Timothy thought, told him one more thing. She didn't think he would last here.

44

CHAPTER FIVE

AUSTIN Pym looked out across the hills from the north side of Colwen Wood, his hand resting for support on the wind-curved trunk of a tree. He coughed softly as his gaze ran along a ridge that merged darkly with the skyline, then looked off to the left, seeing the top of his house in a smoky cluster of other roofs down on Carr Road.

'God's good green earth,' he muttered, and spat.

Austin hated Pencwm. He believed he had hated it for most of his forty-six years. He could certainly remember disliking the drab colours and the mean, twisting contours of the place when he was a boy. The steep rises and windy flat stretches had always irked him, too, especially in his courting days when he could never go for a decent walk, like they did in the romantic stories his mother had concocted round the fireside. Austin and his lady friends had never seemed to get more than ten yards at a time without having to change their pace and angle, which did nothing for his attempts to appear cool and in command. There were no shady glades where a couple could linger, no soft, undulating slopes where they might recline and indulge whatever passion they might have for each other.

He believed he had rested long enough. Turning, he made his way to the path at the bottom end of the wood. He walked with slow, steady steps, breathing carefully, brooding. It had played on his mind a lot lately, that hatred he felt for the place where he was born. It wasn't as if he had ever known anything better. He would have thought a man could grow to some kind of acceptance; there was surely compensation in the simple familiarity of his surroundings. But no. Austin felt trapped and always had. It wasn't just a feeling, either. He

45

definitely was trapped. Sometimes in the night he would wake suddenly, frightened by Pencwm.

It took him twenty minutes to get down to the surgery. In the waiting room he sat staring at his knuckles while the other patients muffled their coughs, shifted their feet and sighed at the walls opposite. It was another twenty minutes before he got in to see the doctor.

Timothy Morris looked up and saw a tall, thin man with reddish, singed-looking hair. He had weary eyes and a tight set to his mouth. As he sat down he nodded curtly.

'It's Mr Pym,' Timothy said, looking at the card. 'Is that right?'

Austin nodded.

'My name's Morris. I'll be standing in for Doctor O'Casey for a while.'

Austin nodded again. 'I heard about you.'

Timothy scanned the lines of high-looped handwriting on the card before him. It had been three weeks since Dr O'Casey left, and in that time Timothy had seen perhaps twenty case cards outlining near-identical patterns of declining health.

'Well then, Mr Pym – how can I help you?'

'I was wondering if you'd let me have some more of the bottle I got last time.' He spoke with the solemnity of a preacher, though his voice had little strength. 'It helped a bit.'

Timothy looked at the card again. Austin had suffered attacks of bronchitis since childhood. As time passed, the weakened lungs became vulnerable to more chronic and disabling conditions. There had been pneumonia when he was twenty, which gave rise later to three distinct types of inflammation, which were further irritated by coal dust. By now, there were clear signs that a long-standing congestion of Austin's lungs was being joined by the miner's curse, pneumoconiosis, which in its turn could transform itself into pulmonary tuberculosis.

'You've had a lot of trouble with your chest,' Timothy said, aware of the understatement. 'Have you noticed any changes lately? I mean, have you felt better, or worse?'

46

'About the same, these past two or three years.'

The card showed that Austin hadn't consulted Dr O'Casey for over two years. 'And why do you think you need some more medicine? You seem to have managed without it for a while.'

'To buck me up, like.'

'So you've not been feeling so good lately.'

'Well . . .' Austin examined his hands. 'There's times I get winded easily, when I'm walking or lifting things, or anything like that.'

Timothy nodded. 'I see you had to take a lighter job at the pit when you were forty-four. Because you were getting breathless all the time. The way you've been feeling lately – is it the same as before?'

After a pause Austin said, 'I suppose it is.'

So he was going into another stage of decline, Timothy thought. Before, it was the effort of his work at the coalface that kept depriving him of breath. Now, even though he did a light job, the attacks were recurring. His lungs were barely coping with the air needed for normal activity.

'Take off your jacket and shirt, Mr Pym. I want to have a listen.'

The stethoscope told a grimmer story than Timothy had expected. Deep rattling sounds in the lungs had been predictable, but not the irregular rhythm of the heart. When Timothy readjusted the angle of the stethoscope he heard a slapping sound, unmistakably the damaged tongue of a valve as it sluggishly tried to cope with the volume of blood.

Timothy stood back, unhooking the stethoscope. 'You can put on your clothes again,' he said. He sat down and waited until Austin had buttoned up his work jacket, then he said, 'How many hours a day do you work?'

'Ten,' Austin said, then added, 'when I'm working.'

'Have you been off, then?'

'Four days.' Austin tapped his chest. 'It's been bad, I'll admit that.'

The stoicism again, Timothy thought. 'You should have come to see me sooner, you know.'

Austin looked at him, visibly trying to analyse the last remark. 'Is it bad then, what I've got?'

'It's never been good. There's a fair amount of fluid building up in your lungs now. The best medicine is rest.'

'But I've got to work, see . . .'

'I know.'

Timothy had learned fast. The British Coal Strike had begun in May of the previous year and hadn't ended until late November. The long struggle had weakened the miners' position and hardened the line taken by the owners. A man with a job knew he was lucky, and the sick among them didn't care to advertise their disability. A miner could always be replaced if he didn't pull his weight, and the benefits for the ill and unemployed amounted to a pittance.

'Mr Pym, I'll put the position to you plainly. If you don't have a long rest you won't be working much longer. You won't be able to.'

In the Kensington practice, that state of affairs would have presented no obstacle to a patient. He would thank Timothy for his advice and go off to the South of France without delay. In this place, the facts presented the most taxing dilemma imaginable, and Timothy knew it. He watched Austin Pym try to cope with what he had said. Inevitably, when Austin spoke it was with the stoic's voice.

'Then I'll just have to work till I drop, Doctor.'

'A month would make a difference.'

Austin stared. 'I couldn't take a month. I'd get laid off.'

Timothy thought about it. A month *might* make a difference. If the heart valve had begun to fail recently, then a regime of rest, plus concentrated therapy for the lung and heart conditions might bring about a reversal, however temporary. On the other hand a month, two months, even six or seven might make no difference at all. But something had to be tried. Good medicine was about preventing disease and fighting back when it threatened to prevail. A passive doctor was no doctor at all.

'What if I had a word with your pit manager?'

Austin blinked, alarmed. 'Oh no, don't go doing that. If he

48

thinks I'm not up to my job that'll be the tin hat on it, for sure.'

'No, no.' Timothy shook his head slowly. 'I wouldn't lead him to think that, Mr Pym. The fact is, you truly aren't up to your job at present. But we can do something about that if we can snatch a month of time.'

Austin still looked uneasy. 'You don't know what he's like, that Mr Lowther. Real heartless bugger – sorry—' He rebuked his lips with a tap of his fingers. 'What I mean is, he wouldn't take no pity on the likes of me. Most of the time he'd sooner do us a hurt than not.' He tugged his ear anxiously. 'Maybe if I just had another touch of the bottle I had before, Doctor . . .'

Timothy spread his hands on the deask. 'That was a simple tonic. A gallon of the stuff wouldn't make any differ-ence to you. You need more than that. Now listen.' He leaned forward, adopting a trace of Dr O'Casey's gritty manner. 'I can guarantee I won't lose you your job. More than that, I can get a special allowance for you and your family while you're off work, so you won't go without. Just take my word for that and let's get on with the business of making you better.' As Austin began to protest again Timothy put up a hand to silence him. 'If I don't talk to your manager, you'll soon be without a job anyway.'

Austin considered the equation. As he sat there gazing at his hands again, Timothy watched the troubled face. He pictured the years of fighting simply to survive. He read the lines of premature age, like troughed scars gained from one dispiriting battle after another. Finally Austin looked up.

'Well?'

'If you reckon you can get me the time . . .'

'It's a promise.'

'In that case . . .' Austin nodded, three sharp movements of his head. 'Thank you very much, Doctor.'

Timothy felt a flutter of emotion as he reached out and grasped the hand Austin had shyly offered him.

Half an hour later Megan was cycling out of Carr Road when she saw Mr Pym turning the corner. He had always

49

struck her as a sullen man, but today he waved and smiled. Megan steered to the edge of the road and stopped. They exchanged hellos and Megan asked how Mrs Pym was keeping. She had attended the woman a number of times the year before, to dress her varicose ulcer.

'She's champion now,' Austin said. 'The leg hardly hurts her a bit.'

'And how about yourself?'

He pointed at his chest. 'Still wheezing away. I've only just been to see the new doctor about it, in fact.'

Megan's smile became fixed. 'Give you something, did he?'

'More than I went for.' Austin explained, between pauses for breath, how Dr Morris had promised to get him time off, and a special sick allowance into the bargain. 'And he's going to give me some special medicine for my chest.'

'That's grand,' Megan said.

'He's a fine man, Nurse – and him an Englishman, too.'

'He's Welsh, Mr Pym. Born in Newport.'

Austin looked surprised. 'You'd never know it, would you? Him talking so posh and all.'

And acting so aloof, Megan thought, *and* lording it over the practice and interfering in her work.

'How long's he stopping here?' Austin asked.

'I'm not too sure,' Megan said. After three weeks of him, she felt another month might be too much for her to withstand. She pointed along the road, towards the parish school. 'I'll have to get going, Mr Pym. No rest for the wicked, eh?'

'Oh, I'm sure wicked's not a word they'll chip into your headstone, Nurse. I'm sure it'll be a long, long time before they put anything on it at all.' He waved to her again as she leaned across the handlebars and pedalled away.

Walking down the cobbles to his little house, Austin sank back into the feeling of quiet buoyancy that had held him since he left the surgery. In all his life, he had never known anyone in authority take any trouble over him, or ever try to help him much. Old Dr O'Casey hadn't been all that bad, he supposed – but that Dr Morris had been a proper tonic, just

50

by his talking and being concerned, and by telling Austin what he was going to do for him.

By his front door he turned and looked up the windy stretch towards Colwen Wood. Scabby old bit of countryside, he thought. Scabby old town altogether. But for the moment, at any rate, Austin found it strangely sufferable.

'So this'll be the last Thursday you do your examinations here,' Miss Pryce said. She blinked delicately behind her big round spectacles as she watched Megan unpack bottles of lotion from her bag. 'I must say Fridays will suit us a great deal better.'

Megan gave her a bewildered look. 'But I'm not changing my days. Who told you I was?'

'Well . . .' Miss Pryce glanced at her office window, as if someone might be there to back her up. 'The doctor agreed it would be better, so I imagined he'd have talked to you about it by now.'

Megan took a slow, deep breath. Her patience was always at a stretch when she was near this woman. Miss Pryce was head teacher at the parish school. Although she took classes regularly, her interest in teaching ran a very poor second to her fetish with administration. After listening to the coals fizzle in the grate for a moment, and after taking a tighter hold on her composure, Megan said, 'You approached Doctor Morris on this matter, did you?'

'Yes.'

'You didn't think it worthwhile to speak to me, since I'm the one directly concerned?'

'Nurse Roberts.' The name was pronounced like the reading of a small indictment. 'It's my view that your fortnightly visits to this school, in order to examine the children for evidence of head lice, scabies and other disorders, is a disruption of our work programme. It can never be anything else, but if you were to visit last thing on a Friday it would be a minimal disruption.'

Megan's hold on her aplomb began to weaken.

51

'I know the examinations are necessary, indeed vital,' Miss Pryce went on, 'but they could be fitted into our pattern much more smoothly than they are at present.'

Megan clasped her hands in front of her. 'I didn't ask for an exposition on the running of the school,' she snapped. 'I asked you why you didn't come directly to me with your suggestion. You see me often enough.'

'It is my understanding, Nurse, that your immediate senior in matters of procedure is the local doctor.'

Megan nodded sharply. 'It was the doctor who told me I should make my own arrangements where school visits are concerned,' Megan pointed out, hating the way Miss Pryce pursed her mouth at her. 'And that's what I did. I worked out a timetable that used my time efficiently – and it suited your predecessor, too.'

'My views on the running of this school,' Miss Pryce intoned, 'are at variance with many of my predecessor's views.' She cleared her throat delicately. 'In much the same way, I daresay, Doctor Morris's opinions on how much free-will you exercise are probably at variance with *his* predecessor's views.'

Megan glared at her. 'What was that mouthful supposed to mean?'

Miss Pryce's eyes widened with owlish affront. She tucked in her chin defensively, causing the baggy skin of her neck to apron over her high collar. 'I will not be spoken to like that in my own office.'

'Let's go out on the playground, then.' Megan's arm shot out, one finger pointing in the general direction of the surgery. 'Are you saying you went behind my back to Doctor Morris, because you had some idea he'd be easier to persuade than myself or Doctor O'Casey?'

'I find your attitude and manner insulting, Nurse Roberts.' Miss Pryce turned away with a rustle of black cotton and stumped behind the security of her desk. Like the bullish Owen Clark, she had little skill at defending herself, because like Clark, she had rarely needed to. Her primary and perhaps only weapon was pedagogic authority. It worked with all the children and most of the adults in Pencwm. She had long suspected it had no effect on Megan Roberts. 'I'll await Doctor Morris's judgement on the matter. I don't wish to discuss it any further.'

'Well I *do* wish to discuss it further.' Megan snapped her bag shut and filled her coat pockets with the bottles of lotion. She never took the black bag into the classroom because it frightened some of the children. At the door she stopped and pointed again in the direction of the surgery. 'I'll discuss it with Doctor Morris – who, incidentally, is not Doctor O'Casey's successor. He's only standing in, so if you're counting on a new broom to sweep things the way you want them, you're wasting your time.'

Late that evening, almost an hour to the minute after he had seen his last patient, Timothy Morris rose from the desk and unlocked the poison cabinet. He took out a half-flask of brandy from the cluster of ribbed blue and green bottles and poured a measure into a medicine glass. He had swallowed half of it when Megan tapped the surgery door and came in.

'Good evening, Nurse.' Timothy held up the glass. 'Care to join me?'

'I'll join you,' Megan said, 'but I can do without the drink.'

'So can I,' Timothy said, locking the cabinet. 'But I choose not to.' He smiled at her. 'I don't know what kind of day you've had, but mine's been rather wearing.' He took his glass to the armchair by the window and sat down, indicating that Megan should take the chair opposite. 'Your button boots must be throbbing, if you've been on your feet until now.'

Megan remained stiffly by the instrument cabinet beside the door. 'I want to talk to you about the school visits.'

'Talk away,' Timothy said with a generous sweep of his hand.

'I understand Miss Pryce came to see you about having the visiting day altered.'

Timothy nodded, his features open and cordial as always. 'I spoke to her on Monday, I believe.' he studied Megan's frown. 'Is there a problem?'

'She never mentioned to me that she wanted the day changed.'

Now Timothy frowned. 'Nurse, something's been troubling me . . .'

'What?'

'Your accent. It's Welsh, I know, but not South Welsh. Not strictly North Welsh, either.'

Megan's jaw ground sideways, once. 'I'm not here to talk about the way I speak, Doctor. I wanted to know why I wasn't consulted about the change of day for the school visits.'

Timothy sipped his brandy and sighed, eyeing the liquid as he swirled it before his eyes. 'I was going to talk to you about it tomorrow. That's when you've always had the little progress and problems chats, isn't it? Or have I been getting it wrong?'

'What were you intending to tell me tomorrow?'

'That Miss Pryce had spoken to me about having the visits shifted to Friday. Beyond that, I'd no plans to *tell* you anything. I thought we might discuss it after that.' He pointed at the other chair again. 'I do wish you'd sit down. You look so uncomfortable standing over there.'

Megan's jaw moved sideways again, a plain indicator of her annoyance. She came forward and sat down, clasping her hands in her lap. 'I'd have thought you'd tell Miss Pryce she could discuss any changes with me, directly.'

Timothy nodded again in the slow, congenial way that infuriated Megan. 'She could, certainly, and I did mention it. But she was at liberty to speak to me instead.'

'And why do you think she did that?'

'I think you daunt her a little,' Timothy said candidly. 'Doctor O'Casey didn't put her too much at her ease, either. It's not anything that Miss Pryce said openly, you understand, I guessed it from her manner and one or two little asides she dropped.'

The room became quiet for a moment, the only sound coming from the mantel clock. Megan stared across at the lamplit desk as her threads of displeasure tangled, instead of twining into a strong rope of indignation, as they should. It

54

was Dr Morris's manner that did it. He was so smoothly wise, so self-contained all the time. He had smilingly deflected every spurt of exasperation she had aimed at him in the past three weeks.

Finally Megan spoke. 'Miss Pryce didn't like talking to Doctor O'Casey,' she said, 'because he wouldn't be bullied by an old biddie who thinks she's automatically to be obeyed. She doesn't talk much to me either. For the same reason.'

Timothy spread his hands. 'There you are then. I was right.' he sipped more brandy, his elbow propped easily on the arm of the chair. 'So, what *is* the problem?'

'Your compliance,' Megan said. 'Miss Pryce came away from here with the impression you would make the change she asked for.'

Timothy's smile played across her nerves again like a wire brush. 'She went away with the wrong impression, then. She explained about last thing Friday being a more convenient arrangement. I had to admit it sounded like a better idea. I said I would speak to you about it. I gave her no assurance, of any kind.' He drained his glass and put it on the floor beside the chair, stirring another of Megan's resentments – the way he made himself so much at ease in Dr O'Casey's consulting rooms. Probably in his bed, too. 'While you're here,' Timothy went on, 'we might as well talk about the Friday thing. What do you think of Miss Pryce's idea?'

Megan was at sea. She had come in here ready to have it out with this complacent outsider, and now he had steered her completely off-course. She felt as if something had been cunningly stolen from her.

'Well?' Timothy prompted.

'If she had asked *me*,' Megan said, 'I'd probably have been inclined to agree with her argument and make changes in my timetable to accomodate her. But . . .'

'But you resent the fact she asked me, instcad of you.'

God, that smile! Megan thought. 'Yes,' she snapped, 'as a matter of fact I do.'

'Because you don't want me interfering in your territory, or diminishing it.' Timothy sat back and crossed his legs. The lamplight winked on his polished boot as he swung one foot slowly back and forth. 'Am I correct?'

'Yes, Doctor, you're correct.' Megan got to her feet, unable to sit there a second longer and be bathed in his poised self-possession. At least now she was physically looking down on him. 'I've a hard enough job as it is, without having to put up with—'

'Interference,' Timothy interrupted, but gently. 'I try not to do that, Nurse. I know what a good job you do. I've Doctor O'Casey's assurance on that point, and I've the evidence of my own eyes. There's no cause for me to interfere, so I don't do it.'

She stared. How could he say that? A dozen times, more than a dozen, he had thwarted her, obstructed her, *harassed* her to the point where she lay awake some nights, seething.

Timothy stood up, cancelling her meagre advantage. 'I haven't been unaware,' he said, holding her eyes steadily, 'that something in my – ah – approach to my job here displeases you. I believe, too, that you've regarded my curiosity and my occasional suggestions as nothing less than meddling.' He smiled, but this time it was different. It was almost self-deprecating. 'I don't have Doctor O'Casey's knowledge of this territory, this kind of medicine. So I have to be curious, I have to nose about. I'm trying to learn, you see. And if I inflict my own opinions from time to time I'm not criticising – I'm observing from my present standpoint, which I've no doubt will change as I learn more.'

Speechless, marooned on silence by his damnable candour and charm, Megan watched Timothy go to the desk and flip shut the case folder lying under the lamp. He yawned as he faced her again. 'I'm very tired, Megan. Do you mind if we discuss the school visits tomorrow, after all?'

She mumbled that she didn't mind at all. Timothy saw her to the door and bade her good night.

Flustered, bewildered, Megan strode up the road to her cottage with her own heel-clicks for company. How could it happen? she wondered. How could she carry so much indignation right up to its target and find there was no target

56

at all? The frustration churned in her like a breaker with no rocks to explode against.

At her front door, with the iron key poised against the lock, she stiffened suddenly, picturing his face in the lamplight as he yawned, then hearing his voice. He had called her Megan. He had used her first name. She rammed the key into the lock, turned it sharply and pushed open the door. 'The damned cheek of the man!' she hissed as Scratch scampered towards her.

CHAPTER SIX

ON a bitingly cold morning in the second week of November Timothy Morris drove his car to the top of Cardower Road and got out, shivering. A thick frost had rimed the gables and put a sparkling cap along walls and gate posts. It had been like that for two days. Timothy had never known anything like it, not even in his Welsh boyhood. He hadn't been out of the surgery for more than ten minutes but already his fingers were turning blue. He rubbed his hands briskly together, hoisted his bag from the front passenger seat and crossed to the Prentices' house. He knocked on the door sharply and waited, wondering if there was any circulation at all in his prickling ears.

Mrs Prentice took a long time to open the door. When she did, she only pulled it wide enough to let her face show at the edge.

'Good morning,' Timothy said brightly. 'I'm Doctor Morris – Doctor O'Casey's replacement, for the time being.' His smile didn't appear to be penetrating the woman's uneasiness. 'You'll be Mrs Prentice?'

'That's right,' she said huskily. There was scuffling movement behind her in the hallway.

'It's about young Gareth I've called.' Timothy took a step closer. 'Do you mind if I have a look at him?'

Mrs Prentice pushed the door forward a fraction. 'He's – he's sleeping just now. I don't want to go disturbing him, like . . .'

Timothy heard the back door bang shut. 'Ah,' he said, frowning. 'Well, perhaps I'll call back later, then.'

Mrs Prentice nodded and closed the door without another word. Timothy turned, dropping his bag on the car's running

58

board and moved sharply to the end of the building. A big, dishevelled woman, a gipsy by the look of her, was moving rapidly away from the direction of the Prentices' back yard.

As Timothy drove back through the town he saw Megan's bicycle outside her house. He parked the car and got out, stiffening himself to encounter more frost on the other side of the little green door.

Megan answered his knock after only a moment, throwing the door wide and simultaneously telling Scratch to stop barking. She looked surprised to see the doctor. 'Oh,' she said. 'I thought you were the postman. He's been getting later these mornings.'

'I was passing and thought it might be an idea to have a word with you.'

Megan stood back, letting him in. The dog began scampering round his ankles as he stepped to the fireplace and held out his hands to the glowing coals. 'You have a nice, cosy place here,' he told Megan, looking round admiringly.

'Yes, it's comfortable.' She pointed to the tray on the table. 'Cup of tea? I'm having one while I can. Heavy morning so far, heavier day ahead.'

'No, no, you carry on.' Timothy stooped, patted the dog, then nodded to the bookshelves. 'Looks more like an academic's room than a nurse's,' he murmured. 'That's quite a library.'

'I've been collecting books since I was a little girl. Hoarding's maybe a better word. I can never bring myself to part with any.' Megan picked up the teapot and looked at him. 'Are you sure you won't have a cup? There's plenty.'

'Well . . .' Timothy shrugged and smiled. 'If it's going begging I'll have one. I could use something to warm my blood.'

'I can't guarantee it'll do that,' Megan said, pouring. 'But it'll create the illusion, at least.' She filled two cups and put down the pot. 'Help yourself to sugar and milk.'

'Thanks.' Gauging her tone, Timothy decided she must be getting used to him. There was still a trace of formality, but this morning the chill was missing from her voice.

59

He spooned a little sugar into his cup and added a trace of milk, then crossed to the bookshelves, taking the cup and saucer with him.

'You seem to have wide-ranging interests.'

There were poets – Keats, Shelley, Burns and Swinburne – thick novels, a battered Mrs Beeton, volumes on Botany and gardening, numerous dictionaries and almanacks, a row of bound nursing journals and two whole shelves of medical text books.

'I was encouraged to be curious,' Megan said. 'The curiosity led to a lot of different enthusiasms, over the years.'

'Ah, look – one of my favourites.' Timothy took down a volume of Aesop's fables bound in wine-red leather. 'I've had a copy since I was twelve.' He flipped carefully through the pages. 'Do you remember the moral of *The Hare With Many Friends?*'

'I don't think so,' Megan said.

' "He that has many friends, has no friends",' Timothy quoted from memory.

It's the summing-up of *The Jackass in Office* I remember best,' Megan said casually. ' "Fools take to themselves the respect that is given to their office." ' I've always found that to be pretty apt.'

Timothy smiled as he returned the book to the shelf. He wasn't always sure when Megan was directing barbs at him; she could look so disarmingly innocent. He sipped his tea, sighing gently as the liquid warmed its way past his throat. 'The reason I dropped in was to talk about Gareth Prentice.'

'What about him?'

Timothy watched Megan's face stiffen. 'I wasn't interfering. Gareth's name is on the list Doctor O'casey left.' The list contained the names of patients who, because of the changeable nature of their illness, had to be seen occasionally by the doctor, even though their routine treatment was the responsibility of the District Nurse. 'I called at the house a few minutes ago, but his mother wasn't keen to let me see the lad.'

'Did you go in, anyway?'

'No. There was something fishy afoot. I could hear someone shuffling about behind Mrs Prentice. As soon as the back door shut I took my leave and managed to catch sight of the visitor. It was a female – she looked tinkerish.'

Megan frowned. 'A big ragbag of a woman? Matted-string hair and clothes like a bundle of flags?'

'Yes, the description fits . . .'

'Nesta Mogg!'

'Doctor O'Casey mentioned her. She's some kind of folk-physician, isn't she?'

'She's a monster!'

Timothy nodded, catching the point from Megan's growl and her loathing expression. 'Are we to presume she's been treating the Prentice boy, then?'

'Oh, no doubt about it,' Megan said. 'He's been trying to persuade his mother to call her in for ages.'

'So this Nesta Mogg – she must have a good reputation among people here. I know of one or two herbal practitioners in London with a fiercely loyal following—'

'Nesta isn't any kind of *practitioner*, herbal or otherwise. She's a criminal. She's used people's fear and superstition to get herself a reputation as a healer. She likes to have power over the folk round here – there's no concern for their welfare.'

'She sounds more like a witch than anything else,' Timothy observed.

'That's how I usually describe her to people. But a lot of them won't listen.' Megan slapped her cup down in the saucer. 'God, if they would only see reason . . .'

'Reason and faith don't mingle,' Timothy said. 'And faith is most often attracted to mystery.'

Megan stared at him. 'Mystery? There's nothing myster-ious about Nesta Mogg's remedies. She makes a poultice with chicken droppings and boiled urine. I *swear* she does. She pricks boils with a dirty pin and rubs in a salve made with river mud and crushed laburnum leaves.'

'Good heavens!'

'That's not the half of it,' Megan grunted. She began to

61

pace in front of the fire, the agitation making her eyes flash. 'Her treatment for ringworm is to slap on a jelly made of rotten apples, sour milk and black treacle. Shingles are no problem for Nesta, either – cow dung, spread on a leather thong and hung round the poor, ignorant sufferer's waist. And do you know what she does for eye infections? She chews sage leaves to a pulp and spits it in the patient's eyes.'

Timothy shook his head. 'I hate to imagine what she's been giving Gareth Prentice.'

'Oh, when it comes to treating weak blood, as she calls it, there's a whole battery of horrors in Nesta's armoury.'

'Should I go back there, right now, and put my foot down? Or do you want to see to the matter?' Nowadays Timothy was careful to give Megan her place at every opportunity. 'I'd be quite happy to read a medical riot act, if you're too busy.'

'No,' Megan said, 'I'll see to it.'

'Well be careful. If the witch is around she might put a spell on you.'

'That'll be nothing to the curse I'll put on her, one of these days,' Megan promised.

As she turned and looked pointedly at the clock Timothy drank up his tea and thanked her. 'Let me know what happens. I'm interested in the case for a special reason, apart from the voodoo feature.' He patted Scratch again and went to the door. 'I read a paper on persistent nutritional deficiencies a while ago. Some bells began ringing when I looked over Gareth Prentice's case notes.'

'Doctor O'Casey researched the condition pretty exhaustively,' Megan said, defensively.

'It was an American paper I read.' Timothy opened the door. 'They've got some interesting new approaches. And a change of therapy wouldn't hurt, since what we've been pumping Gareth doesn't appear to have had much effect.'

Megan couldn't let that go unanswered. She followed Timothy outside, drawing the door close behind her to keep in the heat. 'The boy would start to improve if he'd take his medicine regularly – and if he'd keep himself out of the clutches of Nesta Mogg.'

62

Timothy nodded. 'I daresay that's true. But there's a touch of witchery in *not* trying new remedies, isn't there, Megan? The difference between our kind of medicine and the kind practised by Nesta and her ilk, is that we move forward. Or we should.' He smiled. 'I'll probably see you later at the surgery, eh?'

Megan was frowning again as she went back indoors. The way she saw it, Dr Morris had decided to interfere in a case even though he claimed he was doing nothing of the kind. Dr O'Casey had worked long and hard to diagnose Gareth Prentice's trouble and come up with a regime of therapy. Megan herself had monitored the case for weeks. All that effort, and Dr Morris thought he could simply walk in and take over. Apart from that, she felt there was a criticism of Dr O'Casey in what Dr Morris had said. Wasn't he implying, pretty clearly, that the older doctor hadn't done all he could for his patient?

She checked over her thinking as she tidied away the tea things. She was sure she was being rational and not neurotic, as Morris would undoubtedly read it. She was on the brink of deciding she'd say more on the matter when there was a knock on the door.

Megan opened it and saw Timothy Morris standing on the step.

'Sorry,' he said, 'your tales of witchcraft drove the other thing from my mind – the other thing I wanted to mention.'

'And what's that?' Megan asked stiffly.

'I saw two children in surgery last night and another two this morning.' Timothy took a slip of paper from his pocket and handed it to Megan. 'Those are the names and addresses. I want you to keep a careful eye on them over the next two days – visits in the morning and afternoon, if you can manage it. And watch all the other young children on your rounds, too.'

'Watch them for what, exactly?'

Timothy sighed. 'I hope I'm wrong, but if I'm not, then those youngsters are coming down with whooping cough. We could be facing an epidemic.'

Megan didn't remember him leaving again. She stood in the centre of the room, staring at the fireplace.

'Dear God,' she breathed.

Over the years she had hardened herself to withstand anything that confronted her in the often hideous business of dealing with human suffering. Almost anything. Now she felt her hands begin to tremble as a buried portion of the past was resurrected with cruel, unbearable clarity.

Rose Clark sat in the high backed chair with its dark, shiny wooden handles, watching Gladys Brewster polish and dust the already spotless room. On the table lay the book Megan had given Rose a month ago, and which had rarely been out of her sight since.

'Now remember, won't you,' Gladys said, her arm pumping as her duster put an extra sheen across the mantelpiece, 'there's nothing to be frightened of. Megan's taken care of everything – and when Megan's looking after somebody, they come to no harm at all. Just the opposite.'

Rose nodded and tightened the grip of her fingers on each other. She wore a new blue dress with a pale lilac sash and a lilac ribbon in her hair. In the time since she had been taken from her father's house the darkness had gone from around her eyes. Her skin was clearer and had lost its pallor. The lady who brought her to the Brewsters' house that afternoon said Rose had been enjoying her stay at the Church Home, and had put on weight.

'Mind you,' she added confidentially to Gladys, 'she talked about this house a good deal, and about you and your brother. It's as if she had been here for a long time.'

Rose had spent only five days with the Brewsters, but her leaving had been a wrench strong enough to put tears even in Wyn's eyes. Indeed Wyn had been more affected than Gladys by the girl's presence. They knew nothing of what Rose had gone through, only that she had suffered a great deal. Gladys responded in practical ways, seeing to it that the girl ate well, took plenty of fresh air and had ample to occupy her and keep her from brooding. To Wyn, young Rose was something precious. She was obviously intelligent and had an elfin daintiness about her; in combination, her untapped mental resources and physical grace were what Wyn called the epitome of youthful promise.

'She has it in her to go far, Gladys,' he'd said, sitting by the fire on the second night Rose spent with them. The child had gone to bed after an hour spent listening to Wyn tell her stories about the Knights Templar.

'And what makes you think that?' Gladys had demanded. 'The poor lamb couldn't get a word in sideways.'

'It was all there in the way she listened,' Wyn said. 'Did you see her eyes? She was picturing things, seeing them vividly, building up a store of wonderment and curiosity.'

Privately Gladys believed that her brother had simply been bowled over by a charming child, made all the more appealing because she had been the victim of cruelty. Wyn's capacity for pitying underdogs was vast, and he rarely had the opportunity for indulging it to the extent he had with Rose.

On the day Rose left for the Church Home in West Glamorgan Wyn took himself off up into the hills for the entire afternoon. When he came back he had the look of the bereaved on him. Gladys had made no effort to console him, because she didn't believe in wasting energy. Wyn came round in his own time; in the past week, knowing that Rose was coming back, he had energetically put together a box of books for her, taking some from his own collection, buying others from a shop twenty miles away.

'She'll only be with us for a day or so,' Gladys had warned him. 'Don't go thinking she's settling in for an education.'

'She'll leave here with the makings of an education,' Wyn assured his sister.

'There's more to an education than knowing all about the Crusades,' Gladys pointed out, having read the spines of the books in the box.

Now, as Gladys looked round the living room and decided it would be a cunning speck of dust, indeed, that could have escaped her latest onslaught, Rose cleared her throat and asked when Uncle Wyn would be home.

'Soon, pet. And Megan shouldn't be long, either.'

Gladys had no clear idea what was planned for Rose. All she knew was that Megan had been making plans for the girl's future with someone in North Wales. Seven days ago she had announced that Rose would be going to live near a place called Drynfor, and asked Gladys if she would mind looking after the girl until someone came to take her to her new home.

Wyn came back ten minutes before teatime. He had wanted to be there when Rose arrived, but a meeting of the Pencwm Widows' and Orphans' Aid Association had required his presence that afternoon. As he came into the living room he was already beaming, his hands outstretched to Rose.

'How are you, my petal? My, but you're lookin' fit! They been feedin' you bully beef an' potatoes, eh?'

Rose was clearly delighted to see Wyn. She rested her cheek on the rough material of his coat as he closed his arms briefly around her shoulders.

'It was nice there,' she said, stepping back so Wyn could look at her again.

'Make plenty of pals, did you?'

Rose nodded, self-consciously patting her ribbon. 'I slept in a room with four other girls. They've made me promise to write.'

Wyn sat down, nodding. 'It's terrible important, that, keepin' in touch with your friends. Has anybody told you about this new place you're goin'?'

'Not very much.' Rose frowned. 'It's quite far away, I think.'

'Listen, love,' Gladys called from the kitchen, where she was preparing tea. 'Nowhere's far away when you're close to people that want you.'

Wyn nodded again, glad of his sister's talent for issuing apt remarks at the right moment. 'I can't tell you much about the place myself – but Megan'll tell us all about it when she gets here. He stood up again sharply, realising he was still wearing his overcoat. As he slipped it off he nodded to the cardboard box by his chair. 'That's for you.'

Rose glanced at the box, then at Wyn, her eyes asking permission to look inside.

'On you go,' Wyn said, grinning. He watched, his features softening to a warm smile as the delicate little head bowed over the box and examined the books. When she looked up again she was smiling, too.

'It's all those things you told me about . . .'

'And a lot more.'

As Rose drew her fingers across the books she frowned again. 'Will they let me take them with me – to the new place, I mean?'

'Oh, they're bound to, love. Can't see Megan Roberts lettin' you go somewhere they don't allow books.'

Rose was still on her knees looking through the books when Megan arrived. Blushing with renewed pleasure, the girl showed Megan what Wyn had given her.

'That takes me back,' Megan said. She remembered, more than twenty years before, standing in the midst of open parcels of books, the gifts that had widened her mind and beckoned her into the world. 'Makes my present to you look a bit meagre,' she murmured, glancing at the story book lying on the table.

'I've read it three times,' Rose told her, assuring Megan the book was special to her.

During tea Rose was encouraged to talk about her time in the Church Home. As she told them about the friends she'd made, the supervisor there and the other staff, Megan reflected on the change. In its way it was miraculous, but probably only to Megan, who was making the widest comparison of anyone at that table. She had seen and spoken to Rose when she still lived in the stifling hell enforced by Owen Clark. She had carried the aura of a child who had been damned – Megan could think of it no other way. Now, talking animatedly, smiling and using her hands like lively birds, Rose was the incarnation of happy, untroubled childhood.

67

When the meal was over they sat round the fireside, huddled like a family as Megan explained what she had been doing on Rose's behalf during the past month.

'I knew you would like the Church Home,' she told Rose. 'I've had dealings with them before. But I didn't think it was enough, simply finding you a place to live. Your opportunities in life would have been badly limited – do you understand what I mean?' Rose nodded as Megan thought, *not as limited as they might have been.* 'You need an upbringing that fits you for as full a life as possible. The Church Home couldn't give you that. It's an orphanage and shelter, but not really much more.' She smiled at Rose. 'I decided you deserved more.'

'That she does,' Wyn said. He was sitting back in his chair, arms folded, regarding Rose with the eyes of the proudest uncle.

The moment put another pang of recollection through Megan. One Christmas when she was thirteen and about to go into domestic service, she sat by the fire like this with her family. Wyn's eyes now had the same look as her father's had all those years ago – adoring, with a trace of regret, a fore-echo of loss. Rose reminded Megan of herself at that time, setting her nerve to cross a threshold into a world she didn't know.

'So where's Rose going to?' Gladys prompted, breaking Megan's small reverie.

'To the place I went when I left school.' She saw Wyn lean forward. Gladys, too, looked a trace more alert. She had never spoken to them about her childhood or any other time prior to her training years in Liverpool. She had no doubt they must be curious, but they would never pry. 'It's a house, a beautiful house, two miles south of Drynfor, the slate-mining town where I was born. The house and the estate it stands on are owned by Mrs Pughe-Morgan. I went there as a junior kitchen maid in 1906.'

'Posh kind of name,' Wyn grunted disapprovingly. 'Pughe-Morgan. Very top-drawer.'

'Oh, she is,' Megan said. 'She's also one of the kindest and most intelligent women I've ever met. She gave me my education, Wyn. She taught me to educate *myself*, and she supported me with her enthusiasm every inch of the way.' Wyn looked chided. 'As a matter of fact, I'd never have entered nursing if she hadn't pushed me.' Megan looked at Rose again. 'She's agreed to take you into her service. You'll be working and you'll be paid a wage. But better than that, you'll be part of the family – and it's a grand family, I can tell you.'

For the following ten minutes Megan painted the picture of the life Rose would have in the Pughe-Morgan household. She told her about the old housekeeper, Mrs Foskett, and the delightful gardeners, Jenkin and Griffiths. She talked about the beautiful room Rose would have, the duties she would share with the cook and the other maids. Reminiscences tumbled forth as Megan turned her past into Rose's future. There had been and there would be days filled with hard work and no shortage of laughter.

'The brightest gem of all is Mrs Pughe-Morgan herself, though. She'll shelter you, train you and guide you to your right place in the world, Rose. She won't let you take any other path.'

The girl, though clearly and understandably nervous of what lay ahead, went to bed that night with a glow af anticipation and a promise that she'd never sleep, however hard she tried.

Megan's mood shifted as soon as Rose had left them. The brief sojourn to the past was over. She was back to the present and its aching realities. 'I'll have to be getting back,' she told Gladys and Wyn. 'Lots to do tomorrow.'

Wyn coaxed her to have a glass of port, but Megan declined firmly. She got her coat and as she buttoned it she explained again, that an emissary of Mrs Pughe-Morgan – probably some member of one or other of her charitable committees – would come for Rose some time during the morning.

'Everything's been attended to,' she told Gladys. 'She'll have a hot supper waiting for her and new clothes hanging in her room. I'll try to get round to see her off, but I can't promise. If I don't appear, tell her I'll write soon.'

At the door Wyn said, 'It's marvellous what you've done for the girl, Megan. You've really put yourself out.'

'Well,' Megan said quietly, 'A touch of heaven's no more than she deserves. She's had enough traffic with hell, God knows.' She thanked the Brewsters once again for tea and for looking after Rose, then left them waving on the front step, knowing they would stay there until she was round the corner and out of sight.

On the way down dark, cold streets towards her own house, she silently thanked Gwendolyn Pughe-Morgan for taking yet another young life into her capable, shaping hands. Without that quality of care, Megan knew well, she herself would never have survived. All afternoon she had been assailed with dark, once-buried memories of a time when she had been almost mad with grief. Mrs Pughe-Morgan had pulled her out of that maelstrom; Megan seriously doubted anyone else could have done it.

At her front door she fumbled out her key, sighing at the prospect of the morning. From what she had seen earlier that day, Dr Morris could be right about those children. Tomorrow she would be surer.

'And what if it is an epidemic?' she asked herself, staring up at the pale moon. What if she had to confront *that*? Mrs Pughe-Morgan wouldn't be on hand to point her in the direction of sanity this time.

CHAPTER SEVEN

NESTA Mogg came out on the east side of Colwen Wood, stooping under the weight of the sack she carried on her shoulder. She walked to the grassy margin where the ground rose towards the back of Vaughan Road and put down the sack. Panting softly she braced her hands on her hips and stretched. In spite of the freezing wind there was sweat on her brow and cheeks; she had been digging out roots with her bare fingers for over an hour, tearing at frost-hardened clods of earth to uncover the raw materials of her craft.

Nesta was not old, but she bore no physical traces of youth. Her weather-bronzed face was broad and heavy-featured, like a man's, and the tangle of dark hair only half-concealed a steep, sloping forehead. Her ears protruded nearly two inches from her head and occasionally peeped through her oily curls. When she walked, her lumpish body moved with a rolling action that was aggravated by her bowed calves, the legacy of childhood rickets. People had been calling her 'Old Nesta' for more years than she could remember. Her own estimate of her age, which she kept to herself, was somewhere between thirty-four and thirty-seven. Her birth was not recorded anywhere, and even if it had been, the record would have meant nothing to her, for Nesta couldn't read.

She bent and flipped back the top of the sack, examining the contents. It was a meagre, mud-caked haul, but for winter it was about as good as she could expect. Usually she kept an adequate supply of herbs and roots at her shack down on Powys Cleft, but this year she had been in great demand. People had been coming down with more ailments and in greater numbers than she had ever known. Consequently her summer- and winter-gathered supplies were low. The

71

season for the worst chest afflictions was closing in, there would be rheumatic complaints, too, and in the cold damp months the children produced a crop of sicknesses that always put a heavy strain on Nesta's resources, however large her stocks.

She straightened, gave her back another stretch, then drew her multi-layered, dull-orange shawl about her. Before she had the sack off the ground a voice pierced the air.

'You! Nesta Mogg! I want to talk to you!'

She spun, scowling, and saw the District Nurse coming at her down the slope from Vaughan Road. Nesta narrowed her eyes, hating the sight of that uniform coat, the badge at the woman's throat and the smug set of the hat. The whole ensemble, down to the button boots, represented what Nesta hated most – the official healing woman, the snobby bitch with a mouthful of big words and a hospital smell off her.

Nesta propped her hands at her waist as Megan stepped up to her. 'And what can I be doin' for you, *Nurse?*' She invested Megan's title with all the disdain she could marshal. 'Lookin' a bit hot an' bothered, you are.'

'What have you been feeding Gareth Prentice?' Megan demanded.

'That's for me to know.'

'Lark's droppings and vinegar, something nourishing like that? Or was it one of your cleverer concoctions – like fish scales and nettles, or rat's-blood jelly?'

Nesta let out a growl, as she always did when her craft was mocked. 'He's had a wholesome meal-porridge with basil and fennel root, if you must know. Better for him than that muck you gave him. All it did was make the lad spew.'

'Do you even have any idea what's wrong with Gareth?'

'I know what's up with him, don't you worry on that score.' Nesta wiped a fleck of spittle from her lip. 'You're the one's in the dark, not me. What you've been doin' is pokin' that rubbish into him an' waitin' for nature to make him better. I know all about the way you try to make poor folks believe you know what you're doin'—'

72

'Shut your ignorant mouth and *listen!*'

'I don't have to!'

Nesta snatched up her sack. Megan, eyes blazing, shot out her arm and knocked the sack to the ground. It landed on its side and half the contents spilled out. Nesta took a step back, startled.

'I'll see the Constable about this!'

'If anyone's seeing the Constable it'll be *me!*' Megan promised. 'I ought to have you charged with attempted poisoning. Have you seen the state Gareth's in?'

'He's on the mend.' Nesta was scooping the dirt-clotted roots back into the sack. 'My remedy's what's best for him.'

'On the mend?' Megan was glaring at Nesta's stooping figure as if she might hit her next. 'He's been vomiting and having stomach cramps since last night – since half an hour after you fed him that last bowl of filth. He's so weak he can't get out of his bed. You call that mending, do you?'

'It's the medicine doin' its work,' Nesta said haughtily, rising from the sack and brushing her hair from her eyes. 'The badness is bein' drove out of his body.'

Megan looked at her, exasperated, beseeching harsh justice from thin air. 'So. When my medicine makes the boy sick it's because it's bad for him. When yours does, it's because it's good for him. What blistering logic! Who can win with the likes of you, eh?'

'It's not given to the likes of *you* to understand my ways with healin'.' Nesta had her hands on her hips again. Her lips were drawn back, showing discoloured, uneven teeth. 'You come lordin' it into this town an' think you know everythin', because you've got the fancy clothes an' the gobstopper voice an' a little badge to say you're book-taught on healin'. Truth is you know damn all.'

'And where did you learn your meritorious skills?' Megan demanded shrilly.

'The healin's been in my family for generations! My mam passed the secrets down to me just like her mam did with her!'

'Secrets? *Secrets?*' Megan's anger came to a sudden boil.

73

'You stand there, a misbegotten, pig-ignorant lump of unwashed human debris and call your witchcraft *secrets?*' She stepped very close to Nesta, close enough to smell her, then raised a stiff, warning finger. 'If you take any of your squalid poisons near another patient of mine, ever again, I'll personally make you eat the stuff yourself and stand by while you choke on it. Do you understand that?'

'I'll go where I'm asked to go,' Nesta said sullenly. 'I was here before you, anyroad. My people have been here always. There's them that don't want you pokin' your nose in – most folk in Pencwm'd sooner have me do their healin' than have you interferin'.' She snatched up her sack. 'Folk have a right to get what they want.'

'After they've learned what's good for them and what isn't.' Megan wagged her finger again. 'Just remember what I've told you.'

'And you remember somethin',' Nesta grunted darkly, turning away. 'There's them that's been sorry they tangled with me.'

'Just standing close can be pretty risky,' Megan murmured, unable to keep from scratching herself as Nesta walked away.

Timothy sat forward in the swivel chair behind the desk and adjusted the lamp over the case cards fanned out before him. It was after nine and the wind was beginning to howl through the elders outside the surgery. That day three of the older patients had said it would be snowing by morning. There was a soft pattering on the window that suggested it had started already.

'Hurry up, Megan.' According to the clock she was ten minutes late. Weariness was clouding Timothy's brain. He had been making case notes for two hours and now he suddenly felt useless. The writing of the notes was the last practical move he could make in the cases concerned. Beyond watching and hoping, there was no useful course of action open to him.

He heard Megan in the waiting room and called to her to

74

come in. The glistening flakes on the shoulders of her coat confirmed his suspicion about the snow.

'Blessed crystals, winter's purest jewels,' he said.

'Another quotation?' Megan asked, her voice on the near edge of irritation. She unbuttoned the coat and shook it, making droplets fly like pale sparks. 'If this keeps up, I won't be able to use my bike.' She sat opposite Timothy and spread her hands on her knees. 'I've just been back to see the Thomas baby,' she said. 'It's croup she's got, no doubt about it. But the others . . .' She frowned at the desk.

'I've thirteen here,' Timothy said, waving a hand at the case cards. 'All confirmed. Whooping cough.'

They exchanged helpless looks.

'Nine are at the catarrhal stage,' Timothy went on, as if talking about the cases might somehow open a line of treatment. 'The other four are spasmodic. I'd say at least three are in foreseeable danger, malnourished, ill-housed . . .'

'I've enough camphorated tincture of opium to see us through,' Megan said.

'For all the good it is,' Timothy observed, 'it wouldn't be any disaster if you ran out.'

'It's something,' Megan insisted.

'Yes, you're right. We should clutch at every straw and hang on. It's better than doing nothing.'

They took fifteen minutes to lay down an observation schedule. Megan would make regular calls to a specific two-thirds of the households infected with whooping cough, while Timothy would call twice a day on the remaining third. At each visit they could do no more than check on the progress of the infection and give reassurance to the parents.

The calls would be timed so that each family had a late visit, since the disease was worst at night – it was then, too, that emergencies were most likely to happen. The children's lungs sometimes became inflamed, often with the added complication of infected bronchial tubes; convulsions could occur without warning and there was the ever-present danger of haemorrhage. They were all emergencies that

75

could kill a child weakened to exhaustion by tearing bouts of coughing.

When their separate timetables were drawn up Timothy sat back and yawned. To Megan, he looked as if he had been on his feet for days. It was one more indication, she believed, that the man wasn't up to the punishing pace of a physician's life in a poor, working class community. He should have stayed in the soft, easygoing surroundings of his fashionable London practice. Perhaps – and Megan found a ray of hope in the thought – the professional stresses of this coming winter in Pencwm would drive him back to where he came from.

'Anything else to report, while you're here?' Timothy asked, rubbing his eyes.

'Yes. I'm tired and I'm hungry and I'm going home.' Megan felt that might have been too abrupt, but it was out now so there was nothing she could do. She stood up. 'I'll call in first thing after surgery, in case you've come across any more patients with whooping cough – or in case I have.'

'Or both.' Timothy swung the chair round and got up. 'It's not likely the spread has stopped yet. Nor will it, for a week or two.'

The remark, although it was perfectly true, annoyed Megan. It was as if she were being forced to confront the worst, and she simply didn't want to do that. She wanted, at best, to take each day as it came and try not to think ahead.

'If I don't get to bed soon I'll have to curl up on the carpet.' Timothy walked ahead of Megan to the door and opened it. 'There doesn't seem to be time here for more than work and sleep.'

'That's what life's like, out in the big world.' Again, Megan felt she had put more of an edge on her remark than she had really meant to. She put it down to her own weariness, knowing she was admitting only half of the truth.

When she got home she fussed with Scratch for five minutes then set about making her bedtime cocoa. As she waited for the milk to boil she thought back over the events of the day, trying to keep her mind busy.

76

She had managed, after all, to see Rose off to North Wales. The woman who had come for her was small, rosy-cheeked and friendly. It took no more than minutes for Rose to lose her nervousness of the stranger. By the time they left they were chattering like old friends.

Wyn had looked weepy again. Gladys had difficulty talking past the lump in her throat. For Megan, the thought of Rose entering Mrs Pughe-Morgan's house for the first time produced a sensation close to envy. She recalled her own first sight of the place – 'Like a palace,' her mother had whispered, clutching Megan's hand as they waited in the hall to see the mistress. There were curve-legged mahogany side-tables, an opulent Indian carpet, ivory door-handles and a huge brass dinner gong. Megan remembered the big vase, blue-and-red porcelain and as big as her thirteen-year-old self; as her first years in the Pughe-Morgan house passed she had often observed, with amusement, that the vase was getting smaller.

Inevitably, because her mind was caught by fond memories of a place she loved, the shadows closed in. They hadn't all been lovely days. There had been terrible times. Terrible . . .

Megan snatched up the pan before the milk boiled over and poured it into her mug. The memories were still there, coming forward relentlessly and not to be banished by distraction. She put down the pan again and stared blindly at the wall.

'My poor darling . . .'

With blinding clarity she saw Bronwen's face, smiling, chuckling, sleepily nuzzling, a kaleidoscope of her early years. Bronwen, her own dear daughter. Then the image became too much to bear. Megan shut her eyes tightly, fighting it down, willing it back to the place she had banished it so long ago. But the picture remained, Bronwen blue-faced, choking, her breath rasping like the harsh crinkling of paper. Megan felt her own helplessness as she had struggled, time after time, to take the fear and pain from Bronwen. The nights had seemed endless, long heart-tearing hours hearing that poor, weakened little throat gulp the air in whistling

77

threads. Then came the convulsions, the blue-lipped child jerking uncontrollably as Megan, distraught, fought to unblock her throat . . .

The worst memory of all flared forward – Bronwen lying halfway on her back, her tiny hands calm, her face serene. Death had granted her peace, finally, and embedded torment in her young mother's heart.

It hadn't gone, it would always lurk in Megan and rear up at terrible times like this. She buried her face in her hands as tears slipped forward, wetting her fingers. The sight of any child with whooping cough distressed her; so far she had borne up by bracing herself and putting a fierce, professional clamp on her emotions. But until now she had never had to cope with an epidemic.

Megan moaned softly against her palms as Scratch whimpered at her heels, his head on one side, wondering.

CHAPTER EIGHT

As the snow on Pencwm's roads and pavements deepened until the dividing lines disappeared, the path to Dr Morris's door turned to packed ice with the increased traffic of patients attending morning and evening surgeries. Within four days the number of consultations almost doubled. House visits trebled. Timothy rose at seven and never got to bed before one in the morning. By the time the snow showers gave way to day-long frosts and the hills around the town gleamed white and wind-polished, Miss Williams, who headed the Charity Committee which employed Megan, felt she should talk to Dr Morris on a matter that had been troubling her.

'It's not the sort of thing that comes within the province of my official concerns, Doctor. It's a personal anxiety.'

They were in Miss Williams's elegant, comfortable sitting room, taking afternoon tea. Timothy could scarcely afford the time away from his work, but he knew Miss Williams was no time-waster – if she called him saying she wished to talk something over, it was usually something important. He stood by the broad mantelpiece, watching as she composed herself with a tiny frown and a careful folding of her hands. Miss Williams, a sound organiser and a woman with a strong sense of justice, could be oddly and painfully shy at times.

'It's about Megan Roberts.' Miss Williams looked up from her high-winged chair. She brushed a wisp of pale hair from her face, hesitating over what she would say next. Her timid features winced momentarily, as if she had felt a twinge of pain. 'It's awful, really – I mean talking behind her back like this.'

'What's troubling you?' Timothy prompted. 'I'm sure

Megan wouldn't resent your concern. She thinks very highly of you.'

'Yes. I suppose she does. She's a dear girl.' She reached for her cup and saucer, perched on the wine table by her chair, then changed her mind. 'What worries me, I suppose, is that I could be mistaken about this business . . .'

'You still haven't told me what it is,' Timothy reminded her.

'Heavens, of course . . .' Now she did pick up the cup and saucer and take a tiny sip of tea. 'I've seen Megan three or four times during the past week. Twice I spoke to her, the other times I saw her go past the window.' She concentrated hard for a moment. 'No, I'm not mistaken, Doctor Morris. There is something badly wrong with her.'

'In what way? Do you think she's ill?'

'No, not ill . . .' More concentration, then she said, 'It's in her manner. I'd swear – *somehow*, her personality has diminished. She spoke to me brightly enough, you understand. But it was like someone playing a role, and playing it badly. I got the impression of enormous strain.' She made a small, apologetic smile. 'You must think I'm taking a great deal upon myself to make such assumptions – but I've always been able to detect what lies beneath people's surfaces, especially when there's a concealed strain.'

Timothy didn't doubt her perception. At their first meeting he had thought Miss Williams an insipid woman with a face to match. Now he knew better. Her features and behaviour belied a sensitive and constantly analysing nature.

'You say you've noticed this change only during the past week?'

'Yes, that's right.' Miss Williams gestured vaguely with one hand, as if she were describing smoke. 'I've seen Megan concealing strain before, of course, but this is different. It was even noticeable as she cycled past here. She looked so gaunt and distant. As I said, it's as if her personality has been reduced. The way some sick people appear to lose pieces of their nature . . .'

Timothy knew what she meant. He called it spiritual

dismantling. The chronically and incurably ill often gave the impression that parts of their character were being systematically taken away from them. Timothy knew Megan wasn't ill, but spiritual dismantling was also a sign, in some individuals, of impending nervous breakdown.

'Did you say anything to Megan – about how she felt, I mean?'

Miss Williams nodded. 'I said she looked run down.'

'And no doubt she said she felt fine.'

'Yes, which was what I expected she would say.' Miss Williams took another sip of tea and set the cup and saucer aside. 'I thought I should alert you, Doctor, since you're in a better position to observe her than I am. If she's suffering in some way we'll have to do something about it, won't we?'

'Of course.' Timothy put down his own cup and saucer. 'I'm glad you've told me this, Miss Williams. I've been so busy lately I wouldn't have noticed if our District Nurse had grown horns.'

At the door Miss Williams said, 'I don't think, personally, that confronting Megan with this would be productive . . .'

Timothy smiled at her. 'Don't worry. I'll be discreet. If I said anything to her she'd only bite my face off, anyway.'

As he walked down the path Timothy was observing that, although Miss Williams had smiled at his last remark, she had also blushed. Megan had probably told her exactly how she felt about the interloper from London.

Back at the surgery he began making preparations for the evening's onrush. It was his usual practice to ensure that instruments were sterilised and laid ready, case notes from the morning brought up to date and filed away, the desk tidied and the stove turned up to make the room comfortable. After that he usually made any calls that were outstanding and went home for a light, swift meal, prepared by Dr O'Casey's old housekeeper. Following that hc would go back to the surgery and embark on work that would keep him occupied, one way and another, until after midnight.

Today he decided to change the routine in one small particular. He cleaned the instruments, tidied the desk and turned up the stove. Then he sat down, deferring the hour-long job of entering case and ledger notes. He would use the time, instead, to think.

So far as he could tell, the people of Pencwm were beginning to accept him. He wasn't Dr O'Casey and he never would be; already, a number of regular patients would be remembering O'Casey as a man with much greater skill and stature than he had ever possessed, because in accordance with the Law of Absent Friends, what you had lost was always infinitely better as soon as it was gone. Even so, Timothy felt he was being compared pretty favourably with Pencwm's regular doctor. The only person who held strong misgivings about him was Megan Roberts.

More than misgivings, he thought, smiling. Although there were occasional signs that she was getting a little more used to him, her disapproval, generally, was firm and unwavering. She didn't believe he was the man for the job and she had lots of cause for that view – or she thought she had. There was certainly conflict in their professional relationship.

What other conflicts inhabited Megan's life? Timothy wondered. He put his elbows on the desk and speculated. Patients occasionally infuriated her, petty officials did the same, and Nesta Mogg could easily trigger her aggression. But Megan could cope with that type of pressure; she had the strength of personality to prevail with little or no effort.

'What else could there be? ' Timothy asked himself. Megan lived alone and there wasn't a man in her life – he was sure of that. So there was no domestic or romantic discord. Nothing on the money side either; she had only herself and her dog to fend for – and she was a ferocious saver, according to Dr O'Casey.

For a moment Timothy considered Megan's work load. It was heavy, certainly, but it didn't take much perception to see she thrived on hard work. Inactivity would put a much greater strain on her.

'There we are, then.' Timothy sat back and put his hands behind his head. If Megan was suffering – and he didn't doubt Miss Williams's diagnosis – the cause stemmed either

82

from a factor in her life he knew nothing about, or, more likely, she was finding her professional relationship with Timothy too much to live with.

He stood up and went to the window. It was important, in maintaining his authority, to take a firm stance on matters of policy. Many aspects of his professional stance put Megan's hackles up. But he had been warned long ago, as a student, that if he *gave* anyone an inch, they would soon *take* the rest. So there he was and there he stood, take him or leave him. He tried always to be diplomatic in his dealings with Megan Roberts, but that didn't alter the fact that he had a set of attitudes she resented. As time passed the resentment grew and grew until it was eating into her spirit. That sounded to Timothy like a sound enough appraisal of the situation. But what was to be done?

Observe, he finally decided. Just observe. When he could be sure which aspects of his relationship with Megan put the greatest strain on her, he could perhaps find a remedy.

Sighing, he turned from the window and sat down again. Set beside his own situation, he thought, Megan's was almost trivial. Perhaps if she knew more about him, her resentment wouldn't be so strong. But Timothy was determined that nobody should know more than they had to. He had driven out his pity for himself; he would be mad to invite other people's.

Gareth Prentice was propped in a chair by the fire, a brown blanket covering him from his bony shoulders to his feet. His hair, spiky from the deficiency of vitamins, stood in clumps, giving him an appearance that would have been comic if his expression hadn't been so forbiddingly dour. Beside the chair his mother hovered, hands clasped at her waist, watching as Megan unpacked two brown medicine bottles and a jar of tablets from her bag.

'Doctor Morris got this stuff specially for you, from London,' Megan told Gareth. 'It's new and it's been hard to lay hands on. I'm going to see to it you take every last drop.'

83

She put the bottles on the table. Turning to Mrs Prentice she said, 'You're to mix one tablespoonful from each bottle in a medicine glass, then he's to wash down two tablets with it. Do you understand that?'

The woman nodded, her eyes flicking guardedly towards her son, who was huffily staring at the smouldering coals. 'One spoon out of each bottle,' she repeated, 'wash down two tablets with it.'

'Right,' Megan said. 'Tablespoons, remember.' She stepped across to Gareth, staring at him until he was compelled to look at her. 'Now I want you to listen to me. Carefully. What you did, or what you bullied your mother into doing, was very foolish. The look of Nesta Mogg should be warning enough to anyone with half a brain. She's a filthy mess and so is her medicine.'

'I'd have got better if I'd carried on with it.' Gareth showed Megan his meanest face, pucker-mouthed and slit-eyed, for all the world like an ill-made scarecrow. 'Nesta knows what she's doin'.'

'Oh, she knows that, all right.' Megan was talking through clenched teeth, pushing her face closer at the boy's. 'Taking in poor simple-minded clods like you with her poisons and her mumbo-jumbo, that's what she's doing. She picks her targets carefully, Gareth. She knows who'll put her on a pedestal and worship her criminal bunkum. Always the stupidest souls, always the fools.' Holding on to her temper was out of the question, lately. For more than a week Megan had been telling people precisely what she thought. Now, staring at Gareth's suddenly hurt face, she didn't entertain so much as a twinge of remorse. 'Can't you get it through your thick head? Nothing that woman does can come to any good. Have you not heard the saying – you can't draw sweet water from a foul well?'

Gareth jerked his head at the table. 'An' what's that muck goin' to do for me?'

'It is *not* muck! It's a balanced set of medicines designed to put back the nourishment you've lost and help your body to help itself.'

Glaring at Gareth, feeling an impulse to smack his stupid face, Megan recalled how Dr Morris had yet again taken the wind from her sails. He had simply put the medicines on the desk in front of her and explained clearly what they were supposed to do. Then he had told her he hoped she would get better results from the new medication. No question of interfering. No condescending advice. If anything, that had made Megan resent him a shade more. Why did the man keep depriving her of a grip for her dislike?

Gareth was contemplating the coals again. His mouth was working tightly, trying to formulate a rejection of the help he was being offered. His mother put a hand on his sticklike shoulder.

'It's for the best, son . . .'

He shrugged her hand away. 'I know what's best for me. If some folk'd stop interferin'—'

'Right!' Megan screeched, making Gareth and his mother jump. 'I'll take this lot away with me, eh? Just you call in Nesta Mogg and get yourself some bottles of bat-wing cordial and a cauldron or two of rancid porridge!'

'He doesn't mean it, Nurse . . .'

'Do it, Gareth!' Megan snatched up her bag, opening its jaws wide. 'You know what's best for you, after all! The whole damned lot of you in Pencwm know what's best – that's why you're all so fat and sleek and bursting with health!' She swept the bottles off the table and into her bag, shutting it with a loud snap. 'Hell mend you, Gareth Prentice!'

She was back out on Cardower Road before she knew it, swept on the surge of her anger, slamming her bag into the basket at the front of her bicycle. When she grasped the handlebars her hands were shaking. Knowing she wouldn't be able to steer the machine she pulled it away from the wall and began pushing it.

Why did she bother? she asked herself. Why bring her hard-won experience and qualifications to a community of glowering dullards who would sooner put their faith in tinker quackery than orthodox medicine? Why put herself at the disposal of po-faced idiots when there were plenty of towns

85

where her ability would not only be needed, but appreciated? What was she *doing* with her life, for God's sake?

When she had rounded the corner at the bottom of Cardower Road she stopped, staring ahead at newly-gathering rain clouds, feeling the wind shift to accomodate a thaw.

'We'll be up over our boots in slush, next,' a little man called to her. Megan nodded, trying for a rueful look, but only managing a scowl. She glanced away sharply.

Everything she did lately went wrong. She couldn't remember when she had felt so miserable – or so incapable of sustaining a mood, whether good or bad. Already she was rebuking herself for the unprofessional outburst at the Prentices'. And there was so much more, besides, to rebuke herself for. She felt she was losing all sense of scale in her dealings with other people.

To the unquiet soul all is harsh; no sweetness may enter or go forth. Her father had passed that on to her, a little homily from a big book he used to keep near his chair. Megan had kept the phrase with her over the years, among countless other pieces of wisdom Owen Roberts had bequeathed. That one certainly fitted her present condition. If she had a soul it was as disturbed now as it could ever be, short of disintegrating

Sighing, she leaned the bicycle on a wall and turned up the collar of her coat, wondering vaguely how she could go back to the Prentices and offer an apology that wouldn't commit her to a loss of face.

As she pretended to look for something in her bag, appeasing the curiosity of three women passing on the other side of the road, her father's kindly image came back to her, unbidden, as it often did. He had been a man of great inner strength. Megan believed she had inherited that strength. She wished she could find where she put it just lately, her blessed talent for deflecting life's chafing edge. When she was very young, she had stood with her father's big book open before her and committed to memory a quotation from the work of a foreigner whose name Megan couldn't, at that time, pronounce. She recalled the quotation now, seeing it laid out clearly on the page:

Life is a gift. Cherish it always and learn to master its challenges. The mastery of life is the key to full living, when every true path will show itself and no gate shall ever be barred.

That had been her guiding philosophy since childhood. Her father had prompted her to carry it with her – 'Always remember, Megan, a mastery of life . . .'

Lately she had no mastery of anything, not even her own timetables or temper. She knew what was wrong, but knowing was no cure. The longer she had to face those poor children with their burning lungs and exhausted bodies, the more the past flailed her and crippled her ability to cope with the simplest daily encounters.

'I wish you were with me now, Da.' She pulled the bicycle away from the wall again and began walking back up Cardower Road. Her hands, she noticed, were still shaking. 'A mastery of life,' she murmured, thinking how hollow it sounded. Mastery of life meant just what it said, a command of her existence and control of the influences which touched it most deeply. How, Megan wondered, could she restore such a power? What must she do to regain it, before she broke under the weight of a grief that renewed itself a dozen times a day?

CHAPTER NINE

PAUL Wood was five. He lived with his parents and two other brothers in a three-roomed house on Logan Road, a straggle of miners' cottages in the shadow of a coal tip to the north of Pencwm. Paul had been ill for two days before the doctor was called. What Timothy Morris found was a skinny, fair-haired little boy lying under two blankets on a home-made bed. He blinked warily at Timothy, his throat making a whistling sound as he laboured to breathe.

'We thought it was just a fevery cough he had,' Mrs Wood said, 'just like the young ones get at this time of year, you know? But this mornin' his chest's soundin' bad, an' his throat's terrible sore.'

Timothy felt the child's pulse, then put a hand on his forehead. He was hot and trembling.

'Is he able to speak?'

'Not without it hurtin'.'

'Let's have a look, then.'

Timothy sat on the wobbly bedside stool and opened his bag. Seeing the other two boys standing in the doorway he smiled and nodded to them. They glared back dumbly. Timothy had learned that the children in these parts regarded doctors and priests with the deepest suspicion. Real fear, though, was reserved for the local policeman.

'I'm not going to hurt you, Paul.' Timothy steadied the boy's head and pressed gently on his chin. 'Try to open your mouth for me. Wide as you can.' As the dry lips parted he inserted the end of a spatula and peered at the swollen throat. The inflammation was severe. The membranes beyond the tonsils were stiff and congested; their colour resembled raw beef. There were thick secretions around the vault of the

88

throat and a cherry-red swelling at the root of the tongue.

'All right, Paul, you can close it now.'

The child gulped as Timothy withdrew the spatula. Mrs Wood stepped closer, her eyes questioning. 'His tonsils is it, Doctor? My eldest had tonsil trouble a while back. It was a bit like that, but not so bad.'

'No, it isn't his tonsils.' Timothy was still analysing what he had seen. He believed Paul could be suffering from one of three conditions. The symptoms resembled those of diphtheria, severe croup and a dangerous infection called acute epiglottitis. It was unlikely to be diphtheria; the appearance of the throat tissues wasn't quite the same as those Timothy had seen when he treated diphtheria cases during his houseman days in London. He would have preferred to plump for croup, but the cherry-coloured swelling wasn't typical. Timothy looked at the child again and felt the diagnosis harden. The anxiety in the eyes, the fever, the rasping breath – when those signs were added to the visible evidence in the throat, doubt was banished. Timothy stood up.

'I'm afraid we'll have to get him into hospital.'

Mrs Wood looked instantly frightened. The two boys in the doorway stared at each other as if they had heard a pronouncement of doom.

'Whatever's wrong with him?' Mrs Wood leaned over the bed and touched her son's cheek.

'He's got an infection of the epiglottis,' Timothy said, hurrying to explain further before the big word struck even more fear in the woman's heart. 'It's a piece of elasticky gristle at the back of the tongue – it stops food dropping into the voice box when you swallow. Paul's is very badly inflamed. He needs the kind of careful nursing he can only get in hospital.' Timothy picked up his bag. 'Stay with him and make sure he's kept well wrapped up. I'll telephone the hospital and make arrangements for him to be taken in. I won't be long.'

Out on the street Timothy threw his bag into the car and got behind the wheel. He started the engine and was pulling away when he saw Megan. She was cycling towards him, her head bowed against the wind. Timothy braked and got out, flagging Megan down. When she stopped he explained rapidly about the child he had just examined.

'I'm convinced it's epiglottitis. Which means he's got to be put in very capable hands – very swiftly, too. I'm going to ring the hospital at Llengwyn and arrange to have him admitted. If need be I'll take him there myself, but I'll need your help. He'll have to be watched carefully, all the way.' They both knew that Paul's condition could rapidly turn fatal. Any undue disturbance of the throat tissue, or further swelling, could cause a sudden blockage of the air passages. If such a thing happened before the infection began to reduce, expert treatment would be needed to keep the child alive. 'By the look of things, I got here just in time. Stay with the boy till I get back, will you, Megan? I won't be more than a couple of minutes.'

Megan nodded and without a word she pushed her bicycle across to the Woods' house. As Timothy drove away she knocked the door and identified herself to Mrs Wood. She explained that she would sit with Paul until the doctor came back.

'I've not visited you before, have I?' she said, letting the woman lead her through to the room where young Paul lay.

'No,' Mrs Wood said absently. She shooed her two other boys away from their brother's bedside. 'Put the kettle on, Davey,' she called after one of them as they went into the living room. 'I'm sure the nurse could use a cup of tea. I know I could.' She sighed and shook her head at Paul, who was drowsing. 'Wait till his da hears about this.'

Megan detected self-rebuke. 'It couldn't be helped,' she said. 'You can't see something like this coming.'

'I suppose not,' Mrs Wood said, without conviction. 'Maybe I should've been keepin' more of an eye on him, wrappin' him up a bit warmer when he went out . . .'

Another mother taking the blame, Megan thought. They were certainly encouraged to. *If all men are born free, how is it that all women are born slaves?* It was a remark Mrs Pughe-

90

Morgan had often made, quoting a woman who had first said it as long ago as 1706. Among the working classes it still applied. The boy's illness was his mother's fault, because it was women's work to tend the home and keep the children healthy. Megan had known men openly rebuke their wives for failing to shield a child from infection or accident. For so little in the way of returned love and protection, the women were expected to manage so much. It was heart-rending to see the mothers of children with whooping cough, brought low themselves by anxiety and exhaustion, and often by an unspoken burden of guilt.

Megan gave herself a mental shake. She was doing too much dwelling on things, letting in too much introspection. In truth she was getting sick of herself. She didn't believe she had entertained one uplifting or cheerful thought for weeks.

'Is he goin' to be all right?'

'He'll be in good hands,' Megan said. It was an evasion; another recent change in her, she believed, was that she couldn't hand out convincing reassurances – not when she harboured any doubts. Young Paul's case was fraught with doubt. Even in expert hands he wouldn't be out of danger, not for several days.

'The doctor seems a very smart kind of chap,' Mrs Wood said, as much to comfort herself as make conversation. 'Gives you the feelin' he really knows his business.'

'Oh, he's a smart one all right,' Megan said. A postcard from Dr O'Casey, two days before, had suddenly sharpened her umbrage. How much better things would be if the old doctor were there, instead of his clever-clever locum. She would cope better, she knew she would.

'Nurse . . .' Mrs Wood's voice was a sharp whine of concern. She was standing close to the bed, bent low over the child. 'He's breathin' different . . .'

Megan pushed her firmly aside and drew the blankets away from Paul's shoulders. His eyes were wide open, pleading as his chest rose and fell. With a jolt in her own chest Megan realised there was no sound of breathing.

'Oh God,' Mrs Wood whined. 'Do somethin' for him!'

Megan's mind was in a clamp. This was happening and she had no power to act. The boy's air passages were blocked and a voice in Megan was screaming *this is an emergency!* but she couldn't move.

'Please, Nurse!' Mrs Wood screeched. Her two sons came running from the living room, their faces already twisted with alarm. 'Nurse! Do somethin' for him!'

Action was cancelled by the sight of the child's face. His lips were drawn back, his eyes beginning to roll. Just as Bronwen's must have, when she was left alone to die, her exhausted mother asleep not a yard away . . .

'Get out of the way!' It was a man's voice. Megan felt herself pushed roughly aside. Dr Morris stooped in front of her, took one sharp look at the boy then flung his bag on the bed and jerked it open.

'Bunch the pillow under his neck and shoulders!' he snapped, glaring at Megan.

Still she couldn't move. Something terrible was happening to her. She couldn't tear her eyes from the small mouth turning blue, the eyes showing only white. He was dying. The boy was going to his death in the effigy of Bronwen. Megan felt a whine rise in her throat, echoing the sound coming from Mrs Wood as she frantically clutched her other children to her.

'Nurse!'

Timothy barked the word straight in her face, jarring her into sudden movement. She saw her hands wad up the pillow and push it under the boy's frail shoulders, extending his head. The blue had spread to his cheeks and ears.

'Now hold his head and neck rigidly in line!' Timothy was opening a tracheostomy pouch on the blanket, pulling out a scalpel. *Rigidly*, Nurse!'

The rules of procedure were unrolling coldly in Megan's head, remote from her as she obeyed. *The trachea must be maintained with absolute rigidity in the midline and never allowed to displace to the side . . .*

'Lord, no!' Mrs Wood cried as Timothy brought up the knife blade over Paul's throat.

92

'Stop it!' one of her boys yelled.

Timothy jerked his head at the door. 'Outside! All of you!' He dropped a bundle of gauze swabs beside Megan's hand. 'Be ready with those,' he snapped at her.

'Don't cut him!' Mrs Wood wailed.

'Out!'

As Megan held the slender column of the neck in line Timothy lowered his elbows, trapping the child's arms at his sides. With the point of the scalpel poised over the bulging cartilage of the trachea, he paused for an instant, steadying himself, then put the blade on to the skin and made a swift downward cut.

As blood flowed freely Megan tightened her hold on the child's head, still distantly reciting the procedure to herself. *The rings of the trachea must be exposed. A few drops of cocaine are injected between two of the rings to prevent the violent coughing which occurs when the trachea is opened* . . . She still felt eerily remote, almost as if she were outside herself, watching her own mechanical movements as she held the head with one hand and applied a swab with the other, permitting Timothy to quickly inject the cocaine.

'Now. Keep him absolutely steady . . .'

Panting with concentration, Timothy poised the knife to make the second incision.

A tracheal stenosis may occur if the incision is made too high. The most suitable site for incision is at the level of the second or third tracheal rings . . .

The knife went in and was held there until a small bone dilator was in position. Already Paul was breathing through the opening, the pinkness returning swiftly to his cheeks. Timothy took a curved length of sterilised rubber tubing from a cellophane wrapper and eased it into the slit in the cartilage. Next he fixed the breathing tube in position with tape, then called out to Mrs Wood. When she came in, her eyes red with crying, he told her what had happened.

'Paul's throat closed. I had to make an opening further down for him to breathe through. Now I'm going to take him straight to the hospital. Later today I'll come by and tell you when you can go and see him.'

She nodded mutely, staring at the child. He was semi-conscious but rallying as his blood's oxygen level increased.

'Right, Nurse.' Timothy gave Megan a sharp, appraising glance. 'Let's get him wrapped up for the journey.' As he moved close, collecting his instruments, he murmured, 'Are you all right now?'

'Yes,' Megan said, 'I'm fine.'

She had never felt so odd in her life. The paralysing anguish that had gripped her, watching the boy choke, had gone completely. But what remained was another extreme, a chilling dullness, a fog in which she could move and function without feeling she was really alive any more.

On the way back from Llengwyn Timothy stopped the car on a shoulder of road overlooking a snow-dappled, bowl-shaped valley, perhaps two miles across, dotted sparsely with cottages and outbuildings.

'Care to strecth your legs?' he asked Megan. She was a silhouette beside him, sitting stiffly upright and looking straight ahead, as she had done all the way from the hospital.

'I don't mind,' she said.

They got out and walked to the grass-tufted verge. The sky seemed low at this point, with dark and light streaks of cloud like vast, random brushstrokes. Timothy stared down into the valley, saying nothing for a full minute. Then he turned and looked at Megan. She was staring at the sweep of hills and gullies with a small frown, as if they were a puzzle, though not a very interesting one.

'Is it something you can talk to me about?' Timothy asked.

'What do you mean?' Megan glanced at him quickly, then looked away. It was as if her eyes couldn't meet his. She turned up her coat collar.

'Your odd behaviour today. For a number of weeks, come to that.'

Megan set her mouth tight, staring at the valley now as

94

though it were offending her in some way.

'For a time I believed I was the trouble,' Timothy said. 'But now I don't think so. Are you ill?'

'There's nothing wrong with me, Doctor.'

'Yes, there is,' Timothy sighed. 'And you're bound to know that. Look at you now. Like a sleepwalker.'

Megan turned to him. 'If I have a personal problem, I'll keep it to myself and deal with it myself.'

'It's not that simple.' Timothy combed bluish fingertips through his hair and gazed out over the valley. 'You've been showing signs of strain, very clear signs. I've watched you and I recognise what I've seen. For weeks you've been close to the edge of nervous collapse. Now, I suspect the collapse has begun.'

'I wasn't aware you were a psychiatrist, too,' Megan snapped.

'Functional disorders aren't purely the province of psychiatry. Some factor in your work has brought you to this state, Megan. I'm sure it has. And you can't keep it to yourself and deal with it yourself, as you seem to think you can.'

Megan's eyes widened. 'I've a right to lead my own life and make my own decisions about it. I don't need your interference or anybody else's.'

Timothy was beginning to shiver with the cold, but he remained where he was, still watching the valley as if he wanted to memorise every detail. 'I'll say it again – it's not that simple. I have to interfere. Your present condition of mind is affecting your work. Badly.'

'Are you telling me I'm not doing my job properly?'

'That's exactly what I'm telling you,' Timothy said.

'Well I resent it – and I can't say I place much value on the quality of your judgement, anyway.'

'For weeks,' Timothy said patiently, 'your manner has been erratic and the quality of your work even more so.' He turned and looked at Megan, stepping closer. 'Today your standard of professional performance dropped as far as I'm prepared to let it go.'

95

The change in Megan was startling. From the stiff vagueness of a minute before she had moved quickly to agitated affront. 'You can't obstruct me! No one gave you that right!'

'We're not talking about obstruction—'

'Yes we are! You've been trying to drive me out of my job since you came to Pencwm!' Megan's voice had a hysterical edge that she was obviously trying to suppress, but churning indignation was taking control of her. 'You've thwarted me at every turn and worked just as hard to undermine Doctor O'Casey's reputation! My timetables have been changed, I've been given a heavier work load and I'm questioned on practically every move I make!'

'Calm down, Megan . . .'

'And stop calling me Megan!'

'You're misunderstanding me completely. I've no intention of thwarting you, whatever you think. I'm a doctor whose first concern is the wellbeing of his patients. Every move I make is aimed towards that end. If I seem at times to stand in your way, or re-direct you, I'm doing it in the interests of the patients, not to drive you out of your job.'

Megan was shaking. 'It's easy to say one thing and do another.' She knuckled a tear from her eye. 'I know what you've been doing, don't think I'm stupid . . .'

'Listen to me,' Timothy said quietly. 'You're in a state of thoroughgoing nervous debility. That's a diagnosis I'm standing by. I don't know the reason or reasons, but I know the therapy. Rest. I want you to take time off. I'll arrange it with the Charity Committee. You'll need at least a month to put yourself in order again.'

Megan glared at him. 'I've my work to do! You know I have!'

'You're not capable of it.'

'How dare you!'

'Earlier today,' Timothy said, keeping his voice calm, 'Young Paul would have died, if I hadn't come back when I did. You were frozen with panic. Or *something*.' He watched tears slide along Megan's cheeks. 'I have to consider the patients, primarily. Their wellbeing can be best served, at

96

present, if I deny them the services of a District nurse who clearly isn't up to her duties.'

'You can't force me,' Megan began, then put her hands to her mouth, unable to go on as a sob caught her throat.

'Yes I can. And I will, if I have to. It's for your wellbeing, too. You're ill, for God's sake. There's no saying what'll happen if you don't take a break.'

Megan shook her head defiantly, one hand still covering her mouth.

'The decision's made. You're taking a rest. As of now.' Timothy took her by the elbow and began leading her back to the car. 'No democracy, Nurse Roberts,' he said gently. 'I'm boss.'

CHAPTER TEN

ON November 21st, a gloomy, drizzly Monday as dispiriting as the day before, a letter with a London date stamp arrived at the surgery with the morning post. Timothy recognised the pale blue paper of the envelope and decided to leave it sealed until after the last evening consultation. Since childhood, whether eating, opening presents or reading, he had always tried to leave the good things until last.

As he had guessed, it was a letter from Geoffrey Lloyd, his former partner. Timothy sipped a brandy as he read the neat, curving handwriting and pictured, from time to time, Geoffrey's own tidiness of nature and appearance. After an amusing, rambling first page, in which Geoffrey described developments at the practice since his new partner joined him the tone of the letter became serious

There's no avoiding this, Timothy, and since it's the whole reason for writing the letter I'll get to the point. I've discovered, as would have been inevitable, whatever means you adopted to prevent anyone knowing, just why you took yourself off to that God-forsaken practice. I know why, but I can't pretend to understand. I can't tell you how shaken I was, and after a whole afternoon brooding on the matter I decided I must say this to you. Of all the physicians I've known, you typify the manner of approach and execution in your work which I, a far less talented man, still hold before me as an ideal. I suppose that's a flowery way of saying I admire you greatly. And I miss you.

Can I beseech you to let me visit you? I want to talk to you, to ask you things and tell you others. Before I learned what I now know, I still felt a regular yearning for some time in your company. Now, I feel it is imperative. Please write, Timothy, and please grant my request. Naturally, I would never impose my presence on you uninvited. But I will never know an hour's complete peace of spirit, either, if you should decline to see me.

Avoiding the serious implications of the letter, Timothy embarked on a jocular criticism of Geoffrey's style. The man wrote like a Victorian novelist, he decided. A lady Victorian novelist, at that. He always turned pompous and artificial when he put pen to paper. It was something he couldn't help. In his case notes he had once described a patient's carbuncle as being 'of extreme tuberosity', and another's recovery from shingles as 'coming encouragingly close to analeptic expectations'. Timothy smiled, holding the letter before him, picturing Geoffrey struggling to put it together. 'Beseech' and 'yearning' were words he never used when he spoke, yet there they were. And as for 'you typify the manner of approach and execution' . . .

Timothy put down the letter. There was no point in treating it lightly. Geoffrey had found out why he had left London – which said a lot about the confidentiality of the Medical Appointments Board. Geoffrey knew, and now Timothy wondered how many others did. It was irrelevant, he supposed, though he felt spied-upon, he sensed himself being watched at a distance by countless members of London's medical brotherhood, passing their opinions of his behaviour from one to the other and making flatulent judgements.

Timothy swirled his brandy, watching lamplight skid across the amber whorls. 'Poor old Geoffrey,' he sighed. What did he want to say, and hear? Timothy could guess. He wished his private motives had remained private. Because now a decision was being forced on him.

He stood, walked to the window and peered out at the dark. He saw his own reflection surrounded by the dim halos of street lamps. He hadn't felt so alone for a long time. Usually his own company was enough for him – or lately it had been, anyway. Now he wished he could talk to someone. He needed to make living sound of his argument, so that it could be considered and approved by another human being.

99

What he wanted to say was not for Geoffrey's ears, though. It would only make him more miserable than he undoubtedly was already.

'This I believe. This is the direction I shall take.'

In the quiet room it sounded impressive. It had the solid tones of a man declaring his resolute intention. But who would agree with it, who would find it solid or sensible, given a full explanation?

Megan Roberts might. He couldn't think of anyone else who would. A week ago Megan had gone back to her roots in North Wales, a journey which, whether she believed it yet or not, would restore her personality and strengthen her spiritual muscle. Yes, Timothy thought, in time she would understand, because she was doing precisely what he was doing, and the benefits would be identical.

He turned and crossed the room, deciding on one more brandy before bedtime. It would ease the ache of the decision he had taken as he moved away from the window. He wouldn't grant Geoffrey's request.

'Sorry, Geoffrey, sorry . . .'

It stung, but the pain of the decision wouldn't linger, whether he had a brandy or not. From the stones life had thrown at him in the past few years he had built a fortress around himself. Nothing hurt him now. It was his fervent hope that as time passed, the fortress would continue to hold.

'I've always believed that no matter how well things are going, there's bound to be room for improvement,' Mrs Pughe-Morgan said. She smiled at Megan as they stood by the fireplace in the morning room. 'This past year, in addition to all my other ventures, I've been organising support for the underprivileged children's summer-outings scheme. And I've got myself involved with two more rescue homes and the committee of the Girls of the Realm Guild.'

'What's that?' Megan asked.

'The Guild makes educational grants towards the schooling and training of single girls.' Mrs Pughe-Morgan

100

smiled again. 'There was a time when you would have been eligible.'

'Do you know how many organisations you're attached to? There must be dozens.'

'I stopped counting years ago, my dear. Causes have been a habit with me for as long as you or I can remember – and as I say, whenever I see I'm making headway, I promptly widen my horizons.'

They were the widest horizons Megan knew. At fifty-eight Mrs Pughe-Morgan still had the sharpness and enthusiasm that had impressed the young newcomer to the household nearly twenty-two years before. The mistress, as Megan had known her then, had lost neither her upright deportment nor the lively sparkle of her green eyes. As yet, her high-piled, dark gold hair showed only a few traces of grey.

'If there's one thing I've stopped doing, Megan, it's talking about my work so much. Do you realise you've been here a week and I've only just begun to bore you with chatter about my boards and panels and committees?'

'You know it doesn't bore me.'

For a time, during the Great War, as her housemaid's duties underwent change and she gradually became Mrs Pughe-Morgan's protegée and personal assistant, Megan had been active on a soldiers' relief scheme operated by the mistress. During that time she had also attended educational conferences and seminars and had learned the value of sound organisation. Such efficiency as Megan possessed – and appeared, recently, to have lost – had been gained under the tutorship of Gwendolyn Pughe-Morgan.

'Well I warn you, seriously, as Christmas gets closer you may well revise your kindly view of my compulsive campaigning. I'm giving a few dinner parties for an ungodly number of my cohorts. I'll expect you to attend, since I'll need all the moral support I can muster. You'll meet a few old friends, mind you. That'll be some consolation.'

Megan said, 'It's been a tonic, getting together again with the old friends I have here.'

'Are you truly beginning to feel better?'

'Yes, I am. In a lot of ways.'

On the second day of Megan's visit, she and Mrs Pughe-Morgan had sat down in this room and talked for more than an hour. Megan held back nothing, since she was talking to the one person in the world who knew practically all there was to know about her personality and history. She explained how she had been forced to suspend her work in Pencwm, and admitted that she had probably been unfit to work, anyway. She had poured out her grievances and her frustrations, and explained her deep resentment of Dr Timothy Morris, the cause of them all. Mrs Pughe-Morgan had listened attentively, then said she was glad, terribly glad, that for once Megan had accepted the annual invitation to spend Christmas with her. 'What you need is lots and lots of inactivity, my girl,' she had said. 'A dose of laziness can work wonders.'

As they talked on, Megan began to suspect that Mrs Pughe-Morgan possessed some knowledge of psychological therapy. In the manner of a surgeon cutting out a deep-seated infection, she had encouraged Megan to recall the dark days, the times and events that could still hurt her and, in the case of her dead baby, cause her terrible emotional harm. It was a process of purging that brought Megan to tears at one point, but she felt distinctly better in the ensuing days. It was possible now, a week later, to think of Alun, her dead fiancé, and his baby, Bronwen, without going through the pain and distress she had been suffering in Pencwm.

'Ah,' Mrs Pughe-Morgan said now, glancing at the mantel clock as it chimed. 'Three o'clock.'

They looked across the room expectantly. As the last chime died the door opened and Rose Clark came in, carrying the tray for afternoon tea. She set it on the table and looked at Mrs Pughe-Morgan. 'Shall I pour, Ma'am?'

'Yes my dear. Thank you.'

Megan beamed at Rose. She looked so smart in her black dress and white apron, with her hair tied back and the little white cap perched on top. There was something else today, some additional element to her appeal – Megan strained to detect what it was, then realised that Rose had completely lost the nervousness she'd displayed on the two other occasions when she had served afternoon tea. She handled the silver teapot confidently, stood straight-backed as she poured and appeared altogether calm and in control of herself.

When Rose left them Mrs Pughe-Morgan said, 'She's coming on by leaps and bounds, Megan. I'm glad you sent her to me.'

'She's a lovely child,' Megan said.

'She reminds me of you at that age. Do you know, she's even showing an interest in botany, just as you did? I can scarcely wait for spring.'

Megan stirred her tea slowly, relishing memories. 'Do you remember our trips to gather herbs, and the little albums I used to make up, with dried plants stuck to the pages and the botanical descriptions written underneath?'

'I've forgotten nothing. The walks, the winter sessions with the text books and encyclopedias, the sheer pleasure of watching you learn. I'm looking forward to re-living it all with Rose.'

'Do you think she's over what happened to her?' Megan asked.

'She appears to be happy enough. Doesn't ever seem preoccupied. I hope we can pile on enough affection and lively distraction to bury the awful memories forever.' As she said that Mrs Pughe-Morgan frowned at Megan. 'We both know, however, that some memories won't be obliterated, no matter how we try.'

'I'm beginning to believe they can always be kept tolerably quiet, though,' Megan said, 'so long as we're close to . . .' She paused, the thought crystallising as she spoke. '. . . to reassuring human warmth. I had that here, with you and Mrs Foskett, I had it in Liverpool from a couple of my tutors, and in Pencwm I had Doctor O'Casey to lean on.'

Mrs Pughe-Morgan sipped her tea in silence for a moment, then she said, 'Megan, do you believe that Doctor O'Casey's absence is at the root of your recent troubles – or do you believe it's the presence of the new man?'

'Both. I have friends in Pencwm, of course, but the link

103

with them isn't the same, somehow . . . I'm still not sure what the difference is, but as much as I like Miss Williams and Gladys and Wyn Brewster, I've never felt the same, well – *closeness* I feel towards the doctor.' Megan shook her head. 'It's very difficult to explain.'

'You believe you would have withstood the strain of the whooping-cough outbreak if Doctor O'Casey had been there?'

'I honestly don't know.'

'Well,' Mrs Pughe-Morgan said slowly, 'if I may make the observation, you've grown to be a woman who needs her own realm. I can't imagine you letting anyone into your ordered domain. On the other hand, you need someone strong on the outside – a special touch-stone, perhaps. A criterion to help you maintain your own standards and guidelines – it's only a theory, of course, or the start of one . . .'

As she had often done throughout Megan's life, Mrs Pughe-Morgan had deliberately laid the foundation for fresh self-understanding, creating a base for Megan to build her ideas on.

'That's very astute,' Megan said, smiling.

'Of course it is. I'm a very astute old lady. And uncommonly modest.' Mrs Pughe-Morgan grinned as she set down her cup and saucer. 'Megan, it's time we got ourselves out in the fresh air. All this analysis is giving me a headache. One last thing I'll say, though, if you'll permit me, before we wrap up warm and take to the hills.'

'What?'

'I'm truly indebted to your Doctor Morris.'

Puzzled, Megan said, 'Why's that, for heaven's sake?'

'If it hadn't been for him, you wouldn't be with us for the Christmas festivities. Worse, you might have been locked away in some awful institution for the treatment of nervous disorders.'

As they went out to the hall Megan considered that. It made sense, she decided. But gratitude towards Timothy Morris, on her own part, was out of the question.

104

CHAPTER ELEVEN

EARLY on Christmas Day the cook, Mrs Edgar, began the final preparations for dinner, which this year was to be rather more than a family-and-friends affair. In previous years Mrs Pughe-Morgan and the retired housekeeper Mrs Foskett, who still lived in a cottage in the grounds, would sit down together with a handful of the mistress's friends – usually men and women from the Drynfor Miners' Welfare Committee. Dinner on those occasions was prepared and served by Mrs Pughe-Morgan.

This Christmas marked the tenth anniversary of the Welsh Rural Medical Aid Association, of which Mrs Pughe-Morgan was a founding member. In addition to the usual guests, practically the entire Board of the Association would be present for dinner. Mrs Pughe-Morgan had planned to hire outside help for the occasion, since her own staff always had Christmas Day off. But Mrs Edgar had argued that that she should do the cooking, because she knew the kitchen better than anyone and, more importantly, she was a widow and preferred to be working rather than stuck at home alone. To add persuasive weight to Mrs Edgar's argument, Rose had volunteered to help in the kitchen. So now, at half-past seven on a windy Christmas morning, the stout, elderly cook and her young assistant were busying themselves cheerfully, Mrs Edgar trilling a favourite old song as they fired ovens and set out the turkey, ham, beef, vegetables and other food ready for cooking.

'They're having some fancy foreign stuff for Boxing Day,' Mrs Edgar told Rose as she turned from putting an eleven pound ham on the stove to boil. 'I can't say the names of half the dishes.'

'Why are they having foreign food?' Rose asked.

'It's the mistress's idea. Says it's time we stopped sticking in the mud over Christmas food – over British food altogether, come to that. She's keeping it traditional for today, mind you. But tomorrow I'll have to come to work in a Spanish hat and a French pinnie, just to get in the mood for what I'm doing.'

'Maybe a pair of Dutch clogs too, eh?' Rose giggled.

'And you can strum a mandolin while I'm up to my elbows in chicken livers and plum sauce and the rest of it.'

They were chuckling over the picture that conjured when Megan came in. 'My, there's a festive atmosphere in here this morning,' she said brightly. 'Happy Christmas to you both.' She handed each of them a small packet tied with silver-spangled string.

As she had always done in the past, Mrs Edgar made a frowning show of disapproval, saying Megan shouldn't have gone to the expense of a present for her, frowning harder as she undid the wrapping. Rose, flush-cheeked, took her gift to the draining board by the big sink and stood fingering it a moment before she unknotted the string.

'Oh, Lord save us . . .' Mrs Edgar half-turned to Rose, who was still busy with her own packet, then turned to Megan again, holding up an oval, silver-mounted amber brooch. 'You *shouldn't* have, Megan. It must have cost you a fortune . . .'

'What's important is, do you like it?'

Mrs Edgar held the brooch by its pin, turning it to catch the light. 'It's the loveliest thing I've ever had, and there's a fact.' She looked at Megan. 'Thanks ever so much, pet.'

There was a small cry from Rose. She held up her hand towards Mrs Edgar, showing her a heart-shaped locket dangling from her fingers on its thin gold chain. There was a look of pure wonderment on her face.

'My,' Mrs Edgar breathed, 'you are a fortunate girl.' She glanced at Megan, making a tight mouth and shaking her head sharply, silently saying *you're spoiling the girl.*

Rose stood transfixed as Megan showed her how to open the locket.

'You can put a picture in there, see? Just take out the little frame, cut the photo round the shape of it and pop everything back inside.'

Rose nodded, understanding. 'It's beautiful. Nicer even than the one my Mam had. I don't know what happened to that.'

Sold for drink before the poor woman was cold in her grave, Megan thought. She could feel a grim satisfaction beyond the pleasure of this moment, knowing it would be a long time before Owen Clark would taste his next drop of beer. Megan, as much as Mrs Pughe-Morgan, saw her young self in this child, finding herself every day in a kinder, broader world than she had ever known or hoped to see.

'Thank you ever so much, Megan.' Shyly Rose kissed Megan's cheek. 'Can I have a picture of you to put in here?'

The emotion in that instant, Megan transfixed on the question and Rose looking at her with those large, serious eyes, was too much for Mrs Edgar. Clearing her throat loudly she bustled off to see if the ham had started to boil yet.

'I'll have a look through my snapshots when I get home,' Megan said, 'and I'll find one to send you.'

The back door opened and let in a momentary gust of cold air. Griffiths, the senior gardener, came in quickly, slamming the door behind him. 'Sharp enough out there to cut your ears off,' he said, rubbing his hands. 'Mornin', Megan, mornin' Mrs Edgar. An' how's Rosie this mornin?'

'Fine, thank you, Mr Griffiths.'

'Compliments of the season to you all.'

Rose stepped close to the tubby little man and showed him the locket. 'Megan gave it me.'

'Oh, glory,' Griffiths said, gazing at the trinket. He scratched his whiskered cheek. 'We'll have to see about puttin' stronger locks on the doors, now. Burglars'll be comin' from miles around to lay their hands on somethin' as grand as that.'

'And look what she gave me,' Mrs Edgar said, holding out the brooch. 'Isn't she the terrible one, spendin' her hard-earned money like that?'

107

Griffiths peered at the brooch, fingering it carefully where it lay on Mrs Edgar's palm. He glanced sideways at Megan, his eyes narrowing. 'You know what you've gone an' done here, don't you?'

'What?' Megan asked.

'Jumped the gun on me, that's what.' He shook his head, his face tight with mock reproach. 'I got Mrs Edgar one just like this – I was goin' to present it to her later on.' He sighed. 'I'll just have to give it to somebody else, now.'

'Old rascal,' Mrs Edgar grunted, carefully pocketing the brooch. 'I suppose you've come to scrounge a cup of tea, have you?'

'It wouldn't hurt,' Griffiths said. 'Neither would a bit of somethin' extra in it, on a freezin' mornin' like this.'

'Extra sugar's all you'll get. There'll be no intoxicating drinks served from this kitchen before noon today.'

'Fair enough.' Griffiths looked at Megan with helpless eyes. 'She don't get no softer with age, this one.'

'But *you* get cheekier,' Mrs Edgar snapped.

Smiling broadly, adoring the warmth of these dear people in this dearest of places, Megan reflected that age had changed neither of them in the least. There had been occasions, since she came back, when she entertained the notion that time had passed this estate by, leaving everybody and everything just as they had been back in 1906, when she first came into the household.

Later that morning, as she took morning coffee with Mrs Pughe-Morgan, Megan remarked on the timeless quality of the place.

'The longer I'm here the more I notice it,' she said. 'The other day, I walked over to the Pantmynach Valley with Rose. I wanted to show her the place where I used to gather toadflax in the summer – you remember, there was always a patch near that spinney, a hundred yards or so below the ridge of the valley?'

'I remember it well,' Mrs Pughe-Morgan said.

'Well, the patch is still there. Winter or not, it's impossible to mistake it. Imagine. I first went there – what? Eighteen or

108

nineteen years ago, I suppose. And the archway of laburnums on the Grannog Hill – that's still there, too. Not changed a jot.'

'Change here is very gradual, Megan.'

'It's the people that make it most noticeable. I mean I don't see any difference in Griffiths, Mrs Edgar or even Mrs Foskett. It's eerie, but it's terribly reassuring.'

'The one remains, the many change and pass,' Mrs Pughe-Morgan said.

Megan nodded. 'Shelley. I remember you telling me to read it. It's a lovely thought – this place, these people, timeless and unchanged at the centre of so much turbulence . . .'

'But you remember how the pasage ends, don't you?'

Megan thought for a moment. She hadn't read *Adonais* for years, but it was locked somewhere in her memory. After a moment it came to her. 'Life, like a dome of many-coloured glass,' she recited, 'stains the white radiance of Eternity, until Death tramples it to fragments.' She looked at Mrs Pughe-Morgan. 'Nothing lasts, after all. True enough.'

'And does that trouble you, when you think about it? One day none of this will be here, none of us . . .'

'I could let it bother me, yes.' Megan was aware, again, that Mrs Pughe-Morgan was working some shade of therapy on her. 'Not long ago the thought would have crushed me, along with all the other black reflections.'

'But not now?'

'No. Because that thought isn't the *point*. The thought to hold, I believe, is that if we endure with hope, even though there isn't any real endurance or any hope of it, we live happy lives. We should be hoping even on the day we draw our last breath.'

Mrs Pughe-Morgan beamed at her. 'That sounded just like the old Megan.'

'Perhaps it is her.'

'So she hasn't changed, either. Just wandered aside from her old path for a time.'

Megan nodded. 'I think that might be so.'

109

'In that case,' Mrs Pughe-Morgan said, 'you can apply your restored powers, if you will, to helping me put the final touches to the plans for this afternoon's dinner.'

The meal would be lavish, but it would remain strictly within the traditional mould – 'Though probably for the last time,' Mrs Pughe-Morgan said, 'if I can persuade Mrs Foskett to sit down to Poulet Sauté Demidov next year instead of turkey and ham.' She wasn't at all a snob about food, she was quick to add. She simply felt that people gained nothing, physically or spiritually, by denying themselves novelty and variety.

They would start with brown Windsor soup. For the main course, there would be a plate piled high with sliced turkey at one end of the table and a ham at the other, skinned, crumbed, sprinkled around with parsley and decorated with a paper frill around the shin. The beef, sliced thin, would be in the centre of the table. In tureens there would be boiled and roasted potatoes, carrots and celery stuffing. There would be boats of four different sauces, pots of jelly and decanters of red and white wine. Afterwards, for those who were up to it, there would be the choice of baked apple dumplings, castle pudding, plum pudding or raspberry meringue.

'I believe Mrs Edgar's going to surprise us with something – she keeps throwing a cloth over the mixing bowl every time I stick my head into the kitchen. I do hope it's her custard topped with nutmeg. It's delicious.'

A seating plan was devised that would put no one near anyone they didn't know too well, or anyone they didn't get on with. Megan suggested that she should sit beside the old housekeeper, Mrs Foskett, so that she wouldn't feel herself overwhelmed by strangers.

'Now, the final arrangement,' Mrs Pughe-Morgan said, 'and it's the one to which I'm looking forward least.' She sighed. 'Megan, whatever am I going to wear?'

By the time guests began arriving, Megan was firmly convinced that her choice of dress for Mrs Pughe-Morgan was perfect. The mistress herself had felt the dress was too young for her; she found it hard to accept Megan's reassurance that she had the figure and grace of a woman twenty years younger. The admiring glances of both men *and* women guests were evidence enough that Megan had been right. It was a simple shift dress in pale green silk which reached to just below her knees at the front and slightly lower at the back. A deep-gold silk cord was tied loosely at her waist; she wore flesh-coloured silk stockings and medium-heeled shoes of shiny green leather. At Megan's absolute insistence she had also put on her rope of pearls, even though she thought them miles too ostentatious.

'Doesn't she look a picture?' Mrs Foskett whispered to Megan, when the few necessary introductions had been made and they sat down to start dinner. 'I don't reckon she could look dowdy if she tried, mind you.'

'She's always been the prettiest woman for miles,' Megan agreed. And at times, she thought, the loneliest. It was the great tragedy of Mrs Pughe-Morgan's life that her marriage had failed when she was still in her thirties. Since that time, only Megan and Mrs Foskett had been really close to her. 'She's in such good health, too.'

'That's because I keep an eye on what she eats and what medicine she takes when she gets poorly – not that she often does.' Mrs Foskett had always been fiercely loyal to the mistress. Now that she was retired she saw herself as something of an aunt, maintaining a protective concern with Mrs Pughe-Morgan's health and welfare, and regularly offering opinions and advice. 'She'll have to be careful of draughts in a frock like that, mind you. This dining room's not the warmest in the house.'

In fact the place was warm. The fire had been banked with logs and the heavy drapes were drawn against the night. The atmosphere at the table was warm, too. The guests talked and laughed easily, helped by liberal cups of hot punch on their arrival. In addition to Mrs Pughe-Morgan, Megan and Mrs Foskett, there were seven women and five men – all of them dedicated, unmarried people whose private lives, Megan suspected, were as solitary and virtuous as Mrs Pughe-

111

Morgan's. The single, well-ordered existence seemed to be a pre-requisite for professional committee membership – in Wales, at any rate. Perhaps, Megan mused, she would drift on to a committee or two herself, if her work load ever shrank enough to permit her.

As they finished the soup Mrs Foskett said, 'I'll likely need a drop or two of Pennyroyal after all this eating. I'm not used to big dinners any more.'

It made Megan smile. Mrs Foskett was by no means a Nesta Mogg, but her adherence to herbal medicine had the proportions of an obsession. In her little cottage she kept boxes stuffed with powders, tinctures and infusions made from a bewildering variety of wild plants that she regularly gathered and spent hours preparing, according to ancient rules and formulas she carried in her head. Megan was about to tell her about the witch-woman who was such a menace where she worked when the man on her right spoke.

'Excuse me . . .'

He smiled tentatively as Megan tried to remember his name. She believed it was Halliday. She couldn't recall if she'd been told what he did.

'Earlier, when we were introduced,' he went on, 'I believe Mrs Pughe-Morgan said you're a District Nurse – is that correct?'

'Yes.' Megan returned his smile, observing that he had particularly balanced, honest features, just as Mrs Pughe-Morgan had – and, as in her case, it was difficult to tell his age from his appearance. Similar physical types, Megan had learned, often had similar persuasions and enthusiasms. 'I've a post in South Wales,' she added.

'I've a long-standing connection with the service,' the man murmured. He seemed to have difficulty knowing what to say next. Megan detected shyness, so she decided to ease matters for him.

'Are you connected with one of the District Nursing management committees?'

'Ah, no, no, I'm with the Medical Appointments Board, among other bodies, and I often interview nursing applicants

112

for particular posts within my area of jurisdiction . . .' His voice tailed off again, making Megan think of something she had read about timidity – 'He that handles a nettle tenderly is soonest stung.' Here was a nice man, keen to talk, probably terribly lonely and yet too shy to get a conversation going. She wondered how he managed to get through an interview.

'I would have thought you saw more doctors than nurses, Mr Halliday – it is Mr Halliday, isn't it? I'm bad with names.'

'Yes, yes, Halliday,' he said with a small fluster, 'and yes to the other question – I do see more doctors, but quite a few District Nurses, too.' He looked now as if he might be able to go on talking. His enthusiasm for his work, Megan suspected, could overcome his shyness – which was probably how he managed those interviews. 'It's interesting that you're in South Wales, because I've made many appointments there. Yes, quite a few. That was in the past, of course. I administer an area of London, now.'

'What's your connection with Mrs Pughe-Morgan, exactly?'

'Oh, I'm an adviser to her rural medical aid venture. I make sure they fill in all the right forms and tell them how to take administrative shortcuts – that kind of thing.'

The two extra maids who had been hired for the day were laying out the main course. Halliday watched them for a moment, making Megan suspect he was stuck, again, for something to say.

'Your work must be very interesting.'

He looked at her. 'I suppose it is, yes. But I've always envied the active people I deal with, the ones who do real, substantial things. People like yourself.'

'But we need people like you,' Megan said, even though there had been times when she had cursed administrative bodies aloud and at length.

'I sometimes think there are too many of us and too few of you.' It had a candid ring, and it was said with some force, as if it were something Halliday had wanted to say for a long time. 'I mean, look at the hours you work, with no help at all. I work very short hours and I have all the assistance in the world.'

113

Megan nodded, taking the point. 'A few extra willing hands in Pencwm wouldn't go unappreciated.'

Halliday looked interested. 'Pencwm? That rings a bell.' He mumbled the name to himself a couple of times. 'Ah, yes, of course. Pencwm. That's where young Doctor Morris got himself into locum work, isn't it?'

Megan nodded. 'Do you know him?'

'No, I've never met him, but I know of him, of course.' He made a small gesture with his hand. 'Sad business really, isn't it?'

Megan frowned. 'I'm sorry?'

'About Morris, his . . .' Halliday's face changed. The features became guarded. 'I, um, I think I may have spoken out of turn.' He smiled nervously and began watching the maids again.

He had thought Megan knew something, she realised; something pretty important, too, she guessed. She was on ethically bad ground to find out any more. But she was intrigued. Sad business? What had he meant?

Two hours later, with dinner over, everyone – including Mrs Edgar and Rose – retired to the drawing room where, as they drank wine and cordials, they could either make conversation or listen to a lady from Caernarvon play Gilbert and Sullivan on the piano. At the first opportunity Megan took Mrs Pughe-Morgan aside. She told her what Mr Halliday had said, or had begun to say.

'I'm eaten up with curiosity,' Megan admitted. 'Could you find out anything?'

Mrs Pughe-Morgan shrugged. 'I could, I suppose. Is it that important to you?'

'I'd just like to know,' Megan said.

'I'll use all the guile I can, Megan. Though I must say it doesn't take much with our Mr Halliday.'

Over the next twenty minutes, as Megan exchanged light conversation with one guest after another, she watched as Mrs Pughe-Morgan talked her own way towards Mr Halliday. Finally she had his ear. Megan could hardly keep from staring. She knew, with little sense of shame, that she was hoping to learn something that might be discreditable to smug Dr Morris. Even a *tiny* scrap of scandal would be something to chew on.

Mrs Pughe-Morgan talked with Mr Halliday for five minutes. When she finally excused herself, she made her way back to Megan by a devious route, taking in a chat with two other men and the lady at the piano, who was resting. Finally, she sidled across to where Megan was standing, near the fireplace, pretending to watch the play of the flames on the coals.

'Well?' Megan looked at Mrs Pughe-Morgan with open expectation. 'Did you find out anything?'

'Yes, I did.' Mrs Pughe-Morgan looked very serious, almost sombre. 'Now I rather wish I hadn't.'

'What is it?'

'Megan . . . I'll tell you, of course, and I know how discreet you can be – but please let no one else know about this. Try not to let it affect your work . . .'

Megan stared at her. What did she mean? 'What could affect my work? Has he done something—'

'It's not anything he's done.' Mrs Pughe-Morgan sighed. 'After what you've told me about the man, I get a very confusing picture of him. Mixed feelings, even a pang of guilt for passing a mental judgement here and there . . . Goodness knows how it'll make you feel.'

Megan was becoming visibly agitated. 'What? What is it?'

'Well,' Mrs Pughe-Morgan said slowly, 'your Doctor Morris – it appears that he's a dying man.'

CHAPTER TWELVE

FOLLOWING a tearful leave-taking, with reassurances that she would not stay away so long in future, Megan made her way back to Pencwm in the second week of January, 1928. She was returning as a changed woman, stronger than when she had left, restored in vigour and spirit. She was also coming back determined to make amends for what she now saw as her wilful obstruction of Dr Morris.

As the train chugged steadily along winding valley tracks she stared out at the snowy hillsides, wondering at herself, at her own blindness. It was a reverie that had overtaken her daily since Christmas. How could she have overlooked the obvious? A new man had come to take the old doctor's place. She had resented him simply becaue he wasn't Dr O'Casey, and her resentment had invented reasons for its own existence; Dr Morris was imperious, he was pushy, smug, interfering, overbearing . . .

Megan had deluded herself, and she was thoroughly ashamed. As her mind and will became overbalanced by the whooping-cough epidemic, so her belief in Dr Morris's iniquity had grown. All delusion, she thought – delusion, fallacy and wildest error. The facts, viewed without the discoloration of prejudice and resentment, were plain enough. Dr Morris was a sane, fair-minded doctor, a caring man who did everything he could for his patients. Again, Megan recalled the trouble he had gone to in the case of Austin Pym – getting him time off work, implementing special treatment, arranging a disability grant. And there was the effort he had made with Gareth Prentice and countless others. He had even saved a child's life while she stood staring, unable to do a thing until he *made* her.

'Poor man,' Megan sighed.

His most formidable act on her behalf had been to save her from herself. If Dr Morris hadn't forced her to take time off when he did, if she hadn't taken the holiday with Mrs Pughe-Morgan . . . Her mind shrank from what might have happened. She hadn't simply been brought back to full, robust health, which was blessing enough; she had been rescued from the brink of disaster. And all thanks to Timothy Morris.

There was a strong danger now, Megan knew, that her sympathy for the man would blend into pity. And she knew also that her maudlin pity was the last thing he would want. Instead, she would do her work and remove as much strain from Dr Morris's life as she humanly could.

She went over the details in her mind again as the train rumbled down a narrow, flint-walled cutting. According to Mr Halliday's information, Timothy Morris had suffered from rheumatic fever when he was a child. A heart valve had been damaged as a result, and the doctor was now at a stage in his life when the heart was beginning to fail. Megan knew from experience that there would be numerous complications. In most cases, as he approached forty the sufferer from rheumatic heart disease began to age rapidly. The body deteriorated as the circulation of blood became increasingly sluggish. Energy diminished like the shrinking hours of daylight as winter set in. There were drugs which could slow the process, but the decline was never arrested for long. Early death was practically inevitable.

Megan could recall the signs, and rebuked herself anew for not recognising what was so plain. She had seen Dr Morris exhausted after a day's work, haggard and scarcely able to keep his eyes open. She had noticed how blue his mouth and fingers became after only brief exposure to the cold. None of it had registered at the time, because the evidence could never get past her resentment.

'He's gone home to die,' Mrs Pughe-Morgan had said. 'That might sound a shade sentimental, but I believe it's what he's done, nevertheless.'

117

Timothy Morris had told the Medical Appointments Board that he wished to move to Wales, and he would prefer to do locum work. It was an odd request, coming from a doctor established in a comfortable and lucrative society practice. Members of the Appointments Board had made discreet inquiries. Friends of Dr Morris knew nothing of his reasons – most hadn't even known he wanted to leave London. In time a locum appointment had been found and Dr Morris left for Wales, taking his secret with him. It had been by sheer accident that, during a medical conference, a consultant cardiologist's remark about a patient of his, a doctor, had rung a bell with a member of the Medical Appointments Board. Word had travelled quickly; Morris was in cardiac decline, and he had removed himself and his plight from the eyes of his friends.

Megan suspected there was more to it than that. She had no intention, though, of trying to find out more. The facts she knew were enough. They had given her a sense of proportion and had dramatically changed her view of the doctor. Whereas before she had seen a disturbing ambition in him, she now suspected he was immersing himself in his work to distract his attention from his hopeless condition – a doomed man surely couldn't have much in the way of ambition.

As the train drew round the long curve that would bring it down to Pencwm Station, Megan remembered what she had said to Mrs Pughe-Morgan; *if we endure with hope, even though there isn't any real endurance or any hope of it, we live happy lives.* Did Timothy Morris believe exactly that? Was he that much in tune with Megan's own view of life?

The thought was intriguing. Not only was he not her adversary, there was now the distinct likelihood that he held views which ran directly parallel to her own. She would find it hard, in the light of all she knew and suspected, to keep her new understanding a secret from him. He would be bound to notice a change in her attitude, anyway. She knew she would have to keep in check any outward displays of sympathy towards him.

She smiled faintly, seeing the unlovely huddle of Pencwm

in the distance. Two weeks before, she had celebrated her thirty-fifth birthday. She was coming back to her duties older, wiser. Most importantly, she was coming back with her concerns aimed firmly in the direction they would take from now on – outwards.

'There's a lot of nonsense bein' talked about this Briand-Kellogg pact,' Wyn Brewster announced after Tuesday-night tea. Gladys, sitting opposite him, looked up from her knitting and read a few signs. His arms were folded tightly; his head was thrown back; his right foot was tapping the rug irritably. Something else was troubling his mind, Gladys decided, something he wouldn't talk to her about, so he would channel his annoyance through another topic. The topic was usually politics. International politics had come in for a hammering when he narrowly failed to win a debating medal in Cardiff five years before. He had moaned about politics and politicians when his essay on the Crusade of Louis IX was rejected by the editor of a historical magazine. Gladys couldn't count the times he had behaved that way. Now he was grumbling about politics again, though for what reason Gladys didn't know.

'I don't think I've heard of that, Wyn. What did you call it?'

'The Briand-Kellogg Pact. You should read the papers more, I've always said that.'

'So what about this pact? What is it?'

'It's called after the French Foreign Minister and the American Secretary of State.' Wyn sniffed, making it sound like an opinion. 'The pact's an agreement to be signed by over sixty nations.' He shook his head at the floor and went silent.

Gladys knitted half a row, waiting, then she looked up again. 'What are they agreeing about?'

Wyn had been thinking about something else. He stared back at her. 'What?'

'Those sixty nations you were on about.'

'Oh. Them. They're goin' to agree to renounce war as an instrument of policy.'

119

Gladys thought about that. 'It sounds like a good idea.'

'It's twaddle,' Wyn said flatly. 'Poppycock.'

Whatever was bothering him, it must be something very serious, Gladys decided. He never usually got this grumpy. It was usually a case of spitting out a few condemnations and that was that. Wyn wasn't a brooder.

'Well . . .' Gladys thought about the Briand-Kelogg pact again, purely in the interests of getting this low patch over and done with. Sixty nations agreeing over anything was something of an event. To find them agreeing to abandon war was tantamount to a miracle. 'I have to say, it still sounds like a fine gesture.'

'A hollow gesture, Gladys. Hot air on paper. The pact excludes wars of self-defence, for a start, and there's not one positive proposal for peace anywhere in the text. Not one. What kind of pact is that, I ask you?'

'Well, when you put it that way . . .'

'There's no other way to put it.'

Wyn got out of his chair suddenly and strode to the window. It was pitch dark outside but he stood there gazing out as if he could see for miles.

'Have you started reading that new book you got, yet?' Gladys asked him. Whatever was annoying him, it was sticking. He had been surly all through tea. 'It looks quite interesting.'

'*You* read it, then.'

Gladys stared at his back. That definitely wasn't like him. He never snapped at her, not like that. 'Wyn, what's the matter? And don't tell me nothing is. I can tell with you.'

He turned, his face stiff, ready to issue a denial, then he let out a sigh and went back to his chair. As he sat down he glanced briefly at Gladys, then fixed his gaze on his clasped fingers. 'How long since Megan's been back in Pencwm, would you say?'

For Gladys the mist immediately began to clear. 'Three weeks, thereabouts.'

'An' how often has she been round to see us?'

'She's busy, Wyn. You know that. This is one of the worst

120

winters we've had for folk being taken sick . . .' Gladys had never pinpointed the exact nature of Wyn's regard for Megan, perhaps because she didn't want to. When Megan had been away in the North, though, Gladys had noticed how restless Wyn sometimes became. During that time, too, he had talked a great deal about Megan, more than he ordinarily did.

'She came here to collect the dog the day she got back,' Wyn said, still staring at his hands. 'That's once. She came to tea two nights after, an' had to leave early. That's twice. An' that's it. We haven't seen hide nor hair of her since.'

'It's not her fault,' Gladys said. 'Megan's our friend. She'd be here a lot oftener if she'd the time.'

'I'm not so sure.'

'Oh come on now, Wyn . . .'

'Listen, Gladys. I've seen her a couple of times lately, both times with that Doctor Morris. First time they was standin' outside the surgery. Second time was beside the bridge over the stream to Powys Cleft.' Wyn unfolded his hands and set them on the arms of the chair, like a judge about to make a pronouncement. He looked at Gladys. 'What was it she said about that Morris? What was she *always* sayin', every chance we gave her?'

Gladys frowned. 'How do you mean?'

'Accordin' to Megan the man's an interferin' upstart, he's pushy an' arrogant, he interferes with her work an' undermines her decisions all over the place. Where the practice is concerned, Megan would have us believe Doctor Morris is nothin' less than a usurper. Now isn't that right? Isn't that what she's told us?'

Gladys nodded. 'More or less, I suppose. What are you saying, Wyn?'

'I'm sayin' she don't come here no more because she's changin' her views about a lot of things – us among them, most likely.'

'That's rubbish. What's she changed her views on, I'd like to know? And how would you know, anyway? You've said yourself, we've hardly seen her since she came back.'

121

Wyn scratched his moustache. 'I've got eyes, Gladys. I'm an observer of life. I've observed a highly interestin' change in our Megan's attitude towards fancy Doctor Morris. Oh, have I. Outside the surgery they was beamin' at each other like the oldest of mates, chatterin' away like school kids, as amiable an' pally as you could ask for.'

'That's just putting on a professional front,' Gladys protested. 'They can hardly go squabbling in front of people, can they now?'

'You should have seen them down by the bridge. Both leanin' on it they were, elbows propped, starin' down at the stream an' talkin' again – but this time he seemed to be sayin' most that was to be said. Megan was just lookin' at him, eyes all wide an' respectful, noddin' as he spilled his words of wisdom . . .'

Gladys put down her knitting and leaned forward. 'This just isn't like you, Wyn Brewster. That's spiteful talk. And it's unfair, because you don't know enough to make judgements. You're always saying yourself that folk jump to too many conclusions without getting their facts together and examining them.'

'I'm an experienced enough observer,' Wyn said, 'to understand the firm evidence of my own two eyes.'

Gladys shrugged. 'So? What if you're right? What if Megan *has* changed her views on Doctor Morris? That's her privilege, isn't it? It's nothing to do with you or me.'

Wyn stood up again, looking round the room, his eyes lingering on old framed photographs of their parents, on his two shelves of books. 'I think she's outgrown us, that's what I think. We're not her kind any more.'

'And I think you're cracked.' Gladys got out of her chair, smoothing her apron, shaking her head at her brother. 'If I'd talked to you the way you've just been talking to me, you'd tell me I was making mountains out of molehills.' She moved towards the small kitchen. 'I'm going to make another pot of tea.'

'Say what you like,' Wyn grunted, his eyes fixed on a picture of his father holding a two-year-old Gladys in his

122

arms. 'I know what I know.' He made a snorting, humourless little laugh. 'It's amazin', right enough . . .'

Gladys paused at the kitchen door. 'What is?'

'Amazin',' Wyn repeated, keeping his eyes on the picture. 'What a bit of posh chat an' a nice suit'll do for a bloke. She's had her head turned, has Megan Roberts.'

Gladys went into the kitchen and snatched up the teapot. She was pretty good with the quick judgements herself, she thought. Come to that, any man or woman could have drawn a sharp conclusion, listening to Wyn going on the way he had tonight. Whether his conclusions about Megan were right or wrong, one thing was crystal clear. Gladys had been listening to the words of a very jealous man.

CHAPTER THIRTEEN

THE MORNING of Friday 16th March proved to be the busiest and the most taxing since Timothy Morris had come to Pencwm. After answering an early call to a farm two miles outside of the town, where he treated a labourer with a broken leg and previously undiagnosed scurvy, Timothy returned to take morning surgery and found the waiting room full and at least a dozen people waiting outside on the path.

By ten o'clock he had seen eleven patients; four had chest disorders, three needed treatment for stomach ulcers, two had skin complaints, one was anaemic and one was a pregnant woman with chronic iron deficiency.

After ten o'clock, when Timothy took a ten-minute break for coffee, the catalogue of complaints became more dramatic. There was a man with obsessional neurosis, who was compelled to hum the same tune in his head all day long, while devoting hour after hour to checking the locks and window catches in his house and ensuring that not one cup, saucer, pot, pan or ornament in the house was an inch out of its allotted place. While the patient knew his behaviour was abnormal, there was nothing he could do to stop himself. Timothy arranged an evening visit, when they could take time to talk over the problem; providing a sympathetic ear was the only therapy known to have much effect on the condition.

Then a woman came into the consulting room. In obvious pain, she removed voluminous black woollen gloves to reveal fingers swollen and grotesquely twisted by gout. She had suffered from the condition, she told the doctor timidly, for about five years. During that time she had benefited, she felt, from the purgative Glauber's Salt her mother had used for the same condition. Now, suffering her worst attack ever, she had been forced to seek professional help. Timothy had learned to keep his temper with people in Pencwm who let their ailments turn to emergencies before they visited him. He commiserated with the woman about her disability and promised he could help. He prescribed Colchis, a drug first used around 1500 BC. It was primitive, he observed to himself, but downright sophisticated compared to the barbaric treatment she had prescribed for herself.

There followed a string of patients with saddening, surprising, shocking and often disheartening complaints. A girl of seventeen showed early signs of syphilis; a man in his sixties had an aneurysm, visible as a lump on his chest, which would soon kill him however much he rested; a thirty-five year-old widow proved to be several months pregnant, even though she swore to Timothy that no man had touched her in the three years since her husband died; a young miner revealed a massive hernia which he had kept bound up with a belt so that he could go on working; a baby's nappy rash was so severe that its buttocks were ulcerated and bleeding; an old woman's ears had to be syringed to dislodge chunks of beeswax she had stuck in them, in accordance with a family remedy for headaches; the local cobbler, Gomer Lloyd, swore there was a rat living in his head and it was eating his brain.

A little after eleven Megan came in. She'd had a busy morning, too. 'The whooping cough's definitely on its way out, now,' she told Timothy. 'But all this damp's playing merry hell with the bronchitics.'

'I've four to see after surgery,' Timothy said.

'Five, now.' Megan examined the notes she had made on her early round, listing cases where a visit from the doctor would be necessary. 'Mr Purve, number four Lampeter Crescent. He's in his middle fifties, lungs very congested and he's got a fever.'

Timothy made a note. 'Anything else?'

'Young Mrs Tweedie's got an unidentified lump on her breast. I had to drag the information out of her after her husband told me she'd been brooding about something.'

125

'Her baby's what – two months old?'

'Two and a half.'

'So, she thinks she has cancer, when what she's got is probably mastitis.'

Megan nodded, consulting her notes again. 'Lumley the chimney sweep's got something nasty wrong with one of his eyes – I noticed it when I was round there to change his wife's dressings.'

'What does it look like?'

'Well . . .' Megan gestured at her own eye. 'It's as if he has a large pea under the upper eyelid and a smaller one under the lower lid.'

Timothy thought for only a second, then said, 'Meibomian cysts.'

Megan grinned at him. 'I'd swear sometimes you've had an operation to implant a medical encyclopedia in your brain.'

'Which is a lot better than having a rat in there.' He told her about the visit from the cobbler. 'The man's deranged, of course, but his complaint was easy to treat. I told him it was common enough and simple to cure. That reassured him straight away. He said Nesta Mogg would have nothing to do with him and he was beginning to despair.'

'What did you do?'

'Gave him a bottle of smelling salts. Three sniffs, night and morning, and the rat will evaporate with the fumes.'

Megan laughed. 'You won't be able to get rid of him now. He'll be back with every new delusion that crops up.'

'I suppose so,' Timothy said. 'But he's a nice, harmless old man. I'd sooner sit here dreaming up cures for imaginary complaints than have him committed to an asylum.' He pointed at Megan's notes. 'Anything else I should know?'

'No.' She hesitated, then said, 'Well, yes.' She looked at him, frowning. 'One thing.'

'What?'

'There's egg on your chin.'

Much later, driving back to Dr O'Casey's house for a late

126

lunch, Timothy smiled to himself, recalling how Megan had laughed as he dabbed his chin with a moistened handkerchief. He was accustomed, by now, to her reversal of attitude, but he still had to regard it as a wonder. When she had been away he had once or twice tried to imagine what life would be like when she came back. He had imagined her improved in health and aggressiveness, doing her job efficiently and strengthening the barricades of her bitterness towards him. He'd had no grounds to foresee such a thorough change in her.

On the day she came back she wasted no time tracking him down, sitting herself opposite him and candidly explaining her revised opinion and point of view. Prolonged rest and the time to think had made her realise, she said, that she had been viewing everything back to front. She apologised and made an effort to explain herself. In the process of doing that, Megan had revealed something few other people knew; she had once had a dearly-loved child, a daughter called Bronwen, who had died of whooping-cough. She had also told Timothy about her fiancé, Alun, who had died in the Great War without ever seeing their child.

Timothy had been moved by her story. He had been puzzled, too; there had been no need to tell him, to explain herself at such painful length. He was sure she hadn't disclosed her secret just to gain his sympathy. He had felt, distinctly, as if he were being given one confidence in exchange for another. Which wasn't the case, of course; apart from professional confidences, he had never told Megan anything he would withhold from other people.

Nearly a month had passed since her return. In that time they had put the old relationship behind them and swiftly developed a working harmony. They even found they had a similar sense of humour. It was no exaggeration, Timothy felt, to say that he had never enjoyed working with anyone so much as he did with Megan Roberts. That fact, ironically, had a sad undertow. After taking care to ensure he would have no abiding human attachments when the inevitable dark days came, he was all-but revelling in something that would eventually be a painful loss.

127

He put that firmly from his mind. For the present he was doing nicely. He felt well enough, apart from tiring easily; even that was less of a problem than it had been, now he had learned to pace his days correctly. The present and the near future were his living space, and it was pleasant. He hadn't come here expecting much beyond hard work and time to let the past dwindle to pleasant, painless memories; in the event he had been granted a bonus, and it was wrong to view it as anything less.

'Best bib and tucker,' he murmured, reminding himself to hang out his brown suit and polish his boots. This evening was to be a special occaison. Megan had invited him to dinner.

He swung the car into the drive by the house and got out, whistling softly. He was looking forward to the evening. It was the first time, since coming to Pencwm, that he'd had anything approaching a social engagement. His only misgiving was that he might suffer a sudden onset of weariness, as happened most evenings when he stayed up late. To counter that, he decided he would take an early-evening nap – if the relentless traffic of other people's ills would permit such a luxury.

'You look so fit and well,' Gladys Brewster said. 'I don't know how you manage it, working all the time with sick people.'

'It's my healing powers,' Megan said, rubbing her hands by the black-leaded kitchen stove. 'They work on me, too.' She turned to her bag on the table, opened it and took out a one-pound packet of tea. 'Here – it's about time I put back some of what I've used up.'

'There's no call for that, Megan . . .'

'Go on, take it. Then I won't feel so bad about dropping in for a cup every time I'm passing.'

Gladys took the packet and put it on the shelf above the sink. 'It'd be nice if you did drop in a bit more often,' she said. 'Wyn was saying, not so long ago, that we hardly see you at all these days.' She jiggled the teapot, hurrying the brew. 'I told him you'd likely been too busy, with all the illness that's about.'

'Run off my feet, Gladys. I don't get home some nights until after ten. But today I was passing and I thought, blow it, the timetable can wait. I'll pop in and have a quick cup with Gladys. How have things been, anyway? Wyn keeping well, is he?'

'Things are fine and Wyn's the same.' Busying herself with the cups and spoons, Gladys said, 'Are you getting on any better with Doctor Morris?' She glanced round to catch Megan's reaction. In spite of everything Wyn had said, she expected to see a scowl of displeasure. But Megan smiled.

'To be honest, Gladys, we're getting on like a house on fire.'

'Well, you do surprise me.' Gladys gave the pot another jiggle, then began pouring the tea through a wire-mesh strainer. 'I'd have sworn you'd never get along with that man. You were so dead-set against him . . .'

'I know,' Megan said, still smiling. 'But I was wrong about him. While I was away I had time to think. I hadn't been giving him a chance, I decided. So, since I've been back we've worked as a team – and it's a happy team.'

Gladys didn't look convinced. In truth she wanted to know more. 'All those things you said about him, love – about him lording it over you, changing things, undermining your authority. Were you wrong about all that? It's not like you to misjudge somebody so badly . . .'

'Well, I did. And I said far too much, even though I *did* believe it all at the time. It was unprofessional of me to go on that way about someone I work with.'

'You sounded so sure, though,' Gladys murmured.

'It was sheer huff and resentment,' Megan assured her. 'My only excuse, and it's not a very good one, is that I wasn't very well towards the end of last year. Spite and bad judgement can thrive in people who are feeling run down.'

Gladys said no more about the matter, not until Wyn came home late in the afternoon. While she insisted she didn't believe for a moment that Megan's head had been turned,

129

she had to confess Wyn had been right about the change in her views on the doctor.

'She hasn't a bad word for him, now,' Gladys concluded, after outlining what Megan had said.

Wyn washed his hands in silence and went to read his paper in the living room. When Gladys brought through his dinner five minutes later, he was staring at the far wall, the paper hanging halfway off his knees. Gladys put the plate on the table and tapped his shoulder. 'Come back, from wherever you are. Your meal's on the table and getting colder by the second.'

Wyn stared at his sister for a moment. Then he got up, muttering gruff thanks, and seated himself at the table. He took up his knife and fork and looked down at the plate. He kept on looking, his eyes glassy and distant again.

'It's braised oxtail, parsnips and boiled potatoes,' Gladys said.

Wyn looked at her. 'Pardon?'

'Your dinner. It's what you always have on a Friday. You were looking at it as if it was something you'd never seen before.'

Gladys went back to the kitchen to wash up the pans. She was pouring hot water into the basin when she heard Wyn slam down his cutlery on the table. She went back to the living room, wiping her hands on her apron. 'Whatever's up with you?' she demanded.

'It's damnable!'

'What is?' Gladys waited for an answer, hands on hips, watching Wyn's jaw churn angrily. On and off, since the night he had talked about Megan and her changed relationship with the doctor, he had been having fits of moodiness, unmistakably linked to his wounded regard, or hope, or whatever it was he entertained towards Megan. Gladys was sure this little outburst, and the distracted silence that preceded it, were bedded in the same unrest. It was time, Gladys felt, to have a serious talk to her brother. 'Wyn? Will you explain, this minute, what's wrong?'

'That Doctor Timothy bloody Morris is wrong, that's what!'

'There's no need for swearing.'

'It'd make a saint swear!'

'What would, for heaven's sake? What harm's Doctor Morris done you?'

'Are you blind? Can't you see what he's doin'?' Wyn had gone white with anger. 'He's a wrecker, that one. Not content with marchin' into our town and runnin' things as if he owns the place – he's deliberately broken up a decent friendship with his flattery an' smarmy talk an' his London airs an' graces. It's as bad as havin' somebody breakin' in an' stealin' your valuables.'

'For heaven's sake, you're going on like something demented.' Gladys came and stood by the table, staring at Wyn. 'You're like a little boy, sometimes, the way you get in senseless tempers. Doctor Morris hasn't broken up any friendship. Megan's still our friend. The only change is that the doctor's her friend now, too.'

'Her friend? *Friend?*' Wyn jabbed the table twice with a stiffened finger. 'I wouldn't sully my mind with what he's up to – but I'll tell you this, it's not friendship.'

'Wyn!'

He pushed back his chair and stood up. 'I'm not hungry enough for my dinner. I'll have it later on.' He went to the door and jerked it open.

'Where are you going?'

'For a walk.'

'A walk? In this weather?' Gladys stepped up to him, stern as a scolding mother. 'You'll sit down and eat your dinner!'

'I told you, I—'

'Sit down!'

It had been years, more than she could remember, since she'd had to talk to her brother that way. It was in the days when he'd been young and bull-headed, impatient to have things the way he wanted them. She watched him blush as he lowered his head and shuffled back to the table. He sat down and stared glumly at his plate.

'You're not in charge of yourself,' Gladys said, 'so I'll take charge until you are. Get your dinner down you and think

131

hard while you're doing it. You've got something wrong in your head about Megan. Terribly wrong. Sort it out. If you don't, then you're not half the man I thought you were.' She turned away from him. 'I'm going to the kitchen to wash up. When I come back I want all this to be forgotten.'

'Listen,' Wyn said, but weakly, with no assurance in his voice. 'All I'm sayin' is—'

'I know what you're saying,' Gladys interrupted. 'You're saying more than you know. About yourself. I don't want to hear it. What I want out of you is common sense – and if I can't have that I'll have silence.'

She strode into the kitchen. Wyn stared at his hands, scratching restlessly at the tablecloth.

At nine o'clock Megan uncorked the port bottle and filled two glasses. She passed one to Timothy, sitting opposite her at the small dining table. 'I hope you don't mind me ignoring the etiquette of passing the port and so on,' she said. 'I'm not up to rules at this time of day.'

'Etiquette's always made me smile,' Timothy said. 'There was a lot of it about when I was a boy. All it seemed to do was get in the way of people doing or saying anything meaningful – they were too taken up with getting their procedures right.'

'I grew up with very elaborate etiquette at Mrs Pughe-Morgan's. She used to say, privately, that so-called bad manners were much more interesting and significant.' Megan sipped her drink. 'Are you sure you enjoyed dinner?'

'I swear.' Timothy put a hand solemnly against his heart. 'It's one of the best I've ever had.'

'Oh, come now, there's no need to flatter me. I'd be happy enough to know you enjoyed it.'

'That wasn't flattery, Megan.' Timothy waved his hand at the table, then at the room. 'The meal was superb. The company delightful. The surroundings, right down to the dog sleeping by the fire, couldn't be bettered. So I repeat, it's one of the best dinners I've ever had.' Megan smiled. 'Pea and ham soup, followed by stuffed shoulder of mutton,

132

followed by custard tart, eaten in the company of the District Nurse and her mongrel dog in a poky cottage in Pencwm. If that's your notion of dining in style, you must have led a very sheltered life.'

Timothy laughed. 'As it happens, I had a pretty sophisticated existence in London. Not quite a stage-door Johnny, but I was socially mobile, as they say.'

'Do you miss that?'

'Some of it.'

Megan watched Timothy as he stared at her bookshelves, his eyes roaming across the titles. He was a well-groomed picture of health. For weeks now she had watched him at every opportunity, looking for signs of fatigue, worrying that he might over-reach his strength. So far, she had seen nothing to indicate he was less than he appeared to be – fit, energetic and perfectly able for the taxing requirements of his work. Close observation had revealed that he paced himself carefully, but he did it with such skill, such style, that he seemed to take no particular care of himself at all.

'Do you mind if I have a rummage?' he said, rising. 'You've got some books there I'm dying to dip into.'

'Carry on,' Megan said.

Watching Timothy with an analytical eye had been rewarding; Megan had discovered so much she hadn't set out to look for. He had a much warmer and more sensitive personality than she had suspected. His enthusiasm for his work was enormous, and unlike a lot of doctors Megan had met, he was wise beyond the limits of his professional skill. She had learned that he liked theatre and the cinema, and he had an impressive knowledge of literature. So far he hadn't said anything about women in his life, but Megan was sure there must have been a few. Nobody so urbane, she thought, could ever get that way without a history of romantic involvements.

'Did you enjoy this?' Timothy turned from the shelves, holding up a book. *Gone to Earth*.

'By Mary Webb – is that the one?'

'Yes. It's excellent.'

133

'It was given to me by Miss Williams, at a time when I was too busy to do more than work, eat and sleep. It got put on the shelf and it's been there since.'

'Do read it.'

Timothy replaced the book and made to come back to the table. Megan suggested they sit in the fireside chairs. She brought the glasses and they settled opposite each other, Megan putting her feet beside Scratch where he lay curled on the rug.

Timothy took a slow sip of port and savoured it carefully.

'I suppose you're going to tell me the year it was bottled,' Megan said.

'I don't know much about wine. But I love the flavour of port. Any old port. Reminds me of student days. A glass of port with my tutor, the sound of cricket being played out on the sunlit grass. Ah, my vanished youth . . .' He grinned and took another sip.

'So you're sentimental.'

'Deeply.' Timothy jerked his head at the bookshelves. 'Hence my adoration of the splendid Mary Webb. Have you read *Precious Bane*?'

'No,' Megan said, finding herself soothed by the off-duty mellowness of his voice. 'I haven't heard of it.'

'It came out about two years ago. Mary Webb's master-piece, if you ask me.' He leaned forward, resting his elbows on his knees, the glass between his hands. 'Shall I tell you the story?'

'If you like.' His eyes had startled Megan. Wide, gently penetrating. It was a look she had never seen before. The look of a man with enthusiasm, she thought, a man with a zest for life.

'Well,' Timothy began, 'the story's told by Prudence Sarn, a girl from just north of the Shropshire meres. Susan was born with a harelip, you see, which some people take to be a sign that she's a witch . . .'

It took him nearly ten minutes to tell the story. Megan had never been so enchanted. She gazed at the fire as the pictures formed in her head, carried and conjured there by Timothy's

134

soothing, persuasive voice. Vividly she saw the wizard Beguildy; she pictured his wife and child as they drowned. Just as clearly she saw Pru's terrible plight and all her tribulations, culminating in an attack by an enraged mob, intent on killing her. With a surge of emotion Megan saw the hero, Kester Woodseaves, carry Pru away to safety.

Megan looked at Timothy as the story ended. 'That was beautiful,' she said.

'Oh, she's a marvellous writer.'

'I meant the way you told it. I was entranced.'

Timothy made a tight smile. 'Thank you. I was afraid, halfway through, that I might be boring you. You looked so distant.'

'I was. I was back at the beginning of the nineteenth century.' Megan stood and took Timothy's empty glass. 'You'd make a wonderful uncle, you know. You'd be in permanent demand for bedtime stories.'

The cork was halfway out of the botlle again when there was a knock at the door.

'I should have known this was too good to last.'

Megan went to the door and opened it. A small boy stood on the path, wearing a coat that was too thin for the weather. He blinked up at Megan but said nothing.

'Yes? What is it?'

'Are you Nurse Roberts, please?'

'That's right.' She thought most of the children knew her. She was pretty sure she recognised this one's face, though she couldn't put a name to it.

'My Mam's Mrs Boyle. She said to tell you the baby's comin'.'

'What? But it's not due for weeks yet . . .'

'Well, it's comin', anyroad.'

'Very well,' Megan sighed. 'Run back and tell your mam I'll be there in a few minutes.' As she closed the door it dawned on Megan why the boy hadn't been sure who she was. Very few people in Pencwm had seen her wearing an ordinary dress.

'The party's over,' she said, then felt a jolt of shock. The change in Timothy was awful. A minute before he had been

135

relaxed, smiling. Now he was pale and his eyes appeared sunken. He looked the way people did when they were about to faint. He was rising, averting his eyes.

'It's all right, Megan, I understand. It happens to me all the time.' He moved to the door and took his coat from the hook. Megan stood watching, trying not to show her concern. 'To tell you the truth,' he said, putting on the coat, 'I need an early night, anyway.'

'It's such a pity this had to happen, though,' Megan murmured. She forced herself to move, going to the door and opening it.

'I can give you a lift round to the Boyles',' Timothy offered.

'No, no, I'll be all right.'

'Well . . .' Timothy smiled. He looked so wan, his skin yellowish and waxy. 'Thanks again for a lovely dinner. It was really splendid.'

'Thank you for coming.'

Megan waved from the step and watched until he was inside the car. Back in the house, preparing her bag for a delivery, she fought down the clutching fear. It was nothing, she told herself; he was tired, it happened that way with heart sufferers. But it had frightened her, nevertheless. And saddened her. The fear would pass but the sadness wouldn't. The man had such a relish for living. There were millions who hadn't and would go on living, just the same. Nature cared nothing about justice.

As Megan reached for her coat she realised that what she had felt, seeing the change in Timothy, was not so much fear as a sense of impending loss. He had become such a dear, cherished friend. She hadn't thought of him that way before.

CHAPTER FOURTEEN

THE weeks streamed by and it was May, declaring itself in the fields around Pencwm with flowering patches of gorse, periwinkle and lilac eyebright. As the winds from the west grew drier and sunshine took the damp chill from the ground, children began to play on the streets again, men took excursions into the hills and wives gathered at street corners to talk.

On a clear Sunday morning Harry Benson took himself up past the ruined chapel at Emlyn Hill, cut across a scrubby meadow and followed a path to the top of the crag he called Mystic Hill, though he never called it that out loud.

Harry was thirty and by all accounts a hard man. In boyhood scraps and, later, in the occasional fist fight outside the pit where he worked, he had distinguished himself as a chap with a born boxer's style – light on his feet and always throwing fast, accurate punches. Harry never picked a fight but he had never lost one, either. He was a quiet man with few friends, married to a girl who didn't think he was particularly hard. She knew he liked nothing better than to go walking on the hills, or stand motionless on the edge of a wood, watching the rituals of birds and wild animals. He had no anger in him, no rebellion. Harry accepted his life and did what he could to withstand its limitations. Mystic Hill was a place that made him feel privileged; it proved to him that even a poor coal miner, held by circumstances to a narrow, often bleak way of living, could slip the bonds of grey reality and experience the miraculous.

Harry believed he was the only one who knew the special place to the west of the summit, which could be reached only by clambering over precarious outcrops of rock and swinging

137

in under a broad mossy shelf. He had discovered the beautiful grotto two years before, when he had accidentally cut himself off and had to improvise a way back to the rock path.

Now, on this quiet sabbath, hearing only the sounds of the wind and distant birdsong, Harry stooped under the shelf and gazed into the wondrous hollow. It was a moss-lined chamber enclosing a natural pool, ten feet across, lined with rosy quartz and lit by slanting beams from chinks in the vaulted dome. Harry had found that this was the best time of day to see the place. The sun touched the single, rope-like stream of water that fed the pool, transforming it to crystal. The glittering pinks and reds of the quartz were projected on the walls of the chamber in restless, dazzling variations of streaking light. Harry had never known anything so beautiful. And it was his alone.

He stayed there for ten minutes, breathing the cool moist air and committing to memory, afresh, the dreamlike, otherworldly sight of the rosy pool in its secret cavern.

When he emerged he was dazzled for a moment by the brightness of the sun. He stood beneath the ledge, his feet braced on two boulders, and looked down through narrowed eyes to the spread of buildings and tips that was Pencwm. Reality, he thought. It always had to be faced again. But at least there was this place to come to for the occasional escape.

Harry reached out to his right, hands spread to grip the rock. As he lifted his right foot and shifted his weight the stone beneath his left foot moved. He tried to throw himself forward and sprawl on the rock before the boulder rolled away. He missed and felt himself tumbling sideways. Rockface rushed past as he sailed into open space. His body turned and he flailed his arms, desperate for a handhold. He was still grasping at air as his head struck a huge knuckle of rock. Silver light sparked across his vision and then vanished, leaving nothing but darkness.

The sun was warming his back as he came to. For a moment he lay still, trying to remember. When he moved his hand he felt grass. Turning, feeling the pain like a lead weight in the back of his skull, he sat up. No bones broken, as far as he could tell. Just bruises, on his knees, elbows and backside. And the ostrich egg on the back of his head. Grunting, he stood up. As far as he could tell, he was in a field. He looked up at the expanse of rock; falling that distance, he thought, he was lucky to be alive, let alone in one piece.

The pain in his head was terrible. It overshadowed the jabbing in his legs, arms and back. He turned and began walking back home, reflecting that he had paid dearly for his visit to Mystic Hill.

Two hours later, as the thin smells of Sunday dinners wafted among the huddled backyards of Cardower Road, Mary Benson, Harry's wife, came bustling into their cottage with Nesta Mogg behind her. Nesta was carrying her black cloth drawstring bag, her dank dispensary which she allowed no other person to touch.

'He's on the sofa,' Mary said, brushing back a strand of hair as she pointed to the living room door. She seemed reluctant to go in. 'It frightened me. He just kind of staggered like, then he sat down an' said he felt terrible. A minute after he was groanin' an' wouldn't answer me when I asked what was up. I went to get him a cup of water an' when I came back he was sort of slumped over on the cushion.'

Nesta pushed past Mary and went into the living room. Harry was lying on his side with his knees drawn up. His eyes were half closed and he breathed noisily through his mouth. Nesta bent over him as Mary came timidly to the door.

'Can you hear me, Harry Benson?' Mary shook his shoulder. 'It's Nesta Mogg.' She shook him again. 'Harry!' He didn't respond. Nesta looked across at Mary. 'Has he been scrappin' again, or what? There's fresh bruises on him.'

'He fell when he was out on the hills, he said.'

Nesta sniffed Harry's breath. She felt around his head, fingering the swelling at the base of his skull. 'He's took a bad knock there.' She pulled up one eyelid, then the other. 'Concussion,' she said, standing back.

'Is that bad?'

'Sometimes, sometimes not.' Nesta picked up her bag and

139

drew open the top. She fumbled among the contents and brought out a dirty-looking folded cloth. She opened it out and looked at Mary. 'Get some water on to boil.'

When Mary had brought the water in a pan Nesta dropped the cloth into it. The water began to turn yellow and pungent smelling.

'What is it?' Mary asked.

'The cloth's soaked with rare herbs.' That was all Nesta seemed prepared to reveal. With calloused fingers that didn't appear to feel pain from the scalding water, she fished out the cloth again and wrung it. 'Save the water,' she told Mary. 'He has to drink a cupful every two hours until it's used up.' She wadded the cloth and pressed it to the back of Harry's head. 'See now, lass, you hold it there.'

'Will it bring him round?'

Nesta nodded. 'Sooner or later.'

Mary knelt by the couch and closed her hand over the compress. 'Thank God I found you,' she said to Nesta. 'I'd no idea what to do.'

'I can always be found,' Nesta assured her. She closed the bag and swung it on to her shoulder. 'I'll come back about suppertime an' see how he is.'

'Erm, about payin' you,' Mary said awkwardly. 'I don't know how much it is . . .'

'We'll wait an' see what the job's worth. I might have to do more yet.'

Nesta let herself out. Mary gazed at her husband. She believed his colour was improving. As she watched his lips began to move and he groaned softly. Thank the Lord for Nesta Mogg, Mary thought. It was no wonder people swore by her.

For a time Megan had believed it was in her power to overcome the inescapable. Throughout April, as she assisted Timothy in the surgery and made countless other excuses to lighten his work load and be near him, it appeared that he was actually gaining in strength. She had mentioned this in a letter to Mrs Pughe-Morgan. The reply had encouraged Megan even more:

It has to be said that nothing is inevitable. Your own experience has shown you that some so-called hopeless cases defy science, logic and most of the relevant laws of nature. They survive. Our own Mrs Foskett, you'll recall, wasn't given much time to live after her heart attack. But I've forgotten how many years ago that was.

Your letter prompted me to have a chat with Dr Fry, an eminent enough chap in Harley Street. He told me that in his own experience, many people now alive should have departed this vale of tears long ago, and a number of them suffer from the same condition as Dr Morris. So there you are. Your observations may not be so fanciful as you feared they were. It's astonishing what the force of will can achieve; I have the impression Dr Morris is a man of strong will, and your own will is as stout as any. Who's to say what they can't do in combination, working to the same end?

Now, Megan felt it had all been fanciful, after all. For three days Timothy had looked ill, while steadfastly denying there was anything wrong with him. Megan had been careful not to insist; twice she asked him if perhaps he wanted to rest and twice he had told her, rather brusquely, that he didn't need to. At other times he was friendly and affable, but any suggestion that his health might be less than robust seemed to find a gap in his good nature.

Today being Sunday, Megan had hoped he would have time to rest. But an early emergency had him out of bed before seven and he hadn't returned until noon. Megan had been in the surgery since eleven, doing the filing and instrument cleaning which she now insisted were part of her duties. Timothy had looked in on her and what Megan saw shocked her. He had the appearance of a man who had risen from a sickbed much too soon. His eyes were dark-rimmed and in some way his teeth seemed to protrude when he spoke.

Megan couldn't restrain herself. 'You must rest,' she told him. 'I know you say there's nothing wrong with you but it's obvious there is. You've caught a virus of some kind. It's vital for you to rest, you know that better than most.'

141

His reaction had reminded Megan of her own outburst when Timothy had told her she must take time off. He had blustered, making her fear for him even more. He demanded to know what grounds she had for assuming he was ill, when his own senses told him he was perfectly well.

'Get it into your head, Megan – I'm all right! I'm fitter than anyone you know!'

He had stamped out of the surgery and driven away. Megan, feeling a deep foreboding churn in her, had begun to cry.

Now, back in her cottage, she wondered at herself. On two successive nights there had been dreams, vivid enough to stay with Megan hours after she woke. She had seen herself walking with Timothy, crossing hillsides and meadows she recognised; they were in the Pantmynach Valley, near Mrs Pughe-Morgan's estate. The dreams weren't precisely carefree. There was a serenity in them, a sense of peace, but it seemed to be a peace that existed apart from life. At first Megan avoided an analysis. When finally she gave in and scrutinised the dreams, the meaning came simply, though painfully. Megan harboured a wish to be with Timothy beyond the time he was snatched from life. Although it went against all reason, something in her longed to stay by him, wherever death took him.

'Such rubbish,' she chided herself. But there it was. Dreams told such disarming truths. She could never have imagined herself becoming so attached to another human being. Not since Alun. There had been one man, John Sykes, a solicitor who had fallen in love with her, but Megan had been unable to return his intensity of affection. She had been wounded so deeply by Alun's death that she'd sworn never to expose herself to that measure of pain again. But now . . .

'Stop this!' she told herself sharply, making the dog drop his ears, thinking he was being scolded. Megan patted him, deciding she would find some work to do, something powerful enough to distract her. She couldn't face what her logically-trained mind urged her to acknowledge.

She snatched a book from the shelf. It was one she had

142

been avoiding – *Current Advances in Nursing Care* – but now it would be a valuable diversion. She sat down and opened the thick volume on her knees.

Within minutes her mind was wandering. She recalled recent times with smooth-flowing clarity. 'The theatre's the last outpost of magic,' she heard Timothy's voice say.'Our playwrights are our Merlins.' They had talked about drama, music, literature, Megan being an avid listener for most of the time. She knew the stories of *Precious Bane*, *A Passage to India* and *The Charterhouse of Parma*, all told to her in the same bewitching style. She had listened to descriptions and a few memorised passages from Shaw's *Saint Joan* and O'-Neill's *Beyond the Horizon*. Timothy had even drawn applause from her for his rendition of a George Robey song from the revue *Bubbly*. She had learned so much, and loved the learning . . .

There was a sharp knock at the door. Megan shut the book and crossed the room. She opened the door and found Mary Benson there. She looked distraught.

'Nurse, can you come?'

'What is it?'

'My Harry – he's been took very bad. It's his head. He fell down on the rocks this mornin', an' now he's babblin' an actin' wild . . .'

A job for the doctor, Megan thought. But he might be resting – she prayed he was. 'Hang on, I'll get my coat and bag.'

Megan dashed back into the house, pulled a handful of sterile packets from a cabinet and threw them in her bag. Normally, she mused as she put on her coat, she would be annoyed at being disturbed on a Sunday. Even district nurses were entitled to their occasional days off. Today she found she didn't mind. She needed distraction, and she was sure now she couldn't find it at home.

'Stay, Scratch,' she called to the dog as she left. She banged the door shut and locked it. 'Right then,' she said to Mary. 'Lead on.'

143

CHAPTER FIFTEEN

Timothy had fallen asleep in an armchair in the sitting room. He had been too tired to climb the stairs, undress and get into bed. For long minutes before he slept, he sat sunken down in the chair with his eyes closed, silently rebuking himself for his behaviour towards Megan. He knew she was concerned for him, it showed on her face, but he couldn't keep down his anger when he saw that look. The anger wasn't directed at Megan, it was aimed at himself, at the condition he was in. His failing heart was like a malignant imp, reminding him that the buoyancy he had found would not last long.

He had wondered if he should tell Megan. They were intimates, after all. The question plagued him as he drifted away from consciousnes; he had fallen asleep believing he shouldn't tell her, for fear of arousing her pity. That would be terrible.

'Doctor . . .'

He woke suddenly, startled, blinking at the housekeeper. She was shaking his arm gently, clutching a slip of paper in her other hand. Timothy pushed himself up in the chair.

'Sorry to disturb you. A young woman came to the door with this. She says it's from Nurse Roberts, and it's terribly important.'

'Thanks.'

Timothy took the paper and unfolded it.

'Would you like a cup of tea or something? There's a pot made.' The housekeeper was looking at him with open concern. 'You've not eaten all day, either . . .'

'Tea'll be fine,' Timothy murmured, squinting to read the note. He read it twice, then stood up, rubbing his eyes.

144

'Forget the tea,' he called to the housekeeper.

He arrived at the Bensons' house less than five minutes later. Inside he found a frightened-looking young woman standing in the corner of the living room. Megan was on the couch with both arms clutched around a young man, restraining him. She was red-faced with exertion.

'Thank God,' she panted, looking at Timothy. 'I didn't want to disturb you, but—'

'Did you see Daddo?' Harry Benson yelled, struggling to free his arms. Saliva dribbled from his lips and his eyes rolled from side to side. 'Daddo! On that bogie, he was!'

Timothy put his bag on the couch and knelt beside Harry. 'Hold him tighter, if you can.' He grasped the man's head and turned his face to the light from the window.

'The dementia comes and goes,' Megan said. 'He lapses for a minute or so, looks comatose, then starts ranting again.' She grunted and clutched tighter as Harry began wriggling.

'Clear the bloody props then! Get them moved! Daddo! Daddo!'

'He's as strong as a pit pony,' Megan panted.

Timothy felt the swelling with the fingers of both hands, keeping Harry's head clamped, staring at his eyes. 'Pupils are uneven,' he murmured. 'And his temperature's up – skin feels like hot paper. How long since he got the injury?'

'This morning some time. Four, five hours ago, maybe longer.'

Timothy looked at Mary, who was pressed by a corner cupboard beside the fireplace. 'When did he start behaving like this?'

'Well, when he came in I asked him what was up, like, an' he said he'd had a fall up on the hills. Then he said he had a sore head, then a bit after that he passed out.'

'And then,' Megan said grimly, 'she went out and got hold of Nesta Mogg.' She relaxed her grip on Harry as he went still. 'She put some kind of compress on the swelling and left a panful of muck for him to drink.'

'You should have come for Nurse or myself at once,' Timothy told Mary.

'Nesta and her mother before her have treated everything this chap's had since he was a baby,' Megan said. 'It's a wonder he's survived this long.'

'We've got to get him to hospital.' Timothy looked at Harry's eyes again. 'I'm sure the skull's fractured. He should have been in an operating theatre hours ago.'

As Timothy stood up Harry jerked violently, catching Megan off-guard. He slipped from her grip and landed on his knees on the carpet. On all fours he stared up at Mary. 'They put him in a damn box! Shouldn't have done that! He'll never breathe in there!'

'It's his da he's on about,' Mary said, cringing from her husband. 'He got killed in the pit a week after Harry started workin' there.'

Harry lurched to his feet, turning a full circle. He stared at Megan, his mouth working soundlessly, then suddenly he grasped his head in both hands. 'Jesus!' His knees buckled and he hit the floor.

'Quick!' Timothy stooped and grasped the broad shoulders. 'Get his feet.'

'Careful,' Megan yelped, concern all over her face again.

Timothy knew she was worried as much for him as for Harry. 'Get him on the couch,' he snapped. 'Face down, head over the arm.'

When Harry was positioned Timothy grabbed his bag, which had been pushed on to the floor. 'We'll have to be fast.' He pulled out a long roll of canvas. As he unfurled it along the floor there was a knock at the door, then a shuffling in the lobby. The living-room door swung open. Nesta Mogg stood in the opening, staring.

'Get out of here!' Megan shouted at her. 'Out!'

'What're you doin' to that lad?' Nesta demanded.

'You heard me!' Megan warned. 'Clear off or I'll throw you out myself!'

Nesta was staring at the unrolled canvas. From one of its six pockets Timothy had pulled a Hudson's brace. Still on his knees he snatched out a perforating drill and began attaching it to the chuck.

146

'That's a brace an' bit!' Nesta snapped.

Megan rose from the side of the couch and stamped across to the doorway. She brought up a balled fist and held it under Nesta's nose. 'Out, you witch-bitch! *Out!*'

'That's butchery! He's goin' to drill the lad's head open!' Nesta stared at Mary. 'How can you let them do that?'

'I couldn't find you,' Mary whined. 'I had to get somebody.'

'He's goin' to make a hole in the poor lamb's head!' Nesta stuck out her arm and waggled her finger at Timothy. 'He's got concussion! Nothin' more! There's no call to go butcherin' him like that!'

'He has a haematoma,' Timothy said, levelling his eyes on Nesta's. 'A clot is pressing on his brain. I'm going to relieve the pressure. If I don't he'll die. He might die anyway, because of the delay.'

'Because of *you!*' Megan slapped her hand on the muscle between Nesta's shoulder and neck. 'Get your stinking hulk out of here and let qualified people get on with their work!' She spun the woman and sent her staggering along the lobby. 'I'll see to you later, Nesta Mogg! Don't think I won't!'

Before Nesta was out of the house Megan was back at the couch, positioning Harry's head and steadying it. When Timothy had shaved the hair away from the base of the man's skull he swabbed the skin with iodine and bunched a sterile cloth around the site of the operation.

'Will it hurt him?' Mary squeaked.

Megan shook her head. Harry was so deeply unconscious they could have amputated a limb without him feeling it.

'Here we go then,' Timothy breathed. He looked over his shoulder at Mary. 'Go and make some tea, will you? There's nothing you can do here.'

He raised the drill over Harry's head and poised the spear-shaped tip. He glanced at Megan. 'All right?'

She nodded, recalling the last time they performed an emergency operation together. No paralysis now, she thought. Only worry. For Harry, and for pale, drained Timothy.

'Do you think he's got a chance?' she whispered.

147

'There's a spark of life in there,' Timothy said. 'One spark is enough, Megan.' His eyes were wide, determined. 'We can fan it back into fire.

It was after five when they got to the hospital in Llengwyn. Megan sat with Mary in the little green-painted ante-room while Timothy and the duty surgeon examined Harry in the theatre.

'How bad is he?' Mary asked, after a ten-minute silence, listening to the muffled voices beyond the swing doors.

'Bad enough,' Megan said. 'But Doctor Morris took the pressure off Harry's brain, and his breathing was getting better all the way here. There's hope, Mary. Hang on to it.'

Mary stared at the wall, her face blank, looking as pale as her husband when they wheeled him into the theatre. 'Do you know something, Nurse?'

'What?'

'That's the first time I've ever been in a motor car.'

Megan smiled and squeezed Mary's hand, wondering at the incongruity of things. It wasn't always voiced, like Mary's inapt little remark, but it was always there. As Timothy had knelt in that shabby little living room, removing his bloodied drill from the brace and replacing it with a burr to complete the penetration of Harry's skull, she had thought suddenly, *I would love to kiss his hands*. It had passed through her mind and heart in an orderly, swift way, almost a casual observation. It was a fleeting incongruity. Later, on the drive over to Llengwyn, she realised that in spite of her resistance earlier, her spirit – or soul, or psyche or whatever it was – had adopted the certainty that she loved Timothy Morris. It was pointless to deny it, or to warn herself against something she couldn't resist. Knowing well that she would suffer more pain by submitting to that love, Megan was aware of another inconsistency; she didn't care. Beneath her immediate concern for Timothy's health, she felt oddly happy.

Timothy emerged from the theatre twenty minutes later. He still looked weary and drawn, but Megan fancied the

148

deeper fatigue had left him. Now he was simply a tired-looking man. He stood by the theatre door and nodded to Mary Benson.

'He's going to be fine,' he said. 'The surgeon's patched him nicely and all it'll take is a bit of rest.' He came across and touched her shoulder. 'We were only just in time, mind you. If ever anything serious like this happens again, and let's pray to the Lord there won't be a next time, come to us at once.'

'Yes, Doctor.' Mary said it through tears. Megan took a handkerchief from her pocket and passed it to the girl. She looked at Timothy and smiled, wishing now that she could kiss his mouth.

It was ten minutes past seven by Megan's fob watch when they dropped Mary off at her house on Cardower Road. As she got out and waved to them, Megan noticed Gareth Prentice standing at the door of his parents' house, four doors away. He had put on seventeen pounds in weight since Christmas and looked like an advertisement for cod liver oil.

'Two exceptional success stories on the same street,' Megan said, seeing Timothy looking at the boy. 'You're making your mark round here, aren't you?' She grinned at him and thought, *God, I'm not imagining it, he looks better.* After a day like that, and starting out from a position of such terrible debility, Timothy looked almost as he had the first time she saw him. Even the tiredness appeared to have lifted.

He clasped the steering wheel with both hands and let out a sigh. 'Megan, I'll tell you something. Seeing Harry Benson come back to the living world before my eyes – that's done more to buck me up than I can tell you. One spark, that's all there was. He was on the point of leaving us. One dying spark and we rekindled him. He has the gift of life again.'

Life is a gift. Cherish it always . . . Megan's guiding philosophy echoed Timothy's words, putting a surge of emotion through her. Not in years had she felt that particular tint of fervour, a breathtaking desire, almost a need, to reach out and hold another person.

Timothy took one hand off the wheel and pointed. 'There goes the villain of the piece,' he said.

149

Megan looked. Nesta Mogg was at the bottom of the road, walking away from them with her black dispensary over her shoulder.

'Can I leave my bag with you?' Megan asked. She already had the door halfway open. 'I'll come round and pick it up later.'

'Now Megan,' Timothy warned, 'don't do anything rash. My own impulse today was to strangle the woman, but a sense of proportion's mandatory with us. Bear that in mind.'

'I will.' She stepped on to the road and ducked her head back inside the car for a moment. 'Keeping down disease is part of my job, though. I have to bear that in mind, too.'

Timothy was grinning and shaking his head as he drove away.

Megan caught up with Nesta on the low-walled bridge over the stream that divided Powys Cleft from the rest of the town.

'Right, Hecate, I want words with you.'

Nesta spun, startled. She stared at Megan. 'What's that you called me?'

'Hecate,' Megan repeated, barely parting her teeth. 'Queen of the witches.' She stepped close, driving Nesta against the wall. 'She had three heads, old Hecate. One was a horse, one a dog and the other one a boar. You're the spitting image, with all three rolled into one.'

'You'll pay for your slanders,' Nesta growled. She pushed a swatch of hair away from her eyes. 'An' you'll be called to account for your butchery too, you an' that fancy-talkin' doctor.'

'Harry Benson is going to be all right,' Megan said, spitting the words. 'In spite of your interfering, in spite of your obscene medicine, he's on the mend.' She put her face close to Nesta's. 'I warned you before not to tamper,' didn't I?'

'The wife came to me first,' Nesta said, her eyes wavering. She was used to awe and even reverence, occasionally. Aggression was something she was ill-equipped to tackle. 'I did what was right, too. It was *your* interferin' that did the lad harm.'

'You ghastly heap of filth!'

150

Megan knew she was not strictly in control of herself. On the other hand, her impulse felt trustworthy enough, and highly appropriate. She took a grip on Nesta's shoulder. 'I warned you. You didn't listen.' Her grip tightened as she thought of Timothy's sense of triumph, and what might have happened to him if he had failed to save Harry Benson.

'You're assaultin' me, that's what you're doin'!' Nesta tried to wriggle free and Megan gripped her tighter still. 'Let go of me!' Nesta sniffed deeply, a rumbling sound, and Megan jerked her head aside in time to miss the gobbet of spit.

'You damned animal!'

Tensing herself, with both hands on Nesta's shoulders now, Megan did what she had known for several seconds she was going to do. She pushed forward violently and stepped back. In a flurry of waving legs and filthy underskirts Nesta went over the edge of the bridge and landed face-down in the water.

Megan leaned over the wall, watching the woman drag herself to her knees, drenched, howling, trying to catch her medicine bag as it floated away from her.

'Next time I have to tackle you, Nesta Mogg, you won't get off so lightly! What I'll do to you will make God's wrath look like a tantrum!'

Megan turned and walked away. Her heart was pounding and exultation sang in her veins. She could hardly wait to tell Timothy what she had done. He would disapprove, of course, and it was only right that he should. But he would be delighted, too, whether he showed it or not. What a day this has been! she thought, her step quickening. Later she would dwell on every particle of what had happened. For the moment, though, it was pleasure enough to glide along on the bracing aftermath.

CHAPTER SIXTEEN

THE fourth of June was a Monday. Since Megan had decided it would be inappropriate to declare summer on a Friday, she had waited until the fourth to breeze into the surgery before 'first bell', as it was called, with a bunch of wild flowers for the vase on the window. She tapped the door three times and entered, then froze. Timothy wasn't behind the desk, as he normally was. The man sitting there was Dr O'Casey.

Megan stared.

O'Casey stared back. He pointed at the flowers. 'You heard I'm back, then. I'm touched, Megan.'

She had never seen him look so well, but that observation was submerged by her surprise. 'What are you doing here?'

'Oh, so you didn't know I was back. Well, I am. I got bored. Ireland is a delight, but I've been hankering to get in harness for weeks. So, since I'm fully restored in wind, limb and enthusiasm, I'm freshly ensconced where I belong.'

'Where's Doctor Morris?'

'At this moment,' O'Casey said, removing his pocket watch and peering at it, 'he's probably packing his bags.'

Megan's heart was making uncomfortable movements. 'Packing?'

'For a trip to London.' Dr O'Casey smiled broadly. 'You probably feel a resentment coming on, Megan, but please don't. I know how you hate being kept in the dark. What happened was, I called Morris on Thursday to tell him I couldn't stay away any longer. We talked for quite a time – indeed, I must owe my brother quite a few shillings towards his telephone bill. Morris and I arrived at an arrangement. He's been worked into the ground in my absence, so a few days' leave seemed to be in order – although I had to insist.

152

After his leave he'll work on until the full term of our contract expires.' He nodded towards the window. 'Fit as I feel, it'll take me a few weeks to get back to the pace that brought me to my knees in the first place. So. Young Timothy and I will operate a partnership for a time. I rather look forward to it.'

'And you say he's going to London?' Megan was finding the flowers an embarrassment. 'I'm surprised he didn't say anything to me. I've seen him three or four times since Thursday.'

O'Casey composed his hands on the desk. 'Don't look so hurt. You'll understand everything, soon enough.' He put on a theatrical scowl. 'You haven't even told me you're glad to see me back.'

'Well of course I am. It's just such a surprise.' Megan shook aside the small tumult of remembrance; Lord, how she had missed him in the beginning! Now, although it was a genuine pleasure to see Dr O'Casey, she felt he was intruding. And why hadn't Timothy said anything?

'Who are the flowers for?'

'I . . .' Megan felt herself blush. 'I thought they would brighten up the surgery.'

'Oh, they will.' O'Casey stood up, went to the window and picked up the brown stoneware vase. He took it to the sink and filled it with water. 'There we are.' He took the flowers from Megan and arranged them loosely in the vase, then put it back on the ledge. 'I understand you had to take some time off,' he said, not looking at her. 'Doctor Morris wasn't all that specific – but I gather you were under the weather.'

'Run down,' Megan said, anxious to dispose of the topic. 'I'm fine now.'

'Good.' Dr O'Casey seated himself behind the desk again. 'Morris has kept an admirable record of the case load while I've been away, and your own notes are splendid, as always. Apart from the renewed energy, I hardly feel I've been away.'

Megan knew if she stood there much longer she would start to fidget. 'I'd better be getting out on my rounds,' she said. 'Nice to have you back, anyway.'

'You must come round to the house one evening, so I can

153

bore you with my snapshots. I've a few stories about Greece that'll raise a couple of yawns, too.'

'As long as the sherry bottle's to hand, I'll enjoy myself,' Megan said. Before she left, she told Dr O'Casey, again, that it was a pleasure to have him back.

Throughout the morning she tried not to dwell on what had happened. Apart from her annoyance at not being told the old doctor was returning early, she wondered at the implications. Would Timothy now take a role so minor that their regular contact with each other would be broken? It was even conceivable that their link would be broken completely. Trying to suppress speculation only seemed to strengthen it. And now that Dr O'Casey was back, Megan had to face what she had been steadfastly avoiding – the prospect of Timothy eventually leaving the area. What then?

At eleven o'clock she made her regular call at the Hewletts' to see Denis, who had tuberculosis and believed that Nurse Roberts would be his salvation. Denis was almost sixteen and obviously smitten by Megan. She found it acutely embarrassing, at times, to see the adoration on his face, but in therapeutic terms that was a bonus. Morale in a patient with TB was of paramount importance – good spirits did for the constitution what medicine could not.

'And how are we this morning, Denis?' Megan put her bag on the floor and sat on the chair by the bed. 'Is the cough any easier with the new medicine?'

'I'm miles better, Nurse.' The boy looked old. The skin of his face appeared thin and translucent, clinging like a film to the spare, fragile bones of his skull.

'Good. And are you sleeping any better now we've got the lotion for the sore bits?'

'Like a log,' Denis said. 'I'm better all round.' His smile underlined his desperate affliction. Listlessness and fatigue seemed always to find expression in the eyes; to see a smile being mustered from such frailty, Megan thought, was like encountering a solitary wilting flower in an empty room. 'I even got up to sit in the living room for a while last night,' Denis added. It was said with such pride that he might have

154

been describing a sports-day triumph.

'That's grand.' Megan leaned down, opened her bag and took out a book. 'There.' She laid it on the bed between the boy's hands. 'You're getting through them like lightning – every bit as fast as I used to when I was your age.'

Denis touched the book, picked it up in hands as feeble as a child's and turned it to read the spine. '*Gulliver's Travels.* The one you told me about.' His big dark eyes, rich with gratitude, turned to Megan. 'Thank you very much. I'll take care of it.'

'I know you will. It's nice to know my books are getting read, Denis. They're no use to anyone just decorating a shelf.'

Mrs Hewlett brought in a cup of tea for Megan, as she did each morning. It was always too strong but Megan never refused it.

'What do you make of him this morning, Nurse?'

The question was another part of the ritual. Mrs Hewlett was sustained by rituals. She moved automatically from one pattern of speech and activity to another, leaving little space for chance to put new hardships in her path. Although she was the same age as Megan she looked much older. She was thin and stooped. Her grey hair was swept back and held at the crown with grips; the severity of the style emphasised the deep lines on her forehead and cheeks. Poverty and continual worry had given Mrs Hewlett the appearance of a troll.

'He tells me he's feeling better all round,' Megan said. She took a sip of the tea, which she had privately labelled Essence of Linoleum. The evasiveness of her answer was the only alternative to a lie. Denis was not getting better, he probably never would.

'Could I have a word with you in the front room, Nurse?' Mrs Hewlett wagged a finger at her son as he frowned. 'Don't worry, now, she'll come back and talk to you before she goes.'

'Of course I will.'

Megan stood up and squeezed Denis's hand, then followed his mother through to the living room.

'It's about his birthday,' Mrs Hewlett said, standing by the

155

table, fingering the frayed chenille cover. 'I'm havin' a little tea for him.' A tea was what children in Pencwm had on their birthdays, if they were lucky; the word 'party' was never used, since it betokened the kind of grandeur miners and their families never aspired to. 'Just some cakes an' fizzy pop, like, an' his uncle an' auntie round to visit him. I was wonderin' . . .' She hesitated, as if she were about to make a monumental proposal. 'Well, I wondered, would you come, Nurse? I know it's askin' a lot, but he thinks so highly of you, it'd really make it a champion birthday for him.'

'Of course I'll come,' Megan said. 'I've already got him a present, anyway.'

'Oh, thank you, Nurse.'

'It was kind of you to ask me.'

As she had entered the living room behind Mrs Hewlett, Megan had been sure the private conversation would not touch on Denis's illness. Apart from the usual enquiry about what she made of the boy today, Megan was never asked any questions about his progress. Mrs Hewlett knew that tuber-culosis was a grave condition, everyone in Pencwm did. But she would not countenance what was evident, that her son was steadily growing thinner and weaker, that he was less and less capable of sustaining life as the days passed. Megan saw strong parallels between Mrs Hewlett's attitude and her own refusal, lately, to think about Timothy's illness. It was an instinctive device, she supposed, for staving off pain until it could no longer be avoided.

Megan thought of that again as she left the Hewlett house. There were signs, now, that she could no longer avoid dwelling on Timothy's future, or her own. Shortly after the incident on the bridge with Nesta Mogg, Megan had taken a decision – or, more accurately, an intertwining trio of deci-sions. It would be enough to be near Timothy and to share his work with him, because she drew a powerful sense of emotional harmony from what they did together. She would never put Timothy or herself to the stress of revealing her love for him. And she would not think any more about his health. That path had worked, so far. But now things were

156

changing. Uneasiness was inching forward again.

As she was putting her bag on the bicycle she saw Wyn Brewster walk past on the other side of the road. She waved. Stiffly he raised his hand, barely returning the greeting. There was already a lot of uneasiness in that direction. Twice in a month she had accepted an invitation to tea with the Brewsters; on neither occasion had Wyn done more than exchange civilities. Although Gladys had done what she could to mask her brother's behaviour, it was clear that he was acting like a huffy child. Megan knew it obviously had something to do with her.

She stood on one pedal of the bicycle and freewheeled down to her next call, six doors away from the Hewletts'. She was halfway there when a car came up behind her, its horn honking. Megan stopped, frowning at the car. It was Timothy.

He drew up alongside and poked his head out. 'How do you manage to be so fugitive in a town this size?' he demanded. 'I've been hunting for you all over the place.'

Megan wanted to ask him several things at once – why hadn't he told her Dr O'Casey was coming back, why was he going to London, what would the working arrangement be from now on? She got no chance to ask any of it.

'We haven't got long,' Timothy said, switching off the engine. 'I'm leaving for London first thing in the morning. A three-day break. I want you to come with me.'

Megan stared at him, dumbstruck.

'I've been very sneaky, Megan, and I hope you won't be angry at me. I wanted it all to be a surprise for you. Three days in the Capital. What do you think?.'

Words were difficult to find. 'I – I can't just drop everything and go trailing off to London . . .' *He wanted her to go with him! To London!*

'I've arranged everything,' Timothy said, in a tone she would once have considered smug and infuriating. 'With the Charity Committee, that is – or Miss Williams, to be precise. She thought it was a grand idea. There's a recreational and study clause in your contract, remember?'

157

Megan nodded, her head singing.

'Well, we're invoking it. You haven't done it before, so it's high time you took advantage. All you have to do is submit a three-page summary of how you spent the time – you can do that on the train on the way back – or on the way there, for that matter. Or I'll do it for you – I've a terrific way with waffle.'

'But what about—'

'I've arranged everything, Megan. Doctor O'Casey will be happy to double as District Nurse for a few days. I think he's even looking forward to it.'

'He knows?'

'I put it to him as soon as he got back.'

Megan stared along the road. It was too much to take in. She looked at Timothy again. 'Why? I mean why do you want me to go with you?'

'It's a thank-you.'

'For what?'

'For everything. For your help,' Timothy said. 'And for your understanding – for your contribution to my enjoyment of the time I've been working here.' He stuck his head further from the window. 'For being a marvellous chum,' he said, smiling. 'What do you say? Are you going to chew holes in me for arranging things in such a cavalier fashion, then pedal off into the distance, or are you going to say yes, you'll come?'

'You amaze me,' Megan said. Her heart was brimming, more than she would dare let him know. 'What have you got planned when we get to London?'

'Fun.'

She smiled, knowing she was blushing deep red by now. 'I thought, somehow, that you never wanted to go back there again.'

Timothy nodded. 'I thought so, too.' His eyes had that look again, disarming, quietly penetrating. 'Can I take it you'll come?'

Megan grinned at him, her answer written all over her happy face.

CHAPTER SEVENTEEN

GEOFFREY LLOYD brought two coffee cups to the window seat and handed one to Timothy. 'I suppose the first thing you notice, coming back, is the pace of life here.'

'I'll say.' Timothy glanced around the consulting room. 'That, and all the luxuries that are taken for granted.' Hanging on silk-threaded wallpaper, a formal portrait of Geoffrey Lloyd's father scowled down on an ordered array of coloured bottles, gleaming steel kidney dishes and rubber-banded bundles of sterile needles in glass tubes. A freshly-starched white coat lay folded on the burnished leather examination couch. There was an instrument table, glass-shelved and rubber-wheeled, holding an impressive array of the finest equipment, some of it in leather-bound boxes. The desk was a picture of opulence, with its inlaid morocco, ornate inkstand and regimented silver and gold pencils. 'You should see the surgery I've been working in,' Timothy said. 'Straight out of the ark.'

'Have you found the work as fulfilling as you imagined you would?'

Timothy twirled his cup on the saucer, considering his answer. 'I don't know if I expected it to be all that satisfying, Geoffrey. I said I did, but you know now I was practising a bit of deception.'

'Yes.' Geoffrey glanced out at the street. Timothy had been in the consulting room for less than five minutes. His illness was bound to be mentioned – indeed discussed, but Geoffrey looked as if the topic had been touched upon too soon, before he was prepared.

'But yes,' Timothy went on, 'I have found it fulfilling. I wish to God I'd got into that kind of medicine years ago. It's very basic and it absorbs all the time that's available. Some nights I fall into bed exhausted. Which isn't the point. I feel I'm doing something important and worthwhile. There's not much money in it, but the emotional rewards are considerable.'

'So it wasn't all a falsehood – you did feel you were wasting your time and talents here?'

'Yes, I did. But I didn't particularly believe the answer to my unrest was to go out into the wilds of Wales and do missionary work. I simply wanted to be away from London, before . . .' He shrugged. 'Before I could no longer enjoy what surrounded me, all the people, places, events, everything I had come to love. I wanted that to be put firmly into my past, and I needed to absorb my present with work. Wales is where I came from, it seemed a reasonable alternative.'

'You could have gone into a less taxing practice, though,' Geoffrey pointed out. 'Wales isn't all mining communities, after all. You could have gone to one of the larger towns, with more amenities. . .'

'No, that wouldn't have been right. I specifically wanted locum work. I didn't know how long I would be able to go on, so I could hardly inflict myself on some practice where I'd have to drop out after a year or so. Short bursts in different areas, that's what I was after. In the big towns there are partnerships. But in mining towns and villages they're all modest-income, one-man affairs – so when a doctor has to take time off, he needs a locum. In that category there's no shortage of appointments.'

Geoffrey was frowning out at the street again. 'I find this difficult to talk about.' He glanced at Timothy. 'Why did you change your mind and come to see me? Your letter was pretty firm and final, I thought.'

'Circumstances changed. *I* changed. My glum, dogged, downward spiral stopped. I levelled out and began to climb. Instead of deadening my self-awareness with hard work, I began to enjoy myself. Truly. I then decided, when I knew I could have some time off, that I'd come and see you – if only to reassure you that I'm not wasting away in misery on some windy mountain top.'

'You certainly give the impression of being happy enough,' Geoffrey said. 'What caused the big change?'

'A woman,' Timothy said. 'A very remarkable woman.'

Geoffrey made the trace of a smile. 'Women always did have a profound effect on you.'

'No, no, it's not like that.'

'Then she must be an old woman.'

Timothy shook his head. 'You have a low opinion of my proclivities where women are concerned.'

'No,' Geoffrey said. 'I have an informed, accurate opinion. Who is she?'

'Megan Roberts. She's Pencwm's District Nurse. She's been an angel. At first, mind you, I thought there was a danger she would put something in my tea. Didn't take to me at all. But since early this year she's aided me at every turn, helped fill my few leisure hours, re-designed the timetables to even the loads we carry – and she's thoroughly charming and intelligent.'

'Sounds like the ideal woman.' Geoffrey's eyes narrowed. 'Are you sure this isn't another Beth, or Eleanor, or Lucinda . . .?'

'No,' Timothy said flatly. 'Our relationship is platonic. Transcendent, spiritual at best . . .' He stared at Geoffrey. 'You don't believe me.'

Geoffrey shrugged. 'If you say it's that way, then that's the way it is.'

'Listen to me.' Timothy put down his cup and leaned his elbows on his knees. 'Just to clear the ground and save a lot of hedging about, I'll say this. I'm a man who managed to keep his illness a secret for a long time. I'm sure you never suspected anything.'

'No. Never.'

'Cardiac insufficiency's what it boils down to, Geoffrey. Two years ago I had the first warning that the vigour of youth had lost its delaying power. You know the symptoms. I had them all. So I took the measures we've discussed. Now

161

consider this. Would I, in my condition, let any new relation-
ships develop? I know you've thought me an unprincipled
womaniser in the past?'

'Not at all,' Geoffrey interrupted. 'No woman ever
suffered at your hands, to my knowledge. But you always had
a certain . . .' He paused, searching for the right word.
'Detachment,' he said finally. 'You could walk away from an
affair unbruised. Even when you were the injured party.'

'I couldn't be like that with the estimable Megan Roberts.
If you met her you'd know what I mean. Less than full
commitment would be an insult to her.'

Geoffrey was having trouble keeping the tone of their
discussion so dispassionate. But he was trying – trying to be
unemotional and keep the woman-talk at the level it had
always occupied in the old days. 'Are you saying that, given
other circumstances, you'd be lovers?'

Timothy's eyes flickered. 'I don't know. Megan has no
sexual guile – you know, the unspoken invitation shouted
through the eyes, or the occasional message transmitted in a
not-so-accidental collision of bodies, that kind of thing. All
she ever invites from me is a response to her warmth, which is
distinctly sisterly.' He smiled. 'I don't think she has any
romantic or carnal yearnings where I'm concerned.'

'But you,' Geoffrey insisted, 'how do you feel towards her?
She must have had a profound effect on you. To my diag-
nostic eye you're twice the man you were when you left.'

Timothy was silent for a moment. 'I think I've kept my
thoughts disciplined. I haven't examined my deeper feelings
for her. And it's neither here nor there, anyway. I don't have
the credentials to be a lover any more.'

Geoffrey slapped down his cup and saucer so abruptly they
rattled. 'Damn!'

'What's up?'

'I can't keep this up, Timothy. I . . .' He shook his head
once, violently. '*Damn it to hell!*'

'I should have warned you I was coming and given you time
to prepare yourself.'

'Time would have made no difference,' Geoffrey said

bitterly, fixing his gaze on the street again. 'There are times when I'd like to rebuke God.'

'Maybe the most charitable thing would be to assume He doesn't exist.'

Geoffrey turned his head. 'Is that what you believe? That it's all chance?'

Timothy shrugged. 'I'm too close to an answer to make brash assertions.' He reached out and touched Geoffrey's arm. 'Don't pity me, please. I have a life span, you have a life span. They'll differ in length, that's all. I've packed a lot into mine. Feel jealous of me for that. I can withstand jealousy.'

'But it's all so wrong,' Geoffrey protested. 'You're a brilliant physician, you're a man with a capacity for living life to the full . . .' He passed a hand across his eyes. 'There's so much I want to say to you, but my emotions are getting in the way.'

'Then let me do the talking,' Timothy said. 'I have some anger about what's happening to me, I'll admit that. But I can't be sorry for myself, nor should anyone else. This has been a good life – no, this *is* a good life. In this practice I've had contact with miserable, spoiled, meaningless lives. In Pencwm I see lives beset with the worst desolation. I count myself a fortunate man, compared to all of those. To this day my existence is saturated with good fortune. It's better I leave while I'm still a happy person, than decamp after years of wretchedness and despondency. . .'

'But Timothy—'

'But nothing. Allow a dying man to be a little dogmatic.'

Geoffrey sighed. He looked at Timothy and saw he was smiling. 'I've never known anyone like you, Tim. You're phenomenal.'

'Good God. You called me Tim. You haven't done that for years.'

Geoffrey gave in and smiled. 'More coffee?' he said, rising.

'No, I have to be going soon. I promised to meet Megan outside the British Museum at twelve.'

Geoffrey frowned. 'She's here?'

'Yes. She's sharing my little break.'

163

Geoffrey picked up the cups, watching Timothy's face carefully. 'I thought you said—'

'All above board,' Timothy cut in. 'I wanted to make a gesture of thanks, and this seemed the ideal opportunity.' He rolled his eyes. 'Geoffrey, we're *friends*, Megan and I. Pals. Is that so hard to take in?'

'If we were talking about me and some woman, no. It would be easy to swallow.'

'I told you. I would never let anything special develop. Even an unprincipled libertine like me couldn't be that selfish or inconsiderate, in the circumstances.' Timothy jerked his thumb at the coffee pot. 'Go on, I'll have another cup, after all.' He sat back and composed a smile, conscious that Geoffrey didn't fully believe him. Briefly Timothy wondered what he truly felt towards Megan. The curiosity was immediately swamped by a fierce urge to think about something else.

People in London talked about so many different things, Megan thought. They were interested in so much that lay outside of their own lives and experience. She supposed that was because they lived close to the heart of things, at the churning centre of culture and entertainment and the liveliest variety of incident, and they didn't have hardship to distract them from what was happening – not the people Megan had been encountering, anyway.

That morning, as she had wandered around the various departments of the British Museum – Prints and Drawings, Coins and Medals, Egyptian, Oriental, Greek and Roman Antiquities – she had heard the latest political talk; Italy had returned to the gold standard, Brazil's economy had collapsed because they had produced too much coffee and the USSR had devised a new five-year plan. There was no need for a newspaper or a guide of any kind – Megan had only to keep her ears open.

She began to wish she had brought a notebook, though. There was so much to remember and pursue. Two men, muttering amidst the Elgin Marbles, had aroused her interest in a new book called *Lady Chatterley's Lover*. Later, having a refreshment in the Museum's tea room, she learned by the simplest of eavesdropping that Thomas Hardy had died earlier that year, and so had Earl Haig. It was astonishing how much she had missed in the narrow exclusion of Pencwm. Who were Greta Garbo, Al Jolson and Thornton Wilder? Names flew around her like confetti – Matisse, Stravinsky, Sinclair Lewis, Rex Whistler, Ravel – all of them segments of a culture she began to think was too wide for her to embrace.

'I don't know if I've been elevated or flattened,' she told Timothy as they met on Great Russell Street. 'I feel like a foreigner. All morning I've heard people saying things that half the time meant nothing to me.'

'Cultural small-talk is just a trick, Megan.' He held her elbow gently as they crossed the road. 'So many people are simply catalogues, especially here in Bloomsbury. They drop names and snippets of opinions they've read in newspapers and journals. Very impressive it can sound, too. But if you probe beneath the surface you find they're posturing.' He smiled at her. 'Don't be daunted.'

'I'll try not to be.' Megan watched Timothy hail a cab. 'Where are we going?'

'Chelsea. To a restaurant I know and dearly love.'

It was their first full day in London. They had arrived two hours late the previous afternoon. Timothy had looked very tired. At the hotel in Knightsbridge, as grand as any Megan had ever seen, they had adjacent rooms. Timothy rested until seven, while Megan bought postcards from the foyer and spent an hour telling Mrs Pughe-Morgan, Mrs Foskett, Rose Clark and Gladys and Wyn Brewster about sights and sounds she had only seen, so far, through taxi and hotel-room windows. At seven-thirty she and Timothy had dinner in the hotel, went to see a late revue on Shaftesbury Avenue, then returned to the hotel, happy and weary, a few minutes after midnight.

Now, riding in a taxi through busy streets, Megan stared out at the endless succession of fashionable shops and realised she was as happy as she would ever be. Beside her Timothy kept up a steady commentary on the passing scene, while her mind danced over the myriad novelties that had entered her life in less than twenty-four hours. This is the way to be, she thought. She was enjoying a torrent of experience, in the company of the man who occupied her mind and heart as no one had for years. Nothing could be better.

'How was your ex-partner?' she asked Timothy, as he paused in his spirited narration to gaze out at Sloane Street. 'Was he glad to see you?'

'I think so. We talked about old times as if we hadn't seen each other in years, and we parted with a promise to keep in touch regularly. It was a nice morning.' And a sad morning. As Timothy had left, Geoffrey was visibly close to tears.

'Did he try to coax you back?'

'For a time,' Timothy said, 'until he realised how thoroughly I'm beguiled by Pencwm.'

'Mm. Knightsbridge doesn't have a look-in beside a place like that.'

They both laughed. As Timothy squeezed Megan's hand – a fleeting, thoroughly natural gesture – her heart swelled. She laughed harder as the long-ago, incandescent pleasure of girlhood sprang in her, bringing its unreasoning assurance that the present was eternal.

CHAPTER EIGHTEEN

TIME flew, but their stay in London was crammed with events. At a theatre in Leicester Square they saw the first talking picture, *The Singing Fool*; they attended an exhibition of paintings at the newly opened Kenwood Gallery in Hampstead; like children, they descended on the bookshops of Charing Cross Road, browsing, buying, showing each other the treasures they had found and finally hailing a taxi to take them back to the hotel with bundles of books and periodicals. They walked in Hyde Park and took an impulsive river trip to Kew, where Megan, wide-eyed, explored the botanical wonders while Timothy did his best to keep up with her. Event was piled upon event and memories were lovingly stored.

On their last night in the capital, Timothy announced they would be dining at The Tavistock.

'Where's that?' Megan asked.

'Just outside the boundary of reality. You'll adore it, as long as you can set aside your class principles for a couple of hours. The Tavistock is dedicated to shameless luxury.' Timothy winked. 'So am I, occasionally.'

Megan took an hour to get ready. She combed out her dark hair, arranging it in soft waves on her shoulders, and permitted herself the indulgence of cosmetics – a little powder, a touch of rouge and the merest film of colour on her mouth. She wore a dark blue linen gown, with a silver brooch Mrs Pughe-Morgan had given her on her twentieth birthday. Before she left the room to meet Timothy in the foyer, she stared at herself in the dressing-table mirror. 'You're not all that bad-looking for thirty-five,' she told her reflection, then giggled, feeling more girlish and feminine than she had for years.

The Tavistock was overwhelming. It was high and circular, more like an opulent banqueting room than a restaurant, with arched openings leading to shadowed recesses beyond the perimeter. The walls were covered in dove grey cushioned silk. Crystal chandeliers hung from a mirrored ceiling, casting soft, tinted light on the tables, which resembled damask-covered islands on the expanse of sea-blue carpet.

'Doctor Morris.' A silver-haired man, wearing a dinner jacket similar to Timothy's, approached as they stood in the doorway. He smiled warmly, giving Megan a quick, appraising glance as he extended his hand to Timothy. 'It's a great pleasure to see you again.' His accent was foreign, Megan noticed. 'I heard you had left London – I'm happy to learn I was misinformed.' French, Megan decided.

'Nice to see you, Charles. You weren't misinformed. I live in Wales now, but I thought I'd pop back for a visit, just to remind myself what I'm missing.' Timothy shook the man's hand and introduced him to Megan. 'Charles Dufour, this is my friend, Miss Roberts.' As Dufour made a short bow and respectfully brushed Megan's fingers, Timothy explained that he owned the Tavistock. 'For twenty years he's devoted himself to enhancing the pleasures of the idle rich.'

'We do what we can,' Dufour said, still smiling. He turned and beckoned a waiter, who responded so sharply he might have been struck. Dufour told him to show Dr Morris and his companion to their table. 'Enjoy your evening.' Dufour bowed towards Megan again. 'I hope, by the time you are ready to leave, you will think it worthwhile visiting us again.'

'I'm sure I will,' Megan said.

When they were seated Megan said, 'I'm terribly impressed. You must have been quite the socialite in your London days. He actually knows you. He looks and sounds like the kind who wouldn't waste his breath on anybody less than a millionaire, or at least a duke.'

'Oh, he gets a few of them in here,' Timothy said. 'But he doesn't mind exchanging pleasantries with the odd commoner, from time to time. As a matter of fact, he looked at you as if you might be nobility. I could see the fawning glint as he came across.'

'Don't be daft.'

'But you do look a shade regal tonight. Honestly.'

'I think the surroundings have a lot to do with it.' Megan had a sudden memory – herself, twelve, barefoot and shivering on a winter morning, putting the kettle on as her father got up to go to work in the slate mine. *Look at me now.* On all sides there were elegant ladies and their well-groomed escorts, dripping wealth and privilege. Privation and destitution were only words to these people. In their world hardship would be a broken fingernail, a head cold. And right there, in their very midst, was Megan Roberts, the District Nurse from Pencwm. Megan smiled at an imagined tableau, seeing herself in uniform, her cap square on her head, sitting at that same table with London Society glittering and tinkling all around her.

'Why, *Timothy!*' A young woman with feathery blonde hair and bright scarlet lips had stopped by their table, looking dramatically shocked. 'I thought you'd gone off to Outer Mongolia or some awful place like that!' She stared a moment longer then bent sharply and pecked Timothy's cheek. 'You old fraud! You've been in London all along, haven't you?'

Timothy shook his head. 'Visiting, that's all.' He looked across the table. 'Megan, this is Laura, an old friend.' The women nodded to each other. Laura's eyes, like Dufour's, were sharply appraising. There was a flash of rivalry there, too. Megan wondered what she was thinking. Timothy said, 'What have you been doing with yourself? The last I heard, you were involved in something to do with Sir David Carey's antiques business.'

Laura made a sour face. 'I gave that up. David's a darling of course, but it was miles too exhausting. I had to catalogue everything. Can you imagine? I mean, I thought it would be enough for me to *be* there, you know?' She waved her hand elaborately. 'Selling, or at least explaining things to customers, showing them pieces and so forth. But no. I was expected to keep lists and make tiresome inventories – it was all too much. Women aren't built for that kind of donkey work.' She flashed a metallic smile at Megan. 'Have you been in business, at all? Do I have an ally?'

'I'm a nurse,' Megan said.

The sour face came back. 'Ugh! All that blood and bandages and stuff – I couldn't abide it. However do you cope?'

'She cares about people,' Timothy aid. 'And she thrives on hard work.'

Laura's changed expression showed the message had registered. Megan, she had been told, was her opposite in every way. 'Well . . .' She shrugged. 'It takes all sorts, doesn't it?' She glanced across the room. 'I must dash – Arnold's getting fidgety.' She twitched her mouth at Megan. 'Lovely to have met you.' To Timothy she said, 'Do give me a ring next time you're in town. We can have lunch and a chat.'

Timothy nodded. 'Good to see you again, Laura.'

When she had gone Megan raised her eyebrows at Timothy. 'An old flame?'

'God, no. Laura's one of those girls who are always hanging on to the fringe of one group or another. A parasite, but a harmless one.'

'So she's not the kind of girl you used to go out with?'

Timothy shifted in his chair. 'Megan, do I detect some curiosity about my taste in women?'

She nodded. 'Yes, you do.'

'Well.' He thought for a moment. 'It's hard to give a specification. I like modest, thoughtful girls, I think, but there aren't that many around here. I've done a lot of compromising.'

'A lot?'

Timothy grinned. 'I'm not going to be driven into a confession.'

'I wasn't exactly trying to do that,' Megan said. 'I saw Laura and wondered if that was your kind of girl, the kind you would have married—'

'And *that* bit of speculation arose, I assume, because

170

you've been wondering why I'm not married by now?'

Megan realised she had blundered. She had simply meant to say something lightly teasing, something reflecting the brittle encounter with Laura. She shouldn't have said anything about marriage. Her own belief was that Timothy had remained single because his expectancy of life was so short. The remark about marriage had slipped out. As Megan was on the brink of saying something to divert the talk along another line, the waiter appeared with the menus.

'Right, then,' Timothy said, the conversation forgotten. He opened the large tasseled folder in front of him. 'Let's give shameless greed its head, shall we?'

The meal that followed would occupy a prominent place, Megan felt, in the store of memories she was building from this holiday. 'Think of it as a farewell feast,' Timothy said, putting a small ache in Megan, which she quickly cast aside.

They began with Crème Saint Germaine soup, followed by fried whitebait, accompanied by a bottle of white burgundy – 'Corton-Charlemagne,' Timothy explained. 'Too good to drink, really. They should find a way of making it edible.'

For the main course Megan had Pheasant Mandarin and Timothy chose Tournedos Rossini. The accompanying vegetables – Gratin Dauphinoise, petit pois, Vichy carrots and magnificently spiced red cabbage – would have made a superb meal by themselves, Megan said. The wine, a red Bordeaux called Martillac, was the perfect complement.

They finished with a traditional syllabub and finally sat back, mellowed and satisfied, to wait for coffee and brandy.

'That was downright sinful,' Megan sighed.

'Pleasure's a sin, and sometimes sin's a pleasure.'

Megan frowned. 'I should know who said it. . .'

'I said it,' Timothy said.

'But somebody else said it first.'

Timothy shrugged. 'I can't deceive you, can I?'

Megan's frown vanished. 'Byron,' she said with a flash of triumph. 'It's from Don Juan, right?'

Timothy folded his arms, looking pleased and contented.

171

'Tell me – have you truly enjoyed all this? Coming to London, the things we've done?'

'I shouldn't have thought there was any need to ask. It must have shown.' The wine, Megan thought, was adding its measure to her mood, which was turning softly, sweetly sad. 'I haven't enjoyed myself so much in all my life.' An expansive remark, she believed, not too well considered, but she suspected it was true. 'I can never do anything that'll make it up to you.'

'At the risk of sounding like a tuppenny poet,' Timothy said, 'I have to say you've made it all up to me, and more, by being with me.'

The moment was precious and Megan did nothing to hasten it past. She let her eyes linger on Timothy's, making no attempt to hide the way she felt. *That's love I see*, her mind whispered. They sat transfixed by each other as Megan's sadness and pleasure mingled, crystallising in the thought of snow on the wind. It was an expression she had heard often in childhood, on bright autumn days when a chilling thread would come suddenly on the breeze, foretelling the bleakness ahead.

'Megan, there's something I should tell you.'

Timothy's contentment had shifted towards candour. His eyes had their open look again. Alerted, Megan sat up in her chair, clutching in her mind for a strand of diversion. She knew, without deduction, why he wanted her to know his secret. But he mustn't tell her, it would unbalance so much . . .

'I hope we're not going to be serious,' she said, forcing a joking note of disapproval. 'I'm frankly and happily intoxicated. I'd sooner be silly than serious, if it's all the same to you.'

She saw the danger pass. He was nodding, shifting back to the safe territory of present pleasure. The coffee came, and the brandy.

'It's been a grand evening,' Megan said, raising her glass.

'I'll say.' Timothy swirled his cognac. 'It's a pity it has to end.'

172

'Megan nodded, sharply aware that too many endings, in her life at least, had been sorrowfully at odds with the bright beginnings. But she was determined not to think ahead. No more thoughts of snow on the wind, she told herself. The here-and-now was too fine to contaminate with the yet-to-come.

'I insist,' Timothy said in the hotel foyer, 'and to hell with what anyone thinks. You're coming to my room for a final brandy.'

Megan's first refusal had been tame, her second almost non-existent. Now Timothy was being firm enough, and pretending to be drunk enough, to make it easy for her to give in.

'Just one, then,' she said as they made for the lift. 'What are you doing with brandy in your room, anyway?'

Medicinal use,' he said. 'I'm a doctor, I know all about that kind of thing.' Giggling, he stood aside to let Megan enter the lift before him.

They had walked back from the Tavistock. Passing along quiet Mayfair terraces, enjoying the night air, admiring the architecture and exchanging humorous remarks about weighty cornices and substantial balustrades, they had at some point linked arms; Megan couldn't remember it happening, it was something she suddenly noticed when they were within sight of the hotel. At almost the same moment Timothy had stopped and looked at her. 'We two,' he said, then paused, his face very close to hers. 'We're . . . We're something very special.' Megan nodded and replied, 'To us, anyway.' Timothy looked embarrassed then, as if he had said something he shouldn't. By the time they crossed the hotel steps his mood had turned brisk and jocular.

He behaved the same way as they rose to the third floor in the lift. He tipped the attendant a shilling and ushered Megan lavishly towards his room. When they were inside he turned to her and said, 'Alone at last,' making a joke of it.

As he dug his travelling flask from a suitcase Megan looked

around her, noticing the quietness of the room. It was a quality she hadn't noticed in her own room, even though it was only next door. It could have been the hour of night, she thought, then decided it wasn't that at all. Between them, in spite of Timothy's bustling pretence, they were setting up an atmosphere that seemed to thicken the air.

Timothy brought two little metal cups almost filled with brandy. He handed one to Megan. 'Shall we drink to something?' he asked her.

She shrugged. 'I can't think of anything.'

Timothy rubbed his nose thoughtfully for a moment, then stiffened his back and held out his drink. 'Confusion to the enemies of the King,' he said in a bluff military voice, clinking his cup on Megan's. 'And may they fester in the fiery pit, for good measure.'

They sipped then stood smiling at each other.

'I'm so sorry this'll all be over soon,' Timothy said.

'It's not over yet, though.'

Megan watched Timothy's face. She had said that innocently, meaning don't live ahead. Or she believed she had meant that. Timothy's eyes had narrowed a fraction, as if he had a pain. He put down his drink. Feeling she was responding to something pre-ordained, Megan let him take her drink and set it on the table beside his own. They looked at each other. Timothy stepped nearer, then his eyes shut tightly and he turned aside.

'What's wrong?'

'Megan . . .' He looked at her again. 'I shouldn't have let this happen . . .'

Megan saw no point in pretending she didn't know what he meant. 'We were conspirators,' she said. 'You did nothing on your own.' The wine was mingling with the sudden force of her feelings, making her uncover the truth she had sworn to keep to herself. 'I've loved you for a long time.'

Timothy stared at her. 'And I've . . . Well, I've been refusing to confront what I feel for you. But I suppose I've known, somewhere deep in myself.

Given voice, it seemed now like something they had

174

acknowledged long ago. Again Timothy stepped close to Megan, but the look of pain was still there. 'It's wrong – wrong for a reason I tried to tell you. . .'

'Can the reason undo the way you feel, or the way I feel?'

Timothy shook his head. 'No, it can't, but—'

'Don't tell me, then.' They were so close now that Megan could feel Timothy's breath on her cheek. She heard herself say, 'Please kiss me.'

The contact of their mouths began a delirious, dizzying swirl in Megan. Her heart pounded as she allowed Timothy to enclose her in his arms. She moaned as urgency took him. By the bed, in a frenzy of movement she found herself helping him to undress her, then lying beside him, holding to his body as he covered her breasts with kisses. At the last moment he froze, arms propped on either side of her.

'Megan. . .'

She thrust herself at him, holding his hips with her thighs. 'Does this make you unhappy? Can it hurt either of us?'

'No. But it's unfair – I—'

She drew down his head and kissed him fiercely. As his body began to move on hers she sighed and whispered, 'An act of sheer love makes no wound.' She didn't know who had said that first, and for the moment she didn't care.

CHAPTER NINETEEN

GLADYS BREWSTER had the tea ready when Wyn got back from his committee meeting. It was a dull afternoon, with thunder rumbling over to the west. Wyn had taken his best cap and the long macintosh that had been his father's. When he came in he looked boiled.

'If the flamin' weather would make its mind up,' he said, hooking his cap on the back of the kitchen door and unbelting the coat, 'folk wouldn't have to go takin' contingency measures. I'd have sworn it would be pourin' by now.'

'Better safe than sorry,' Gladys murmured. 'How did the meeting go?'

'A waste of time, as usual.' Since Wyn's recent and unsuccessful bid to gain the chairmanship of the Pencwm Widows' and Orphans' Aid Association, his patience with other committee members had become shallow. 'Three motions were put forward and three were adopted.'

'Well, that's progress, isn't it?' Gladys handed Wyn a cup of tea and leaned on the edge of the sink, rotating a spoon in her own cup.

'No, Gladys, it's not progress. It's meaningless repetition. The same three motions, in a different form, were adopted six months ago. Nothin' was done about implementin' them then, an' nothin'll get done this time, either. So we wasted two hours an' had no time left for practical matters – such as gettin' the food supplement scheme goin', arrangin' the kids' Christmas party, an' a half dozen other matters that need seein' to.'

Gladys watched Wyn sip his tea and wrinkle his nose. It would either be too hot, or too sweet, or not sweet enough. There was no pleasing him nowadays. He was turning into a

176

grumpy old man, and he wasn't even forty yet. He glared at the window as Scratch barked out in the yard.

'No sign of her yet, then?'

'She'll be here soon, I imagine,' Gladys said.

'We should charge her board for that dog of hers. Eats us out of house an' home, it does, an' all day long it's either barkin' or sleepin'. Useless thing, a dog.'

Gladys sighed. 'Stop talking nonsense, will you? Megan always gives me money to feed the dog when she leaves him here, and he's no trouble to anybody. You used to enjoy having him about the place.'

'I used to put up with him,' Wyn snapped. 'After all, when you know you can help somebody, you put yourself out, like. It's the thing you do for friends. But there's a world of difference between helpin' somebody out of a fix, an' havin' your good nature abused.'

'Now don't you start that again,' Gladys warned him.

'It's the truth, damn it. I mean, what's our Nurse Roberts been doin' these past three or four days? Gallivantin', that's what. With Doctor hoity-toity Morris.' Wyn wrinkled his nose at the tea again and put the cup on the table. 'There's a few stories goin' around about just what they've been up to, an' all.'

'Wyn! Will you stop it? When you go on like that you're no better than a gossiping old woman. How would anybody round here know the whys and wherefores of what Megan's been doing? She got a chance to go to London and she took it. Knowing her, I'd guess she's spent most of her time in bookshops and museums.' Gladys paused, then said, 'Any other guessing, the kind you're indulging in, is just dirty-minded spite.'

Wyn turned and stumped through to the living room. How many times, Gladys wondered, had that happened lately? When he was a boy he had gone through a phase when girls' lack of response to his chat and charm disturbed him so much there was no way to reason with him. He was like that now. Megan Roberts was his friend, but that wasn't enough for Wyn – not now that another man appeared to take up so much of her time and attention.

Scratch barked again. It was different this time, an excited yelp. Gladys turned and looked through the window. The yard gate was swung wide and Megan was crouching in the opening, fussing with the dog.

Gladys hurried through to the living room, where Wyn sat at the table with a book open in front of him. He was glaring at the page as if it had offended him.

'Megan's here,' Gladys said.

'So?'

'So I want you to straighten your face and act like a human being while she's here.'

Wyn looked up. 'Frightened I'll speak my mind, are you?'

Gladys felt like slapping him. 'Just see you behave – and don't go into one of your big-baby huffs, either. Try and look pleased to see the girl.'

Wyn bowed his head over the book again, sniffing. Gladys sighed and went back to the kitchen. She opened the back door just as Megan reached for the knob. Scratch bounded in, still yelping.

'So you're back!' They embraced for a moment, then Gladys stood back. 'My, that's a pretty coat.'

'It's my Sunday best,' Megan said, bending to flick dog hairs from the hem. 'I haven't worn it in ages. I took it with me so I could come back to Pencwm with a bit of a flourish.'

'You're looking grand.' Gladys shut the door and went straight to the teapot. 'Have a cup and tell me all about it.'

Megan put her canvas shopping bag on the table. 'I brought you both presents. Is Wyn here?'

'He's in the living room.' Gladys went to the door. 'Wyn!' She called loud enough to hail someone twenty yards away. 'Megan's here! She's got something for you!' She turned and watched Megan rummaging. 'I've told you before, you shouldn't go wasting your money on presents for us.'

'I enjoy doing it, Gladys.' Megan hoisted a thick parcel from the bag. 'That's yours.'

Gladys put the bundle on the table and began gingerly unwrapping it.

178

'Don't worry,' Megan said. 'It's not fragile.'

Gladys peeled back the layers of tissue paper. 'Oh!' she clapped a hand to her cheek. 'It's what I've been wanting for goodness knows how long!' As Wyn came into the kitchen, his face sultry, she showed him her present. It was a red-enamelled coffee pot with a silver-and-black Ridges' label on its lid. 'Isn't that marvellous?' She tapped the label. 'It's the best make, too.'

'Very nice,' Wyn mumbled.

'How have you been, Wyn?' Megan asked brightly.

'The same as usual.'

'Here's a little something for you.'

Wyn took the oblong parcel and frowned at the wrapping. 'No need for this. . .'

'Well you've got it and you're stuck with it. Go on, open it up.'

Wyn put the parcel on the table and undid the string, folded back the paper and took out a book bound in scarlet leather. He examined the gold edging, fingering its sheen, then looked at the title. It was *The Rights of Man*, by Thomas Payne. He looked at Megan. 'I've been after this for a while. . .'

'I know,' Megan said.

'It's nice of you . . .' Wyn stared at the book, not opening it. 'Many thanks.'

'So tell Wyn and me what happened,' Gladys said, warning her brother with her eyes, telling him he'd better stay where he was, or else.

Megan sat down at the narrow table as Gladys poured her a cup of tea. 'I don't know where to begin. I did so much, saw so much.'

'Museums and the like?' Gladys said.

'Oh, I went to the British Museum one morning, but that was the only one I visited. I went to Kew, to the botanical gardens, I raided a few bookshops – but to tell you the truth, I spent more time in theatres and restaurants than anywhere else.'

Gladys was dividing her attention between Megan and

179

Wyn. 'Did you go on your own – to the shows, I mean? I suppose Doctor Morris would be too busy. . .'

'No, no,' Megan said, 'we went just about everywhere together. He took me places and showed me things I'd never have uncovered by myself. It was marvellous. Like having three holidays packed into one.'

'Some folk are lucky to get just one,' Wyn said. The tone of his voice betrayed his hesitancy; he had to say what he was thinking, but he couldn't make it quite biting enough – he'd just been given a present, after all.

'That's true,' Megan said. 'I know how lucky I was – I kept thinking that. Even when I was wrapped up in something, I'd remind myself. We are at a show with this very funny man in it, Max Wall he's called, and right in the middle, laughing my head off, I thought, Lord, I'm the lucky one, sitting here, being entertained in one of the best theatres in the world.'

'You deserved every minute,' Gladys said, glaring at Wyn, who was rolling his eyes at the ceiling.

'It's been a time to remember.' Megan leaned forward and patted Scratch, who was practically sitting on her toes. 'I was just saying to Timothy—'

'Oh!' Wyn suddenly lost his grip on himself. He was staring at the window, as if someone was there. 'So it's *Timothy* now, is it?'

Both women looked at him.

'He's really led you on, hasn't he?'

'Wyn!' Gladys screeched. 'Megan's a guest in this house! If you can't guard your tongue you can go outside, this minute!'

'I'll be happy to go.' Wyn put the book on the table beside Megan. 'On reflection,' he said, blushing furiously, not meeting her eyes, 'I can't accept this. I don't think Tom Payne would approve of his work bein' turned out all fancy an' expensive. Give it to your upper-crust crony. He'll appreciate somethin' nice an' showy.' Wyn turned and strode into the living room. A moment later the front door slammed shut.

180

Gladys put her hands over her eyes. 'Megan, I'm so sorry .
. . . I don't know what's got into him. . .'

'It's not for you to apologise.' Megan stood up. 'I think we both know what the trouble is with Wyn, but there's no sense embarrassing ourselves talking about it.'

'He's such a . . .' Gladys's voice tailed off in a groan.

'I'll tell you what,' Megan said, 'I'll come round and see you tomorrow. We'll have a chat about my London sojourn then.'

At the door Gladys apologised again. Megan squeezed her hand and told her not to fret. With Scratch at her heels she took the path round the side of the house and out on to Vaughan Road. She had been walking less than a minute when she saw Wyn, standing at the foot of the road. He was facing the hills to the south, his hands stuck deep in his pockets.

'Wyn!'

He turned and stared at her for a moment, then began to walk off towards the pub.

'Hold on!' Megan called to him. 'I want to talk to you!'

He stopped by a lamp post, head down and wry-mouthed, like an ill-tempered child. Scratch reached him first, sniffing and wagging his tail.

'This won't take long to say,' Megan promised, coming at Wyn with her head tilted, forcing him to look up.

'I don't know as there's anythin' to be said.'

'By me, there is.' Megan looked along the road, making sure they were not being overheard. 'You can look on this as a professional act on my part. I want to lance a boil.'

Wyn blinked at her.

'You know what I mean. I'd sooner spare us both the awkwardness of this, but matters have got to be put straight.'

'Don't know what you're on about, I'm sure,' Wyn said gruffly.

'Yes you do. Your behaviour, which I'll call your symptoms, make diagnosis very easy. And don't look at me as if you're stupid and can't follow what I'm on about. You've been harbouring your jealousy so long it's begun to poison you.'

181

Wyn's face stiffened with affront. 'Jealous? What have I got to be jealous about?'

'Do you really want me to spell it out?'

'I'm not listenin' to any more of this.' Wyn made to walk off but Megan grasped his sleeve.

'I'll make a scene on the street if I have to,' she warned him. He drew his arm free and stuck his hands in his pockets again. 'Now listen to me. I've known for a while how you feel about me. And I won't deny this – I've been flattered by your regard. But I don't have the same feelings towards you. In you and in Gladys I see two friends. Dear friends. But I'm entitled to other friendships. Timothy Morris is a friend of mine and it's a fact you'll have to accept.'

'A friend, you say?' Wyn made an attempt at a haughty sneer.

'That's what I said, yes. Are you implying he's less than a friend?'

'Not *less* than one, no. . .'

Megan took a deep breath, pushing down the impulse to shout. 'I don't think I'd like to see inside your mind, Wyn.'

'An' what about his mind? What's been goin' on in there?' The words were strangled, as if Wyn were reluctant to let them out. 'That man's connived at leadin' you off the straight an' narrow – an' he's not found it hard, either. Talk about willin' victims. . .'

'Right.' Megan pushed her face close to Wyn's. 'Not another word. I thought I could make you see sense, Wyn Brewster, but that's obviously out of the question. So I'll tell you this instead. You've insulted me and you've insulted Doctor Morris. You're petty and spiteful and you're not half the man I believed you were. I don't want to be in your thoughts, Wyn. Not ever again.'

As she strode away with the dog at her heels she felt the sharp sting of tears. How could one person's happiness make someone else so wretched? And why did Wyn's misery make her feel so hollow, suddenly – so bereft? It was as if she had come back from London to a reality that was necessarily miserable. And she couldn't escape the feeling that she was

182

being made to pay for something. She wished Timothy was with her. She wished, with a sudden swelling in her throat, that he could always be with her.

> In hell you move from one agony to the next.
> There is no interval of peace.

Dr O'Casey stared at the words, feeling like an interloper, but unable not to look. He should never have read anything in the notebook. There was no point in excusing himself, explaining to his conscience that he had looked inside because he wanted to know whose it was; only Timothy Morris would bring anything so elegant to Pencwm – it had a black crocodile cover with gilt metal corners; the pages were expensively smooth and receptive to the penstrokes.

O'Casey had found the book in the corner behind the waste basket the day after Timothy and Megan had left for London. Things were always landing in that corner, because it was adjacent to the low box where fresh sheets for the examination couch were kept, and a man's pockets emptied themselves easily when he bent down so far. Had Timothy missed the book? O'Casey felt sure he must have. Anything so personal, so revealing of a man's struggle to cope with life, would surely be missed.

There were dozens of entries, set down randomly, undated. Although they had no obvious connection, they painted a painfully clear picture. The first page contained a quotation from a medical text with which O'Casey was familiar:

Mitral valve disease, when it is rheumatic in origin, may be said to have no cure, other than the intervening death of the host.

Following that, page after page carried increasingly bleak observations on the obscenity of dying before one's time. Each time Dr O'Casey looked at the book, its purpose struck him sharply. Timothy Morris had been setting down his fear, anger and occasional despair so that he could examine them

183

coldly and come to terms with them. No good doctor, given the determination, would do less.

I shall probably never see forty, yet men that age and older look to me to cure them of their mortality.

When Dr O'Casey had left for Greece, his own health concerns had eliminated any curiosity he might have had about Timothy. The young man came well recommended, and that was that. As a subject for speculation, his motive in coming to Pencwm had been neither here nor there. Over the months, though, as O'Casey's stamina grew and his self-concern dwindled, he had begun to wonder. Now he knew.

It made him very sad. The little book was a unique testament of bravery – it was a man's confession of his dread, certainly, but ultimately it was an assertion of himself in the face of the hopeless. And in the most recent entries, it was clear that Timothy Morris had found a strong measure of consolation in the person of Megan Roberts.

There are days when I feel so desperately tired, yet she can revive me by simply walking into the room. If there is such a thing as a spiritual tonic, Megan Roberts embodies it splendidly.

Dr O'Casey looked at his watch. Timothy had gone to the house to unpack. He would be back soon. The book would be returned to him – left in the pocket of a jacket he kept at the surgery, so he would think he had never lost it – and it was O'Casey's fervent hope that his own behaviour would never reveal that he knew anything of the diary's existence.

O'Casey went and stood by the window. He wondered if Megan knew that Timothy was ill. He wondered if Megan and Timothy were lovers. Then he wondered why he wanted to know.

'Because I'm as much of an old woman as the rest of the people in Pencwm,' he murmured at the glass.

Poor Timothy. Poor Megan. O'Casey sighed and went back to the desk. He picked up the book, took it to the coat stand and dropped it into Timothy's jacket pocket. Perhaps it hadn't been missed, after all. The very last entry described a memorable dinner at Megan's, and gave the impression of having been written back in the winter or early spring. Perhaps Timothy had found, in Megan, a substitute for the journal. He had come here to take his mind away from himself – but the book had obviously been necessary, even so. Until Megan decided to bestow her warmth on him. It was a nice thought, O'Casey decided. Or as nice as any thought could be, given its tragic framework.

CHAPTER TWENTY

EARLY on a Friday morning in August, Megan was called to the home of Denis Hewlett. In the night, she was told, he had suffered a fever, which had raged for about an hour. Afterwards, as he grew cooler and less disturbed, he became delirious, calling out for Nurse Roberts, singing breathlessly from time to time and repeating passages from books she had loaned him.

When Megan reached the house Denis was propped up on two pillows, wide-awake, looking tiny and shrunken in the fresh nightshirt his mother had put on him. He gave Megan his skull-like smile as she sat on the side of the bed.

'It's a nice sunny day out there,' he said. It was nearly a year since he had felt sunlight on his skin. 'Wouldn't mind sittin' out in it.'

'Maybe you will,' Megan said. 'But not today, Denis. You had a bit of a fever last night, didn't you? Best thing is to rest indoors for a day or so when that happens. We can talk about you going outside some time at the beginning of next week.'

Sunlight was the last thing a tuberculosis sufferer should have, since it was believed to accelerate the disease. But already large areas of Denis's lungs had been excavated by the spread of infection; making the most of life was more important now, than trying to stop the spread of his illness.

'If you don't have any more fevers, and if the weather stays nice, we'll get you out in that back yard by Tuesday or Wednesday.'

'Will I be able to stay out long?'

'An hour or so.' To avoid making any firmer promise than that, Megan changed the subject. 'How are you getting along with the book?' She had given Denis a copy of *Dombey and*

186

Son for his birthday. 'You're not finding it hard going, are you?'

'No, not at all.' He pointed a thin finger at the book where it lay on the bedside table. His bookmark – leather, another gift from Megan – protruded halfway down the book's thickness. 'I feel sorry for the daughter, Florence. But I'm sure it'll turn out right for her – don't tell me if it does, though. It'd spoil the story for me.'

'I promise,' Megan said, putting her hand over her heart. She noticed Denis's nostrils flare as he smothered a yawn. Even the act of holding a simple conversation was enough to tire him. 'I'm going to have a word with your mother now. You just lie there and rest. Before I go I'll read you a bit from the book, eh?'

'That'd be grand.' Denis yawned again. As Megan left the room she heard him cough. It was a disheartening sound, like cinders being trampled.

In the living room Mrs Hewlett had the usual over-strong cup of tea waiting. 'I'm sorry I got you out so early,' she said, handing Megan the cup. 'I thought it was best, though, since you did say I should let you know if he had a fever or anythin' like that.'

'You did the right thing,' Megan assured her.

'I said to his da, mind you, that it's likely just the change in the weather that made him bad. Not good for chestiness this muggy weather, is it?'

'No, not very good at all.'

Chestiness, Megan thought. That was like calling a ruptured stomach ulcer a touch of indigestion. But Mrs Hewlett would hang on to her illusions to the last, like Megan's own mother had done, until the starkest reality had forced her to accept that her husband was dying. Thought of illusions sent Megan's mind veering along another channel. Her own illusions didn't bear confessing, much less examining. In the weeks since they had returned from London, Timothy's health had appeared excellent. So, against all her down-to-earth knowledge and instincts, Megan had begun believing again, that the inevitable was being thwarted. She believed it without ever

187

analysing her belief, just as the intensely religious never examined their faith.

'He was talkin' about maybe sittin' out in the sun,' Mrs Hewlett said.

'Yes, he mentioned it to me. I told him he could perhaps do it next week.' Megan opened her bag and took out a bottle of medicine. 'Give him this three times a day. It'll ease his chest during this heavy spell.' The decongestant was practically useless, Megan knew. Even if an efficient one had existed, it would only help clear out the debris created by the disease. But she knew the boy liked the taste and genuinely believed the stuff did him good. Another illusion, Megan thought. Life needed so many, just to make it sufferable.

She gulped down the tea and stood up, putting the cup on the table. 'I'll look in again on Monday,' she said, reflecting that she wouldn't be looking in many more times. 'I've promised to read to him before I go.'

When she got to the bedroom Denis was asleep. The book was lying open and ready on the bed beside him. Megan went back to the living room and told Mrs Hewlett that she wouldn't disturb him. 'He'll be disappointed, but tell him I promise I'll read twice as much to him on Monday.'

Cycling away from the house Megan was caught by the thought of children and their wonderment. All she could give Denis was the wonderment; she could hold fictional dramas and marvels before him, taking his attention from himself. That was all. It was much more comforting to think of Rose Clark, living in a world of real wonders, a child delivered from abomination to beatitude. But Rose's salvation put little consolation in Megan's heart. Not for long, anyway. It was no more than a diversion. Denis Hewlett was still irrevocably doomed, and that was sheerest tragedy.

'Stop dwelling on it,' Megan hissed into the air humming past her ears. It paid to dwell on nothing, just lately. Concentrating on the sparse solaces of her life only served, in the end, to remind her how many avenues of despair lay open. Better to hang on to the illusions, until the time they fell through – despair, after all, was one powerful example of a bridge that should be crossed only when a person came to it.

Dr O'Casey was surprised by his own shock. He had been prepared, after all. He knew how suddenly these things could happen. But the sight of Timothy Morris, gasping, blue-mouthed, had paralysed the old doctor for a moment.

When he had gathered his wits he got Timothy's jacket off, laid him back in the swivel chair, loosened his tie and rolled up one of his shirtsleeves. The injection of digitalis worked swiftly; within a minute some colour had come back to Timothy's face and he was breathing more easily.

'I think an explanation's in order, Doctor O'Casey,' he panted.

'Don't talk. Put your head back and breathe deeply.'

Timothy did as he was told. After a couple of minutes, with O'Casey sitting on the edge of the desk watching him, he glanced across at the clock. It was getting late. He had been on the point of starting evening surgery when the attack hit him. The waiting room would be full by now.

'People are waiting,' he said, making to push himself out of the chair.

'Let them bloody wait,' O'Casey snapped. 'How do you feel?'

'Better.'

'Is this the first attack of its kind?'

Timothy nodded. 'I'd expected something less spectacu-lar . . .'

'It can happen this way. How long have you known about your condition?' The diary had revealed nothing about the duration of the complaint. O'Casey felt his question did nothing to betray what he did know.

'Since I was a boy. Rheumatic fever.'

O'Casey stood up. 'I'm going to get you to hospital.'

'No. Please don't do that.'

'But you're ill, man. Your heart's fluttering around in your chest like a trapped bird. You need special care.'

Timothy sat forward. 'I've arranged for that already.'

189

O'Casey frowned at him. 'How did you do that, pray tell?'

'I've an aunt in Newport. She lives in the house that was left to me by my father. She's prepared for my, ah, home-coming – has been for a long time. There's a telephone number.' Timothy pointed at his jacket. 'In my breast pocket there.'

Dr O'Casey fished out the slip of paper.

'If you wouldn't mind calling her. . .'

'But can she cope? You'll need a lot of convalescent care. This kind of thing doesn't just pass off after a few hours, as you damned-well know. . .'

'She can cope,' Timothy said. 'She's big, buxom and strong as a Cardiff barman. And she's a retired hospital matron.' He smiled wanly. 'Apart from my dicky heart, my life's pretty well organised. Aunt Dilys will send a car. All you have to do is explain what's happened.'

Dr O'Casey picked up the telephone, then paused. 'What about Megan? I'll have to let her know.'

'Later. When I've gone. There's a letter for her, I'll leave it with you.'

'You don't want to see her?'

Timothy stared down at the desk top, panting softly. 'I want to see her desperately. But I mustn't.' He looked up. 'You've surmised a good deal, I take it? I don't see how you couldn't.'

O'Casey shrugged. 'I've gathered enough, I suppose. . .'

'Enough to know I won't put Megan through what's to come. And it's been good of you, Doctor, to suppress what you've known of my condition for so long.'

Dr O'Casey stared at him, colouring slightly.

'Simple detective work,' Timothy explained. 'I never did keep my dark little journal in that jacket. And if *I'd* found something like that, I wouldn't have been able to resist looking inside, either.'

After a moment's silence Dr O'Casey sighed and looked at the piece of paper again. 'You're a remarkable man, Timothy Morris,' he murmured, dialling the first number.

Dearest Megan,
I'll be gone by the time you read this. I beg you to read it carefully and take seriously what I say, bearing in mind that I love you more dearly than I've loved anyone.

The sunlight beyond the window had died to a deep orange at the margin of hills and skyline. Megan stood in the lamplight from the desk, her hand shaking as she held the letter, trying to take in the words. She looked up and Dr O'Casey, behind the desk, immediately lifted his paperknife and twiddled with it.

'Why can't you tell me where he's gone?'

Dr O'Casey said nothing.

'I've a right to know!'

'He asked me to give you the letter. Perhaps if you read it, you'll understand.'

Megan looked at the page again, blinking back angered, fearful tears.

I have been ill for a long time, and in the past few weeks I've come to realise that you know. I believe Dr O'Casey does, too, though I doubt if you learned from the same source, or confided in each other. I won't dwell on what my trouble is – all I want to do is apologise, and reassure. First, I am sorry for putting you to the pain this separation must cause; I should never have let my feelings carry me so far beyond the point of decent responsibility. Second, I wish you to know that I will never truly be separated from you. You will be in my heart – my all-too-feeble heart – until the very end.

There was more but Megan couldn't read it. 'You have to tell me . . .'

'Megan . . .' Dr O'Casey spread his hands. 'I have to respect his wishes. And frankly I think he's right. What can you do for him? What would you be doing to yourself? He's reached the stage where . . .'

'He's gone into decline,' Megan said, her voice wavering. 'So it's happened and I knew it would. So why can't I see him?'

'I don't think he wants you to see him like that. He'd rather, well . . .'

'He'd rather I remembered him the way he was. Well I can face him the way he *is*. Doctor, I'm begging you, tell me where he's gone.'

O'Casey put his hands to his face.

'*Please!*'

'I gave him my word.'

'Then I'll find him for myself!' Megan bunched the letter into her pocket and strode to the door.

'Megan, how can you possibly do that? Think of it, for God's sake – think what you're saying.' O'Casey stood up and came round the desk. 'Think of your responsibilities here, while you're at it.'

Megan marched out into the purpling twilight, her step brisk, her heart sinking. By the gate she stopped, putting her face to the stone pillar and letting the tears out. 'Damn you, Timothy Morris,' she whimpered, picturing his beloved face as anguish surged over her, splintering her dearest illusion forever.

CHAPTER TWENTY-ONE

EVERY Saturday morning Dilys Carter took a feather duster to her sitting room. For twenty minutes she rearranged the dust on her inherited collection of Victorian ornaments. Following an unvarying pattern, she wielded her feathers across tables, shelves and sideboards from one side of the room to the other, drawing tinkling music from the pendants of ruby and clear-glass candle-lustres, twitching onward across papier maché trays and boxes, matched porcelain oil lamps, cross-stitch face screens, commemorative mugs, an ivory-bound bible, domes covering clustered spun-glass birds and a trio of enamelled silver vases. The ritual, which did nothing to keep the collection clean, was nevertheless soothing and reassuring. Dilys always felt better afterwards.

This Saturday, though, she felt as agitated when she'd finished as she had when she began. No amount of compassion, sympathy or sorrow – which she felt in plenty – could quell her fundamental displeasure. Her training and long experience had made her a very practical woman, and a waste of life was something that angered her as much as it made her sad.

Out in the broad, dark-carpeted hall she stopped by the foot of the stairs, listening, though for what she didn't know. Timothy was asleep in his room on the first floor. He had been asleep since an hour after his arrival the night before. Now it was almost noon. From the look of him, Dilys guessed he would sleep for most of the day. She had seen that quality of desperate exhaustion before, though usually on much older men.

The door knocker rapped sharply, making her jump. She turned and stared at the door, hoping whoever it was would go away. She didn't like callers. There was another rap, harder this time. Dilys sensed determination and some urgency. She went forward and opened the door.

There was a woman on the step, pretty, rather pale, clutching a small leather case in one black-gloved hand.

'Yes?'

'Miss Carter?'

'That's correct.'

'My name is Megan Roberts.'

Dilys frowned. Was the name supposed to mean something to her? 'I'm afraid I don't—'

'I'm a friend of your nephew, Timothy.'

Now Dilys became very cautious. 'What can I do for you?'

'I'd like to see Timothy, please.'

'And what makes you think he's here?' Dilys had switched on her matron's stern face and imperious tone. *No visitors at all.* Timothy had insisted on that. He wanted to see no one.

'I'm sure he's here, Miss Carter. You're his only surviving relative. He's talked to me about you, and about this house. He told me he would come back to live here one day.'

This woman's personality was striking Dilys in fragments. She saw firmness of will, honesty and a directness similar to her own. She also sensed anxious compulsion. None of it was conveyed by her carefully measured speech, but it was evident from her eyes and the intensity of her expression.

'How do you come to know Timothy, may I ask?'

'I worked with him in Pencwm. I'm the District Nurse there.'

District Nurse. That gave Dilys something to hold to. This person was a nurse. Dilys had been a matron. She felt herself on surer ground. The face and tone didn't have to be used as a shield now. They were her instinctive weapon. 'I'm afraid I can't help you,' she said with chilling finality. 'I haven't seen Timothy for at least two years. Now if you'll excuse me . . .'

'I insist on seeing him,' Megan said.

'Insist?' The firmness of will, Dilys noticed, was extraordinarily well-developed. 'You've heard what I have to say. Now will you please leave?'

194

'No. I know Timothy's here and I'll stay on this step, if I have to, until you're compelled to let me see him.'

Dilys pulled herself to her full formidable height and let her breadth show. 'Now look here, young woman—'

'I'm not daunted by matrons,' Megan snapped. 'I've been practising out in the jungle too long to let any institution-alised bully frighten me. Hard-faced, bloody-minded colliers and their ilk are my daily fare. Where I'm from, Miss Carter, *I'm* the bully.'

Without wanting to, Dilys had taken a step back. This was a hard woman she was confronting. 'Do I have to call the police?' Her voice had gone too high, she thought. She sounded far too unsure of herself. 'I won't be trespassed upon in this fashion.'

'Call who you like,' Megan said. 'Timothy is here, I'm sure he is. And I'm going to see him.'

'Why? What special right do you have?'

'I love the man and he loves me!' Shouting now, Megan thumped the side of her fist on the door jamb. 'He went away without saying goodbye to me! I won't have that!'

Dilys observed the anger, the unshakable determination. And the terrible hurt. She stepped back, pulling the door wider. 'You'd better come in,' she said.

Dilys made coffee. An unspoken understanding grew between them as they waited for the pot to boil. After looking in on Timothy and making sure he was still asleep, then reassuring Megan that his condition was stable again, Dilys took the coffee to the sitting room and they talked for an hour. At the centre of that odd room – like a Victorian mausoleum, Megan thought – she sat transfixed, listening to an old woman pour out her heart. There was no doubt that Timothy Morris was her treasure. There was as little doubt that he had kept himself deliberately from her doting care until he had no choice.

'I looked after that boy like a mother would. Better than his own ever did. She ran off with a barrister when he was sixteen – my own sister, doing a thing like that. I got re-appointed to the infirmary here in Newport, so I could live with him and his father and look after them both. I encouraged Tim to go through medical school, helped him with his studies . . .'

'You knew about his heart condition at that time, did you?'

'Oh yes. And I knew how he could preserve himself from . . .' Dilys sighed. 'From what's happened now.' Megan watched her brush aside a strand of wiry white hair. 'With his ability he could take the choice of going into clinical lecturing, or joining a nice easygoing practice. He agreed with me – he was never one to put his head in the sand, he knew he would have to look after himself.'

'He went into a quiet practice,' Megan pointed out. 'His condition still deteriorated.'

'Because of the way he lived,' Dilys said. 'I wanted him to get into a practice here, where I could keep an eye on him and see to it he didn't squander the precious little strength he had. But no, he wanted London. The bright lights. It wore him out, that place.' She tutted. 'Wine, women and song. Carousing half the night, every night. I knew it was going on, the few times I visited him. If he had lived more carefully, if he had kept himself within the measure of his allotted daily stamina . . .'

Megan could tell the old woman had a seriously outdated understanding of human physiology, but she didn't interrupt.

'And then,' Dilys went on, when the first signs of serious decline came, instead of coming home and arresting the process, he went to Pen-wherever-it-is and worked harder than he ever had in his life before – at a time when he was least able for it. So now look at him. He's deliberately squandered himself. It makes me so mad . . .' She looked at Megan suddenly, her eyes softening. 'I'm sorry, this can't be helping you any. But it had to be said, to somebody. I don't often get a chance to let off steam.'

Megan sat back in her chair. 'I know how you feel. I talk to my dog sometimes, just to bring down my temper.'

'He'll be angry that I let you into the house,' Dilys said. 'No visitors. He was so firm about it he sounded like a fugitive. Thinking about it, I'm sure it was you, in particular, that he didn't want to see. Or, rather, be seen by.'

196

'I didn't think he would do anything like this,' Megan said. 'Surely he knows it would make no difference if I saw him weak and ill . . .'

'It would make a difference to him, my dear.' Dilys looked hard at Megan for a moment. 'You must love him very much.'

The day before, Megan might have said she loved Timothy more than she'd loved anyone, but she'd had time, on the journey here, to think that over. She had decided her love for Alun was the identical love she felt for Timothy – he was its new, living focus. 'He means more to me than anyone in the world,' she told Dilys.

'How long have you known about his heart?'

'Since a short time after I met him.'

'He told you, did he?'

'No. I found out by accident.' Megan thought of the letter again. 'I never told him I knew, not directly, anyway.'

Out across the hall, in the kitchen, a bell sounded.

'That's him,' Dilys said, standing. 'There's a bell-push over his bed.' She went to the door. 'I'll see how he is. If I think he's up to knowing it, I'll tell him you're here.'

'And please tell him I won't be put off.'

Dilys was gone for several minutes. When she came back she stood in the open doorway and beckoned to Megan. 'He's feeling better. I had to argue with him, but he'll see you.'

Megan followed the old woman up the stairs. At the bedroom door Dilys said, 'I know I shouldn't have to warn you, but please don't let him tire himself. He's still very unwell.'

Megan went in. Timothy was propped up, his hair freshly combed, his hands folded on the coverlet. At first Megan scarcely recognised him. She had seen him last on Thursday. In two days he appeared to have aged ten years. The light above the headboard emphasised his pallor and the odd prominence of his cheekbones. He was frowning, which made him look older still.

'I told you not to come, Megan.'

'I know you did.' She crossed and kissed his forehead, then

sat on the chair by the bedside. 'You must have known it was pointless to tell me that.'

Timothy stared silently at his hands for a minute, then he said, 'None of this should have happened – you and me, I mean . . .'

'You've said that before. The point is, it did happen.'

'It was irresponsible—'

'Of both of us.'

'I could have stopped it. Right there in London, it was up to me . . .'

'I told you then,' Megan said softly, 'we were conspirators. Don't blame yourself for anything. To be thoroughly honest, I was the one who forced issues all along, so you were less than a conspirator. A hapless victim, that would be nearer the truth.'

Timothy shook his head slowly. 'You stopped me telling you, didn't you? Were you stopping me from making you face the truth?'

'No. I was stopping the truth from putting a scar on our happiness. We were entitled to that happiness, Timothy. And we're the better for it.'

'Certain kinds of happiness are advance payment for misery, Megan . . .'

'That's only one way of looking at it. It's Alexander Pope's way – remember? "You purchase pain—" ' Megan stopped suddenly.

'Don't be embarrassed,' Timothy told her. 'I'm familiar enough with the lines, and their sentiment.' He put his head back on the pillows. ' "You purchase pain with all that joy can give, and die of nothing but a rage to live." '

'But we weren't buying extra pain for ourselves,' Megan said.

'Weren't we?'

'No. I'm amazed you can think that.' Megan leaned forward and reached for his hand. 'I've had something I'll cherish, always – your love, your companionship, the laughter you've given me.'

Timothy sighed.

'What is it?'

198

'I was going to be stern with you. You're making it impossible.' He closed his eyes. 'Megan, Megan . . . Why did you come here?'

'I love you. You love me. That makes us the two halves of a unit. How can I possibly be separate from you?'

'That's sentimental, and we can't afford sentimentality. Not now. You know what's happening to me, for God's sake.'

'You need nursing,' Megan said flatly. 'And that's a very unsentimental reason for me being here.'

'Megan, you can't be serious.' Timothy was staring at her, his fingers tightening on hers. 'You have a job, a career, *duties*. It's madness to think you can turn your back on all that, just to nurse me. I have my aunt, anyway.'

'The duty is rightly mine. And it's the only duty that matters to me now, I might add. I'm determined, Timothy. You won't talk me out of it.'

Weak as he was, Timothy drew his hand away from Megan's, dug his elbows into the pillows and pushed himself forward. 'Listen to me,' he said, panting from the exertion. 'And don't interrupt me.' He took a few deep breaths and moistened his lips. 'I've reached a point where my heart is going into sharp decline. There are no doubts about that. It's a fact. It is also a fact that nothing can be done to improve my health. Whatever the quality of care I receive, I will never get better.' He paused, seeing tears begin to form in the corners of Megan's eyes. 'Please, *please*, don't do that. Don't cry. You'll make it impossible for me to say what I have to say.'

Megan snatched out her handkerchief and dabbed her eyes.

'There's another reason why you mustn't stay here. You saw your daughter die and it's haunted you ever since. You were spared the sight of Alun dying and his absence from life is a fact you've found easier to countenance. Do you seriously want to mutilate your mind and spirit by watching me turn into a gasping, emaciated wreck, choking to death right before your eyes—'

'Stop it!' Megan screamed.

'I *have* to say it – and you have to listen. I'm approaching

199

the lingering stage, Megan. I could go on for weeks, perhaps months. During that time, while you tend me to no good purpose, people who need you, people it's your duty to care for, could die – in fact some of them certainly will die without your help. Now is that fair? Does it make any kind of sense?'

Megan was sobbing into her handkerchief. Timothy reached forward and put his hands on her shoulders. 'Leave me my good memories, Megan,' he said softly. 'Spare me the pain of knowing you're neglecting your people and watching me turn into a husk.'

'You're . . . You're tearing me apart!' Megan sobbed.

'The tearing's between your love for me and your professional conscience. Believe me, darling, there's no need to inflict that agony on yourself. Let reason hold sway – it's your way of doing things, after all. Stay with me for this weekend, then go back to Pencwm. It'll make me as happy as I can be – and in the end it'll be the same for you.'

Megan raised herself and leaned across the bed, putting her wet cheek against Timothy's. 'My precious, precious . . .' She held him tightly, using his breathing presence to blot out her pain.

CHAPTER TWENTY-TWO

ON Monday it rained. Gladys Brewster had put out the washing on the line at eight o'clock, and had to bring it all back in again at half-past nine. When she had finished stringing the clothes on the pulley in the kitchen she made herself a consoling cup of tea, then stood nursing it at the living room window, watching the downpour. Along the streaming length of Vaughan Road she saw people scurrying from one shelter to another, huddling in shop doorways and under the eaves of the Methodist chapel. Smoke from the pit buildings, brought low by the rain, swirled across rooftops and into yards. At times, Gladys thought, summer in Pencwm could be more disheartening than the winter.

She heard a soft whimper and turned. Scratch was curled up asleep under the table. His paws twitched and one eye flickered open and shut.

'Dreaming,' Gladys murmured. Dreaming about running, or whatever dogs dreamed about. She wondered if the dog found it odd, being brought here to stay from time to time. This time Gladys herself found it strange. There had been no explanation. Megan had said she had to leave Pencwm for a while. She didn't say for how long – Gladys had the feeling she didn't really know.

The kitchen door opened and banged shut again. Gladys went through. Wyn was standing by the sink, taking off his sopping jacket.

'Glory be – look at you. You're wringing.'

'Rain'll do it every time, Gladys.' Wyn unwound his work muffler and dropped it into the sink.

'What're you doing home at this time?'

'Rain.' He began undoing his bootlaces. 'The whole face is

floodin'. Management's been cuttin' corners again. They didn't drain the idle shaft above ours the last time it flooded, so all it took was an hour of this deluge an' it overflowed. The water was up past my waist before I got out.'

'Goodness, you could have been drowned.'

'True enough,' Wyn grunted, easing off a boot. 'The bosses knew it, an' all. So to placate us, like, they've told us we can have the rest of the shift off, an' our pay won't get docked.'

'Decent of them, I'm sure.' Wyn put down her teacup. 'I'll get you some dry clothes.'

'Hang on.' Wyn leaned on the wall, mopping his face with the towel off the back of the door. 'There's somethin' I want to tell you. It's somethin' that shames me, so I better get it over an' done with.'

Gladys picked up her cup again.

'You know Mrs Colville, the one that cleans the doctor's surgery?'

Gladys nodded. 'She's got a son works along with you.'

'That's the one. Well, you know you've been wonderin' about Megan – where she's gone off to, why she looked as if she was frettin' over somethin'? I think I know, thanks to Mrs Colville's gossipin'.' Wyn shook his head sadly. 'It's terrible, that's what it is.'

'What is?'

'Young Colville told me when we were goin' down at the start of the shift. On Friday, it seems, Dr Morris had a heart attack.'

'Goodness gracious!'

'A bit of a shock, eh? He was taken away to a relative's place at Newport. Sounds like it was pretty serious.'

'The poor man . . .'

'There's more to it, though.' Wyn folded the towel over the edge of the sink. 'Mrs Colville was earwiggin' when Doctor O'Casey was talkin' to some official or other on the phone. He said, apparently, that Doctor Morris had been sufferin' with his heart for years – practically since he was a boy. His chances of lastin' past forty are slim. Very slim.'

202

'Oh, Wyn. . .' Gladys tutted softly. 'Do you think Megan would have known – before, I mean?'

'That's what I'm thinkin',' Wyn said.

They looked at each other, filling the space between them with remorse.

'The things I thought,' Gladys said. 'God forgive me.'

'And what about me?' Wyn stared at the wall. 'I should have known, or at least suspected it was somethin' other than infatuation, or devilry on his part. At least I could have held back from judgin' Megan for the want of evidence – Lord knows, her compassion is as big as a house, and it dominates just about every important move she makes.'

'And a man's jealousy is powerful enough to blind him,' Gladys said. 'Don't blame yourself too much for your behaviour, Wyn. It was hard to live with, but in my heart I could understand. You were a victim of something you couldn't control.'

'I don't know how I'll face her.'

'The poor lamb. I do think she loves him, mind you . . .'

Wyn nodded. 'I think so, too. That poor devil – she's likely been the only consolation he's had.' He was talking like himself again, Gladys noticed. He was being reasonable, charitable. 'This news,' he went on, 'It's started me thinkin' about why he came here. I've heard of men doin' things like that. Good men, forsakin' the easy way for the hard, puttin' austerity between themselves an' . . . an' nemesis. For distraction. A lot of Crusaders did it.'

'And you were so hard on Doctor Morris . . .'

Wyn nodded slowly. 'It's damned odd, you know – I never did dislike him. I knew I didn't, even when I was ragin' about what a swine he was. Some imp in me concocted ways of turnin' reasons for likin' him into excuses for despisin' him.'

Gladys gave Wyn her chiding look. 'An imp? You're a rational man, you've told me often enough. You don't believe in imps.'

'Well, let's say an imp called jealousy – because if there *are* imps, against all reasonable odds, then jealousy's one for sure.'

203

Gladys turned to the living room door. 'I'll get you some dry things before you catch pneumonia.' She paused. 'We'll have to treat Megan with a bit more consideration when she gets back.'

'That we will. I'll make things up to her, Gladys. I promise you.'

She smiled at him. 'That's the big brother I like listening to.' She looked at the window as the rain began to fall harder. 'What are you going to do with the rest of the day, now you've got all this free time on your hands?'

'I've got it all worked out,' Wyn said. 'I'm goin' to have a cup of hot, strong, sweet tea, just to drive the chill out of my bones, then I'm goin' to sit down in there an' write a long letter to young Rose.' He grinned. 'It's been a long time since she heard from her Uncle Wyn.'

'I had this terrible feeling,' Dr O'Casey said, 'that you'd run away from us for good. Or at least for a long time. I didn't know what I was going to do. There was panic clawing in my chest, Megan.' He smiled gently, squeezing her shoulder as he pointed to the chair in front of his desk. 'Sit down. I'll get you a sherry.'

It was after four and still raining. Megan had come straight to the surgery from the railway station. She had already taken off her wet coat and hung it up. 'I had only one plan when I left,' she said, sitting down. 'To be with Timothy. To nurse him.'

'But you changed your mind.' O'Casey put a glass of tawny in front of her and poured one for himself. 'Why was that?'

'He talked me into it.'.

The doctor dropped into his swivel chair and studied his drink. 'He's a fine man.'

'Yes. The finest.'

'How is he now?'

'Weak. But as strong in spirit as ever.'

O'Casey watched Megan sip the sherry. She looked as if she hadn't slept for a long time. 'Will you be visiting him?'

Megan shook her head. 'He gave me sound enough reasons for not doing that.' She swallowed more sherry and put down the glass. 'It's going to be difficult for me, but I'm going to do as Timothy says. Get on with my work. Rivet my mind and energies to my duty.'

'I'll be all the help I can, Megan.'

'Has anything special happened since I've been away?'

'Well . . .' Dr O'Casey watched her hardening, forcing herself back into her role. 'Young Denis Hewlett, he had another fever on Saturday night . . .'

'I promised to read to him today,' Megan said with a sigh. 'I said we'd talk about him getting out in the open air as well . . .' She looked at the rain streaking down the window. 'Not much chance of that, if this keeps up.'

'Megan. Denis died yesterday morning.'

Her face was blank for a moment. She blinked twice, then her hands flew to her forehead. 'Sweet God . . .'

'You couldn't have done anything to prevent it.'

Megan groaned. 'Was he frightened?'

'He never came out of the fever. If you promised to read to him today, it was still something he looked forward to. You didn't fail him.'

'But I might have.'

Dr O'Casey pointed at the sherry glass. 'Drink that up,' he said sharply. 'All of it. Then go home, rest, and start work as early tomorrow morning as you can manage. If you think you're sliding off the rails let me know – at any time at all. I'll see you through.' He had summarised his concern for her and outlined the treatment. 'Put any guilt or grief from your mind. Be harsh with yourself.'

Megan picked up the glass and drained it. She looked squarely at Dr O'Casey. 'I'm sick to my soul with all the tragedy I've lived through,' she said. 'It's dogged my heels all my life.'

'It's an old companion of mine, too,' O'Casey pointed out. 'People like us, who've given so much of ourselves to others, spending our days struggling to preserve life – we're bound to have a steady acquaintance with tragedy and death. It's the

205

path we've chosen, Megan. And if we're to live with ourselves, we have to stick to that path.'

Minutes later, as Megan made her way up Vaughan Road to fetch her dog, she paused and turned, looking towards the bridge over the stream, the bridge where she'd stood and talked so often with Timothy – the bridge she knocked Nesta Mogg flying from. She wiped the rain from her face, not seeing the bridge now. She saw Timothy's face, the last dear image she had brought back with her. He had been smiling, showing her his spirit, his love for her.

She began walking up the road again, her head down against the rain. Dr O'Casey had been right. Her chosen life entailed a constant traffic with heartbreak, so she should learn to cope with it better than other people could. She was a District Nurse and she was never likely to be anything else. Like O'Casey, she hoped to end her days in harness.

Gradually, she felt the approach of a true consolation. It would be a long time before it was hard enough to support her, but she suspected it would, nevertheless. Her life had been enriched – far beyond any measure she could have imagined – by knowing Timothy Morris, and by having his love. Surely that was consolation of a very rich order?

The heavy sadness of the past few days edged aside at the memory of Timothy's glowing triumph, the day he saved the life of Harry Benson. 'One spark,' he had said. One spark, fanned to glowing life. That had given him such joy. Megan smiled against the rain. She was certain that her beloved Timothy would draw all the fire he could from the remaining dim sparks of his own life.

THE END